Possession Obsession

Blue Moon Sacramento - Book 6

Alex Gates, Steve Higgs

Contents

The Tour.
Monday,
September 4th.
1402hrs.

Douglas Kosar turned from the patch-marked, pot-holed, graying country road onto a narrow, rutted driveway. A thin layer of gravel remained over the hard-packed dirt, but most of the original aggregate base had loosened and slid to the weed-lined shoulder. Trees grew on either side, bare and brittle, like splintered ribs jutting from a corpse.

Doug's sunburned, drinking-age Ford bounced and jostled along the quarter-mile stretch of driveway at a crawl meant to avoid kicking up dust. At the end of the stretch stood the two-story manor, like a chipped and weathered headstone.

Two square wooden columns, like decayed fangs, held up the front porch ceiling. Atop it sat a second-floor balcony that slightly sagged. Plywood covered every window on the face of the house. The roof tiles, though faded and chipped, remained mostly intact.

Doug's eyes were those of a child in a toy store after being allowed permission to spend a crisp one-hundred-dollar bill on anything he desired.

From the passenger seat, Kathleen, his wife, hugged her arms across her chest. "I don't like it."

"Open mind, remember?" Doug tapped the side of his head.

"We can't live there. Look at the place. It's falling apart."

"Kathy, we have the RV for a reason. You green lit that purchase for this possibility." Doug parked his dinosaur truck behind a sparkling Lexus sedan.

"For a fixer-upper," Kathy said.

"What do you think this is?"

"A demolition project. A complete rebuild that needs permitting. This doesn't look like we would just spruce up the place, knock down a useless wall, and replace the finishes." She reached into the cupholder for her afternoon iced coffee. "Doug, I have an open mind, but look at the house. It's not a month-long investment project. It's a money pit and a time suck. We'll be living in the RV for six months." She glanced over her shoulder toward the backseat.

Kathleen didn't have to speak her mind for Doug to know what the simple turn of her head suggested. They couldn't live in an RV and support Emily, Kathleen's fourteen-year-old daughter, medical costs.

Doug, staring at his wife with a mixed look of sympathy and pleading, gasped at a sudden sharp noise. He bolted his attention out the windshield.

A woman in her early twenties had slammed her door and now stood beside the silver Lexus in the front yard, which was a combination of barren hard soil and overgrown weeds. She wore blue jeans, a black blazer over a white blouse, and heels. She continually glanced over her shoulders, as if seeing shadows she couldn't quite track.

"She looks nervous," Kathleen said.

"Young, too."

"First showing?"

Doug frowned. He had spoken to Lexi Delbrugge over the phone, and she had seemed less than excited to show them the house. In the driveway, standing beside her Lexus, the young woman appeared fearful.

"Maybe," Doug said after a breath. "More likely, it's her first house way out in the country. We're strangers to her, and she's alone. I doubt that's a comforting thought."

Kathleen slowly nodded, as his words seemed to resonate with her. A young, small woman meeting strangers out in the middle of nowhere would feel uncomfortable in the best of situations.

Lexi raised a ring-covered hand and waved at the truck, forcing a small, fleeting smile across her youthful face.

Douglas nodded in return.

"There aren't any stairs," Kathleen said.

"What do you mean?"

"Look at the front porch."

The covered porch raised three feet off the ground; steps didn't lead upward, though. There wasn't a ramp, either.

Douglas glanced into the backseat. Emily wore headphones and stared out the tinted window at the flat acreage covered in weeds and wild-flowers. He reached back and gently flicked her kneecap. When her eyes snapped over to him, he pantomimed taking off the headphones.

Emily obliged. "What?" she asked, her voice tinged with the impatience of a teenager having to respond to an adult.

"We're getting out to look at the house."

"Okay."

"Do you want to join us?"

"No."

"Emily," Kathleen said, turning her head to look at her daughter.

The teenage virus had hit Emily hard over the past month or two. Douglas and Kathleen spent many nights discussing her new attitude, how to approach her, how to discipline her, how much freedom and space to allow her.

Doug advocated for his stepdaughter, believing she needed room to grow. "Like a foot in a shoe," he said, speaking around his toothbrush and mouthful of toothpaste. "She's cramped, growing, but without space to breathe."

Kathleen saw it differently—with Emily, she saw everything differently than anyone else. "She can't walk, Doug. She can't eat without taking pills first. She can't use the bathroom without help. She can't dress herself. She can't shower without me there. What space can we give her? Space for her could mean a tragic accident."

The discussion always circled back to Emily's health—what it permitted and disallowed her to do.

"What?" Emily said, glaring at her mother. "How do you expect me to get across the dirt and gravel to the raised balcony? Should I climb up there?"

"Doug can carry you."

"I don't want Doug carrying me."

"I can carry you."

"I don't want anyone to carry me." Emily pulled her headphones back over her ears and furiously tapped the side of her phone, turning the volume up loud enough for Doug to hear from the front seat.

He glanced at his wife with exasperation. "She can wait in the truck. It's not like she's going to contribute financially to whatever house we decide to buy."

"Her opinion still matters."

"Sure, her opinion matters, but, at the end of the day, it's not weighted that heavily. Besides," he lowered his voice, though the music still roared from Emily's headphones, "it's not like she can run away."

Kathleen punched his shoulder. "Douglas Terrance Kosar." She brandished an amused smirk, though. "Fine. We'll look without her."

"And keep an open mind."

Kathleen rolled her eyes.

"I know it looks like a lot of work and money, but you have to imagine how it can look in a year."

"That's what I'm afraid of. A year."

"It'll be worth it."

Doug and Kathleen had met shortly after her first husband's death two years prior, and their romance was a whirlwind that ended in a secret marriage six months after their first date. In more ways than not, the two of them still spent a lot of time and conversation getting to know each other.

"Do you trust me?" Doug asked.

Kathleen sighed, reached across the truck's cab, and grabbed her husband's hand. "I do."

Doug lifted her hand to his lips and kissed her three times. He stepped out of the truck, spread his arms as if hugging the property, and he smiled at Lexi. "Wow. Look at this place."

The young real estate agent forced a smile. "It's quite... breathtaking."

Doug crossed the distance between them and reached out a hand to greet her. "Nice to meet you in person. I'm Doug Kosar." He gestured behind him. "She, who is taking her sweet time, which explains why we're late, is my lovely wife, Kathy."

Lexi released Doug's hand and waved at Kathleen.

"It's a pleasure to meet you," Kathleen said, her footsteps marking her slow approach.

Doug scanned the decrepit house—the plywood used to board the windows, the faded paint, the overgrown shrubbery encroaching on the base of the home.

"She's quite the fixer-upper, eh?"

"There are good bones, as they say," Lexi said. "My fiancé is an appraiser. We met on the job." She barked out a quick, uncomfortable laugh, a sharp punctuating sound. "He came out here a month ago and said if it didn't sell before the new year, we had to buy it to flip it."

Doug crossed his arms and nodded with interest. He understood the temptation to buy the property just to flip it. With any other house or property, and as a general contractor, he would have considered the same investment. Except, the three overgrown acres and rundown house had sat on the market for over a year. Why hadn't any property investors swooped in, especially when considering the price point?

The seller had listed the house for half of the market value.

Doug held his tongue, not asking the mock question that popped through his mind.

Is it haunted?

Kathleen was prone to superstition and conspiracy, including ghosts and spirits and all other paranormal nonsense—one of those late-learned truths he discovered after their rushed marriage.

She had asked him about the low price point the night before, but Doug had prepared himself for the question. He rattled off a response he hoped, because of her inexperience with the subject, would assuage her concerns.

"It needs a complete facelift, and a lot of internal reconstruction. The bones are good, though. If we add up all the remodeling or demolition costs... well, any investor would likely lose money on the transaction. Because of its poor condition, a typical buyer can't live in it. So, it's stuck in a no-man's-land of uninhabitable and not worth investing in. Also, with only three-ish acres of land, it's useless to farm."

"So why do we want it?"

"It's half the market price, Kathy. I can do the work myself, meaning we're saving on labor. And I'm not sure I want to sell it. We'll have three acres. It's a big house. We can turn it into our dream."

The conversation on the matter stalled for the time, but Doug knew it hadn't ended.

His eyes climbed the face of the house to the second-story balcony, to the attic nestled near the roofline. A circular window, one not covered with plywood, overlooked the front yard. Behind the dark, dirty glass, even from the distance he stood, Doug noticed his reflection—or that's what he thought.

He leaned forward, as if getting a few inches closer might provide him a zoomed in view, and he squinted his eyes to focus.

He saw a face, and not the face of his reflection.

Doug saw a stranger's face.

He blinked.

It was gone.

His heart rate spiked and his palms went sweaty. "Is there someone currently here?" he asked, not taking his eyes off the attic window.

"No," Lexi said. "I mean, there shouldn't be. The house has been abandoned for," she glanced at the sky and clicked her tongue, "nearly three years. That's not to say squatters haven't had their fair run at it. I've heard rumors that teenagers sneak out here at night, drinking, smoking, fornicating."

Doug inwardly chuckled at the use of the word fornicating.

"Look at this place," Lexi said. "I'm sure it makes a scary dare to have someone wander around out here in the dead of night."

"Why do you ask?" Kathleen asked.

"Hm?" Doug turned to his wife.

"Why did you ask if someone was here?"

He softly shook his head, reeling to come up with a reason for his question without making Kathleen more nervous than she appeared. "I meant, like, a squatter. There are laws about evicting someone from a home, even if they earned their residence by trespassing."

It was a lame answer, but not an entirely unbelievable one. It didn't seem like too many real estate agents had business at the house, and the poor state of the place evidenced that no one cared for the property.

Still, believable or not, Doug pushed forward to change the subject. "You said no one has lived here for three years?"

Lexi licked her lips. "The owners, only last year, put it on the market. According to them, no one has lived here for three years."

"Why not?" Kathleen asked. "I mean, why not, at least, rent it out?"

"The house switched through an inheritance. I'm not sure why the owners never rented it out or lived in it, but they recently passed away—last year. The house was inherited again, and the new owner immediately placed it on the market. I'm not sure about other details regarding its abandonment. I'm sorry."

The sun sat high and hot in the blue sky.

Doug wiped sweat off his brow and cleared his throat. "Should we go into the house?"

Lexi tucked a strand of hair behind her ear and sported a nervous smile. "Sure." She led them to the front porch and took a giant step, climbing the three feet to the wooden planks. The deck groaned beneath her minimal weight.

For a terrible second, Doug thought the rotted boards would give and the real estate agent would plummet into the crawlspace beneath.

The porch planks held steady, though.

Lexi, moving as if crossing a frayed foot bridge, stopped before the eight-foot-tall front door. She fiddled with the lockbox dangling from the handle, retrieving a key.

Doug assisted Kathleen onto the deck. As with Lexi, the old boards groaned in protest to her added weight.

"They feel sturdy enough," Kathleen said, though her tone hinted that she wished to be anywhere else but on the decrepit porch.

Doug hopped up and stood like a surfer riding the tail-end of a wave—stance broad and arms outstretched.

The porch miraculously held the three of them.

Doug chuckled with disbelief.

The deadbolt clicked. Lexi twisted the knob; with her other hand, she crossed herself and muttered something beneath her breath.

A prayer? Doug wondered.

The agent opened the door and stepped inside the old, dilapidated home.

Doug and Kathleen followed quickly on her heels.

Despite the air conditioning unit not running for at least a year, and despite the intense heat, a breath of frigid air enveloped Doug upon entry—like stepping into a grocery store during the summer.

"It's freezing in here," Kathleen said, hugging her arms to her shoulders.

"Probably poor insulation and a faulty HVAC," Doug said, stepping ahead of his wife and the agent, scoping the genuine hardwood floors, the ugly yellow floral wallpaper peeling on the edges, and the custom-carved trim on the ceiling. "Highly custom finishes, huh?"

"A reputable contractor built the house in 1953. Apparently, from what I understand, he specialized in carpentry."

"A man after Jesus," Doug said.

Lexi released an unnerving laugh. "To our left is the living room." She allowed her arms, which remained tight to her body, to venture wayward a hand length as she gestured to her left.

Doug first noticed the dusty drop cloths covering old furniture. "Does it come with the furniture?" he asked.

"Yes."

He nudged his wife with his elbow. "We can sell our couch and make a few extra bucks."

Kathleen held her tongue.

Lexi flicked the light switch. Nothing happened.

"Faulty wiring?" Kathleen asked.

"The owners don't pay for electrical to the house. No utilities."

Kathleen squeezed Doug's hand. "It's a dump."

Doug tapped on his head. "Open mind, remember? We have to have vision." With the lack of electricity and the boarded window, a gray darkness filled the house. Broken rays of sunshine worked through the split, uneven boards, providing enough light so they didn't stand in absolute darkness.

Doug activated his phone's flashlight and stepped forward and inspected the living room—the fireplace first, or rather, the mantle. Someone had carved intricate patterns into it. The entire piece—hearth to mantle shelf—could have belonged in a European museum. Hardwood ran across the expanse of the floor. The lower half of the walls were wooden, with more ornate patterns carved into them, and the upper half had more floral wallpaper. The ceiling was custom, a checkerboard of concave squares, each fully trimmed. A massive picture window stretched nearly across the entire wall with sheets of plywood covering it.

"Shall we continue?" Lexi asked, as if hurrying them through the tour.

They crossed through the entry hallway and stepped into the room to the right.

"The dining room," Lexi said.

Once again, the custom-built room had furniture covered in drop cloths. The walls possessed a carpenter's touch—wood panels with amazing filigree designs. The ceiling, no longer checkerboard but spiraled in figure eights, also boasted of a master in charge of his craft. Dangling from the center circle, like a spider descending from its web, its eight legs curling upward, was a massive, double-decked chandelier with dark diamonds raining around it.

The tour continued.

Lexi spent less and less time in each successive room.

They viewed the kitchen—the cabinetry throughout it boasted of first-class woodwork. They moved into the office, which had a floor-to-ceiling bookshelf across one wall, and a boarded window that, if visible, would overlook the side yard. The master bedroom was the last of the downstairs rooms.

Without having viewed the second story, Doug was ready to make an offer. He was head over heels for the house.

He saw himself sitting in the office; the bookshelf stuffed with true crime books, as moonlight poured through the window, flooding over his desk while he worked on his manuscript—the meticulously researched account of the Vampire of Sacramento or the Dream Demon Killings in Santa Cruz. He would have to write at night, since he had to work during the day to pay their bills.

Until his book sold millions of copies.

Then he could wave adios with both middle fingers. Sayonara. Hasta la vista, baby. See you in Hell.

The upstairs rooms were a collection of two bedrooms, two bathrooms, and an expansive playroom.

"What about Emily?" Kathleen asked, whispering into her husband's ear.

"What about her?"

"She can't have an upstairs bedroom."

"We live in a second-story apartment right now."

"That's different. There's an elevator."

"We could install one of those stair lifts."

Kathleen sighed, exasperated. "That's just more money that we don't have."

"Quit worrying about the finances. We're fine."

Doug controlled their finances. Kathleen didn't know how little disposable income they had, especially after the monthly costs of Emily's medications. A mortgage would cost less than their rent, though, so that would help.

As they moved through the bedrooms and hallways on the second floor, a thumping, like clumsy footsteps, skittered across the ceiling, followed by a falling cloud of dust.

Kathleen jumped and leaned into her husband, her eyes scanning the ceiling. "What was that?"

Doug watched the debris slowly drift to the hardwood floor and listened for another burst of noise. He thought of the face he had seen in the window. "Where's the attic access?"

Lexi's face blanched to the color of spilled milk. She glanced at the stairwell leading downstairs and back out of the house.

"What was that?" Kathleen asked again.

"Probably a rodent," Doug said. He neglected to mention probably a big rodent, like a rat, raccoon, possum, or human, though the words filled his mouth. He swallowed them back. "Where's the attic access door?"

"I don't know," Lexi said, her voice tight and quiet.

Doug stripped himself of Kathleen's grasp and scoured the upstairs for a hatch that led into the attic. He found it in the hallway, right outside a bathroom. He didn't have a ladder or a chair, or any means to open the hatch and climb into the attic.

"Kathy," he whisper-yelled. "I need your help."

Kathleen appeared around the corner a few seconds later, Lexi in tow.

"I'm going to prop you up."

"No."

"Kathy, just hear me out. I'm going to prop you up, and you're going to open the access door. Once you have it open, I'll lower you to the ground."

"I don't want to. I'm scared. Doug, this place scares me. Can we just leave?"

Doug shifted his attention to Lexi. She appeared sick, like she had spent the past three days in the bathroom. He sighed. "I need one of you to open the access door. That's it. I'll do the rest."

"What are you going to do?"

"See what's up there?" Doug glanced at the ceiling, as if he could see through the plaster.

"Why?" Kathleen asked. "Let's just... let's go downstairs and climb in the truck and leave. There are plenty of other houses for us."

"None as perfect as this one," Doug said. "I'm buying this house, Kathy." He hadn't meant to blurt the statement, especially not in front of Lexi, but his fear and frustration had hijacked his rational thought.

"I don't want to live here," Kathy said. "It's gross, and I don't like it. It scares me."

"Forget it," Doug said. "I'll do it myself."

"I... I'll help," Lexi said, her voice so quiet Doug barely heard her over his screaming thoughts. "It's my job to allow you to view the entire home."

Doug hoisted Lexi upward. She planted her palms on the square hatch and pushed. It lifted an inch, and she guided it over to the side. When the hole appeared, Doug lowered her to the ground.

Though the ceilings were ten feet high on the first floor, they were only eight feet high on the second level. It didn't take a miraculous leap for Doug, at a hair over six-feet in height, to jump and grab the ledge of the hatch. He wriggled, kicking his feet to propel his momentum through the pull-up. A pair of familiar hands pressed against his bottom, pushing him upward.

With the reluctant help of his wife, Doug slithered into the attic.

Sunlight cut through the exposed, circular window, providing enough light for Doug to discern a general layout. He also removed his cell phone and clicked on the flashlight.

The attic was more of a loft than anything else. It had solid flooring and insulated walls. Though nothing was up there but dust, cobwebs, and mouse droppings, it would serve as a perfect storage room. First, he would have to replace the access door with dropdown stairs.

"Do you see anything?" Kathy called from the second floor.

Doug narrowed his eyes and scoured the open attic. The emptiness should have relieved the initial fear he felt from seeing the face in the window. Instead, it deepened his discomfort. Doug's body seemed to compress, squeezing his heart and lungs.

What had he seen in the window? More importantly, where had it gone?

Move-In Day. Friday, October 6th. 1123hrs.

THE HEAT HAD FADED over the preceding five weeks, succumbing to the fall weather. The sun sat bright and high in a blue sky laced with skinny streaks of wispy clouds. A cool, gentle breeze played through the afternoon.

The seller and Doug agreed on a short escrow, only two weeks. On the day the escrow closed, Doug spent his evening, late into the night, working on the remodel. Kathleen refused to live in the RV until she absolutely had to, which meant she had stayed in the apartment with Emily until their lease expired at the end of September.

Over the past week, Doug replaced windows, dry rot, and sections of the roof, and he cleaned the interior of the home, making it inhabit-able. Kathleen bunkered in the RV with Emily, hesitant to step onto the property, disinclined to help Doug with the remodel.

Doug paused in his current task of creating a wheelchair ramp to wipe sweat off his brow before it dripped into his eyes. He placed his other hand on his hip and watched his wife.

He had positioned the RV to the side of the house, in a dead area where grass would one day grow, hopefully sooner rather than later. With the house repaired and cleaned enough to live in, Doug had declared the day move-in day. So, Kathleen had ventured from her hiding, and she emptied the RV, boxing their belongings, transferring them outside, and stacking them in the yard.

Emily sat in her wheelchair and tossed a muddy, sopping-wet tennis ball to Frank, her overweight Rottweiler. She didn't have a big throwing arm, but Frank didn't have a big tolerance for exercise. They made perfect playmates.

Doug worked in the driveway, where he had set up a station to fabricate a wheelchair ramp leading up the front porch.

Over the past week, Doug had also tackled the house in sections, tiered in importance by practicality and livability. To him, the process felt like he lived in a dream. He had always wanted an old, run-down home to morph and mold into his vision.

Kathy was less enthused. Over the past week, she had constantly complained about Doug's decision to purchase the home. She hated the idea of living in the RV, even for a week while Doug made the home livable.

"It's not just the inconvenience," Kathy said as they lay in bed one night, muting the television to not interrupt their argument. She brought up the complaint the night Doug signed the papers. "It's the impracticality. What will I do with Emily?"

"I thought you would see that as a positive."

"What does that mean?"

Doug massaged the corners of his eyes. "Nothing."

"What's it mean?"

"You're just... you're always suffocating her. I thought living in an RV, in that close of proximity, would make your parenting style more convenient."

"Excuse me? My parenting style? My daughter is sick."

"With what?"

Kathy threw the blankets off and jumped out of the bed. "With what?"

"The doctors don't know what's wrong with her. Everything they try seems to make her worse."

"Just because they can't figure it out doesn't mean she's not sick."

"That's not what I meant."

"What did you mean?"

"Just…" Doug sighed and shook his head, unsure of how he had dug himself into that specific hole. "I don't know. I'm tired, and I don't know what I meant."

"I don't want to live there. Neither does Emily."

"We can't live here anymore. Our lease is up. I already purchased the house, depleting all our savings. We have no other options."

"Quit saying we. You did this outside of how I felt."

"Well, it's the perfect place for our family."

"Says you."

"Yeah, says the only person in this house who has an income."

"My job is to care for Emily. Don't throw that in my face. Don't you dare." She sat on the edge of the bed. "Besides, that place is evil."

The wind gusted, pushing a cold exhale across Doug's face, pulling him from his thoughts. In the end, Kathy had no choice but to divorce him or agree to live in the house. So, she begged for a compromise—call in a priest to bless the home before they moved in.

"I refuse to live in that home until it's blessed and cleansed."

"Cleansed of what?" Doug asked. "Demons?"

"Yes. Malevolent spirits. You toured the house and felt the cold spots, right? You heard those steps in the attic, but found nothing in there. There's something not right with the place, and I refuse to step foot inside that home. I refuse to allow Emily inside that home until it's blessed and cleansed by a man of God."

Doug scheduled Father Hartke to arrive that afternoon, before the first night he, Kathy, and Emily slept in their forever house.

He picked up the wheelchair ramp and carried it to the front porch, where he attached it. He walked up it, down it, pausing in the center and jumping up and down to test its durability.

Satisfied with his work, he circled to the side yard to help his wife.

Though she emptied the RV, she placed their belongings just outside, not daring to cross the threshold and carry them into the house.

Doug didn't have any such qualms. He scooped a box labeled 'KITCHEN' and trudged to the front of the house, up the ramp he installed seconds prior, and through the front door.

As he passed the living room, movement danced in his periphery. He slowed and turned his attention to one of the many rooms he hadn't yet revamped.

On first inspection, nothing appeared out of the ordinary. A thin layer of dust covered the floor and the walls of the vast empty room. The picture window overlooked the front yard and driveway. He had pried off the plywood, allowing natural light to pour into the room.

He momentarily dismissed the dancing movement and stepped toward the kitchen. Again, from his periphery, the gentle swaying caught his eye. It came from the fireplace at the far end of the room.

Flames burned old, petrified wood and crinkled, blackening newspapers.

Doug nearly dropped the box.

Kathy refused to enter the home until a priest blessed and cleansed it. Emily had no access, at least not until a couple of minutes ago—not enough time for her to wheel herself into the house, start a fire, and disappear. Doug hadn't stoked the flames, either.

He stared at the burning fireplace, as if the answer might pop into his head the longer and harder he looked.

Who had started the fire?

Doug placed the packing box on the hallway floor and retreated from the house. He stepped into the RV and found Kathy preparing lunch.

"I hope you're hungry," she said. "I know it's a little early, but I wanted to clear out this kitchen. Bacon, avocado sandwiches. Your favorite." She looked at him and smiled, a warm, bright expression differing from the cold, dreary attitude of the past month.

"Were you in the house?"

Kathy cocked her head. "No, why?"

Doug pursed his lips and shook his head. He didn't want to specify; he didn't want to build on her concerns about the home being haunted or corrupted.

"Why?" she asked again.

"I was curious to see what you thought about the improvements I made."

"Oh. Well, after Father Hartke purifies the home, I'll go in there." She abandoned her station at the counter and approached her husband, wrapping her arms around his waist, tiptoeing upward, and kissing him. "You seem off. Everything okay?"

Doug forced a restrained nod. "Just a lot of stress leading up to today." He kissed her forehead. "Thank you for helping."

"You really think we can make this house a home?"

"I do."

"Even though it's a murder home." The statement and speaker came from outside the RV.

Doug glanced over his shoulder at Emily. She scratched Frank's head and stared up at Doug and her mother.

"A what?" Kathy asked.

"A murder home. That's why we snagged it for so cheap."

"What do you mean?" Kathy asked.

"A few years ago, a family lived in the home and experienced strange occurrences. At first, they chalked them up to an old house playing tricks on them, but they couldn't make that excuse for too long... not after a series of unexplainable events."

"You're scaring me," Kathy said.

"It's true," Emily said. "Every word. Look it up. I did. Apparently, I'm the only person in this house who knows how to use a computer."

"It's all legend and folktale," Doug said, his stomach twisting with anger. "There's no factual basis for those claims. There aren't even survivors from the incident to corroborate or falsify those statements."

"You knew about this?" Kathy's warmth turned into an inferno fueled by rage. "You knew about the murders that happened inside those walls?"

"Not until recently," Doug said.

"What happened? Tell me what happened."

Doug sighed and massaged the back of his neck. "Kathy—"

"Tell me."

Doug planted his palm on the counter. "A family of four rented the house from the previous owner. There are conflicting reports about the events leading up to the incident."

"Is the house haunted?" Kathy asked.

"Of course not."

"They experienced unexplainable things," Emily said.

"Again, conjecture. There was also speculation about mental illness. About a husband learning his wife might leave him, take the kids with her, and he wouldn't allow that. There's a thousand theories swirling around the Internet. So, Emily, how about we stick to the facts?"

"Which are what?"

"They sat down for dinner one evening, as a family, and they never stood up again. The father poisoned them."

Kathy covered her mouth and stared wide-eyed at Doug. "Why didn't you tell me?"

He shrugged in annoyance. "Listen, Kathy, people die all the time and everywhere. Someone had a heart attack inside that diner we love, but we still eat there. Someone else was shot and killed at that Target you're always going to, that you're still always going to."

"This is our home, Douglas! You sank all our money into the purchase and rebuild of—"

"My."

"Excuse me?"

"My money. Not our money. My money."

Kathleen fumed. For a second, she simmered, building up to boiling. Then she exploded. She wheeled around and reached for the counter, grabbing the sliced bread and slimy, uncooked bacon, and she threw them at Doug. She grabbed the half avocado and chucked that at him.

He stood there and took his punishment, food slinking down his body.

Kathleen leaned over the counter and panted, dropping her head and fighting against sobs. "I'm not sleeping in there. Never."

"Father Hartke will be here soon," Doug said, using the hem of his shirt to wipe bacon sludge from his face. "He'll cleanse and bless the house."

Kathleen kept her gaze fixed on the floor.

"If he senses evil, or anything malicious, I promise you, Kathy, we'll stay in a hotel until I figure something else out." Doug didn't dare step nearer to his wife or reach out a hand and touch her, for fear he might set her off again.

Kathleen spoke, her voice low and strained. "Even if Father Hartke clears the home, offers his blessing on it, I want to sage it, too."

Doug nodded. "Of course. We'll go through any purification process or practice you think is necessary."

The simple truth he refused to share was that, even at half the market price, the house and the remodel had stolen all of their savings. Tragic history, haunted house, faces in the windows, fireplaces that burned with no one lighting them didn't matter when compared to the alternative option—nowhere to live. Besides, what little income remained went directly to bills, food, gas, and medicine for Emily. They couldn't afford a hotel room, let alone a new home. Doug had inquired about selling the property after his remodel, but that route seemed less than promising. The house had sat for two years before Doug snatched it. Even if he spruced the place up to livability, he wouldn't make a dime on the transaction; he would most likely lose money given the history of the home.

Tires crunched on the driveway as a vehicle approached. Father Hartke.

Kathleen lifted her eyes and stared out the open front door at her daughter. "What do you think we should do? I mean, Em, given your health, I don't want to subject you to any unnecessary stress."

"Unnecessary stress is us living homeless, in a hotel, without access to the necessities she needs," Doug said.

"I'm not talking to you," Kathleen said, her words like daggers toward her husband. "Em?"

A car door closed as Father Hartke stepped out of his vehicle.

"I think we give it a shot. Doug is right, as much as I hate to admit it. An old house with a grim history might be better than living out of a suitcase."

"The inspectors didn't detect mold," Doug said. "Apart from the accumulated dust throughout the house, there's nothing to compromise her immune system. This is our best bet, Kathy. Father Hartke is here. We'll do the sage thing, along with anything else you think is necessary for you to feel comfortable."

Kathleen closed her eyes and sighed in defeat and surrender. "Okay."

Doug exploded into a booming laugh. "You hear that, Em? We're moving in!"

Medieval Deeds. Sunday, October 22nd. 1142hrs.

A BROADSWORD ARCED THROUGH the air, slashing at my clavicle to slice me in half, shoulder-to-hip style. At the last possible second, I raised my arm.

The thick blade met the thin fabric of my shirtsleeve.

My arm dropped boneless to the side.

The man wielding the broadsword—a burly, red-bearded man who stank of Cheetos dust and microwaved farts—bellowed a deep howl of laughter. He cocked his impressive sword back once more and hacked downward, his excitement fueling the force of his strike.

The foam blade connected with the base of my neck.

I shrugged at the man with annoyance. "Really?" I asked, massaging my neck where he made contact. "You chopped off both my arms. You had to hit me that hard in the neck, too?"

"The dead don't talk, unless spoken to through an elaborate, painstaking—"

An axe head flashed horizontally through the air, connecting with the redhead's tubular torso, accompanied by a barbaric roar.

Fred stood at the end of the toy great axe, bubbling with laughter.

"I told you, Ira, I was coming for you. Now, my pet worms will never be hungry again!" Fred turned to me, a wide smile stretched across his beaming face. He wore bracers on his arms, a shield on his bare back, and no shirt—his chiseled, muscular chest an anomaly amongst the other live-action role players battling in the open field.

"Dude, that hurt," Ira said, rubbing his ribs.

"Oh, shoot. My bad," Fred said. "I was a little excited, both because you killed my friend and I saw a chance to kill you. Let's be honest, with your combat superiority, I couldn't defeat you face-to-face."

Ira glanced at me. "You were a pawn?"

I offered a closed-lip smirk. "I agreed to die to exit the battle as quickly as possible."

"With Ira the Indomitable slain, the tide of battle has shifted, and a new warrior stands fearsome and superior above all others." Fred turned away from Ira and me and shouted at the battlefield, raising his voice to compete with those who screamed in a war-frenzy. "Brave warriors of Otnemarcas, attack without reservation! Run them down! Show them no mercy! Take no prisoners!" He screamed and waded back into the thick of battle.

Arcane users pointed their wands or raised their staffs, casting spells. Archers hid behind trees or up in trees, shooting arrows. Knights in full armor parried with frenzied warriors in nothing more than leather straps.

I looked at Ira. "What do we do now?"

"We hang out right here. People can loot our gear to use in the battle. Also, if there's a cleric amongst your ranks, they could raise one of us from the dead if they're at a high enough level."

I sat on a mound of dirt and stared up at the blue October sky, contemplating how I had wound up in the LARP event. As with most of my ruminating about sticky, ridiculous situations, the answer revolved around Fred or Maya as the culprits, as the initiators.

Maya, currently working twenty-five hours a day, eight days a week, launching her journalistic enterprise, which corresponded with the Sacramento branch of the Blue Moon Agency. She had nothing to do with my current predicament.

Fred, honestly, had little to do with me sitting as a living corpse on an imaginary battlefield, either. He had always wanted to LARP, but he couldn't ever find anyone to go with—not even Maya would stoop to the depths of live action role playing for him.

As an early birthday present for Fred, which landed on Halloween, I bit the bullet, researched different days we could attend an event, and settled on a Sunday morning a week before his thirty-third birthday because it also coincided with a Renaissance fair.

I couldn't think of a better gift than fighting a war with Fred, eating meat off of a stick, then driving him home after he drank four too many mugs of ale.

Also, my latest case with the Blue Moon Investigative Agency brought me out here.

Yes, Fred knew about my dual intentions with the LARP experience.

After everything with Daniel Quinn settled, I took some much-needed time off of work to rest. It quickly turned into three months of doing nothing. During that time, I caught up on a lot of horror movies based on Alina's recommendation, and I read a lot of books that had sat on my to-be-read list for far too long.

If you're interested in knowing about my romantic life, well, it went stagnant fast.

Glacia refused to move out of Oregon. Though temptation flirted with me, persuading me to move out of Sacramento, I couldn't leave.

Maya signed a contract for my branch of Blue Moon, making us business and professional associates and stripping away any romantic ideations. She investigated supposed paranormal happenings around the country, discovered the truth behind the supernatural, and wrote about them in her blog, posted them on her TikTok, did the whole

21st century journalism thing. Through her ever-expanding audience, she would (though, from my time off, I had not allowed her to yet) bump business over to me. I would pay Maya a finder's fee.

A little over two weeks ago, I met with Detective Kyle Vanek from the Sacramento Sheriff's Department. He sat me down and offered me a consulting gig, where he explained in excruciating and boring detail that Sacramento County covers 994 square miles and houses one-and-a-half million people, half of whom are some strand of crazy. The skinny detective snapped a small smile after that comment.

"Now that Daniel Quinn's tactics have gone public, he has a cult following. We've seen a drastic spike in supernatural crimes." Vanek finger-quoted the word supernatural, which made me feel warm and fuzzy. "Given my connection to Blue Moon Agency, the higher-ups assigned me as the lead of a new task force, and the only, to be clear, detective of a division they denoted as Special Investigations."

I sipped my coffee, feigning disinterest, though he had my attention.

It didn't take long to settle on an agreed-upon rate, one which would allow me to avoid taking jobs from private citizens forever, if I so chose. It allowed me the freedom to pick my private cases.

The caveat, though—Vanek needed me to start right away.

"We've had a series of robberies carried out in a variety of locations, usually in popular chain stores. The perpetrator somehow sneaks into the store after closing, steals the cash made throughout the day, and... well, disappears."

"Steals the cash? Isn't it stored in a safe?" I asked.

"It is."

"The perpetrator knows the combinations to different stores?"

"Yes."

"I'm assuming you asked the retailers about current or previous employees?"

"Correct."

I sucked on my teeth. "What do you mean by disappears?"

"The perpetrator first appears, as if from thin air, then vanishes after taking the cash. If you watch security footage, it almost appears doctored, like the person is teleporting."

I signed the contract to consult, and I spent the next two weeks investigating the disappearing thief with no help apart from Vanek.

Fred now spent a lot of time away from the office, but any client calls forwarded to his cell phone. Daphne, his wife, made the leap to create a food truck business. She still worked her full-time job, which meant Fred spent more of his time helping Daphne's dream come true throughout the day.

Alina waffled on her decision to enter an independent study program, choosing to give high school a committed shot. After all the abnormal things that had happened in her life, she wanted to feel normal—to fret over classes, friends, and boys. So, she went to school five days a week, seven hours a day.

Everyone moving on to pursue their personal greatness played a part in my agreeing to Vanek's offer.

"How do you know Fred?" I asked, turning my attention back to Ira.

Around us, the grunts and screams and slashing sounds of battle waged beneath the warm, blue October sky.

"Who?"

"Ghan," I said, uttering Fred's character's name. "How do you know Ghan?"

"Oh."

With a lack of interest, Ira simply shrugged his shoulders. "I don't. I mean, I do, but only from today."

I inwardly chuckled, not surprised at Fred's ability to make connections with strangers so easily. "Is your name really Ira?" I asked after a second of spectating the battle. "Or is that your character name?"

"Character name. I'm Will."

"August," I said.

"Nice to meet you. And I'm sorry I killed you."

"Sorry for distracting you and getting you killed. We didn't really trick you, you know? At least, we didn't mean to. Fred and I didn't have a plan or strategy to sacrifice me, or anything like that." I was rambling, but I didn't know what to say to him.

"Are you a pirate?"

I lowered my gaze and glanced at my getup, which I had bought from a costume store. "Captain Sack Jarrow."

He snickered. "What's your backstory?"

Fred had prepared me for that question, so I had a half-baked answer. "A rival pirate gang took over my ship and killed all my crew. They forced me to walk the plank. Either I survived and lived with the knowledge of having failed my ship and crew, or the ocean swallowed me up."

"I'm sorry for your loss."

I scrunched my face, wandering if Ira actually thought my character backstory reflected my real life. Not caring to correct him, I tossed a question his way. "I like your costume. Where did you get it?"

Ira, or Will, dressed as a knight. He wore black-painted plate mail, including a breastplate, greaves, and gauntlets.

A look of pure pride washed over him. His chest puffed out, his posture straightened, and his chin lifted an inch. "I made it myself."

"Really? That's incredible. How long did it take?"

"Nearly six months."

My eyebrows raised as I whistled. "Will you sell it?"

"This?" He rapped his knuckles against the breastplate, which had a brilliant depiction of a three-headed dragon. "I don't think so. This is my paladin armor. I'm building the entire *Dungeons and Dragons* class set. The barbarian and monk classes were pretty simple—just a lot of sewing and leatherwork. I finished a druid costume late last year, and a bard costume earlier this year. That was my build before this one. It was pretty simple, apart from the lyre. I crafted that from scratch."

I shook my head, not having to work hard at expressing my amazement. I could barely color inside the lines of a coloring book, yet Will could piece together entire armor sets. "That's impressive."

"Thank you."

"So, the lyre? You also create weapons and objects?"

"A few, yeah." He hefted his broadsword, an impressive foam weapon obsessed with detail. "I made this sword and the lyre. I made a staff for my monk costume and a great axe for my barbarian." He spoke like an actor getting interviewed for their latest movie release. Excitement filled his voice like air in a balloon.

On the battlefield, some magic-based character cast a spell by reaching into a leather pouch on their hip, grabbing a handful of colorful sand (no glitter, confetti, or other pollutants allowed) and tossing it into the air.

I pointed at the scene. "What about something like that? Can you create magical effects more believable than colorful dust?"

Ira nodded, his red beard bouncing up and down. "I'm working on my next build. A rogue. The design is all studded leather with a hooded cloak over the top. Anyway, the character, like most rogues, is a thief. So, I wanted to build that into the design."

"What do you mean?"

"Dark brown and black for a color scheme. Light-weight weapons, like daggers and darts. A way to disappear."

"Disappear?"

"Like, into the shadows."

"Turn invisible?" I asked.

Ira shrugged, noncommittal to answering my question.

"How would you do that, or is that just something…" I chuckled and nodded at the magic caster throwing colorful sand. "A cloud of smoke, or a handful of sand, you know? Something that represents invisibility, but doesn't actually make you invisible."

Ira cocked his head and regarded me for a second. "Really? You think that little of me?"

My heart picked up pace, sprinting against my chest. I hadn't done this in months, and a seed of doubt sprouted within me. Had I lost my touch? "It's not possible to become invisible. I'm just curious how you would implement the feature into the costume."

Ira's deadpan glare softened, and he shook his head and released a low-burning chuckle. "My friend, though I love to imagine living in a medieval, fantasy-based world where magic rules and technology drools—"

Yes, that's what he said, verbatim.

"—we live in a technological world. Things that only magic could accomplish yesteryear are now commonplace. I may not look like it, but I have quite the scientific mind."

"Which I'm sure helps when you're designing your costumes."

"Exactly."

"So, you were saying science, not magic, can turn things invisible?"

Ira winked at me. "When used in combination—science and magic—things can become invisible."

"I don't understand."

"There's technology already developed to disguise stationary items. The military could cloak weapons and tanks from enemy surveillance. It's like the invisibility cloak from *Harry Potter*, except it doesn't do well hiding moving objects."

"Okay," I said, responding to show I followed but didn't fully understand his explanation.

"Magic is based on misdirection. You look here," Ira snapped his fingers high in the air, "while I do something over here." In his off-hand, he produced a gold coin. "So, for my rogue build, I'll use the art of misdirection to enhance or complement..." he trailed off, opting for a bright grin.

It took a beat for me to realize he waited for me to fill in the blank.

I gasped, truly in shock. "No."

Ira nodded.

"You built an invisibility cloak? Does it work? What? How?" I purposely piled the questions one on top of the other, stoking the fires of his ego, pumping him up with hot air.

"It works as well as I could've hoped. Would you like to see it?"

"Um, no. Let's just sit here and talk about it. Yes, I would love nothing more than to see an invisibility cloak!"

That's all it took. Often in these types of affairs, stroking someone's ego proves the most effective tactic to bring them down.

Will led me through the Renaissance Fair and out to the parking lot.

Kyle Vanek, along with a uniformed deputy sheriff, waited near Will's ancient Toyota Avalon. Vanek was rail thin and pale as the Horseman of Death. He had an angular physique, much like a praying mantis, and piercing blue eyes, though an unexplainable softness exuded from him.

If Will felt nervous about law enforcement, he didn't show any signs. He continued to walk toward his vehicle without hesitation, stopping only when he stood a few feet away from Vanek.

"Can I help you, officer?"

"Detective," Vanek said.

"I'm sorry. Can I help you with something, detective?"

Vanek had his arms looped behind his back. He pulled one forward, dangling a pair of handcuffs. "You could kindly not resist arrest."

Will turned to me. A look of pleading splashed across his face, as if I could help him, as if I hadn't set him up. "I don't know what's going on."

"I'm not a hundred percent sure about what's going on, either," I said. "Though I have a fair idea. You sneak your invisibility cloak into certain retail stores, don it in a spot blind to cameras when no one is looking, and wear it, standing statue still, until the place closes for the night. Once you are alone, you peel off the cloak and make your way to the manager's office."

I waited for Will to explode into a flurry of denials, or to say something cliche, like, "I would've gotten away with it, too, if it weren't for you meddling… investigators." Instead, the man wearing a picture-perfect paladin costume said nothing.

"That's what I'm not so sure about," I said, picking up where I had left off. "How did you enter a locked room without breaking in? Did you have a key? How? More confounding. How did you unlock the safe to steal the money?"

"I don't know what you're talking about," Will said, opting to speak, since I had given him an opening for denial.

I snapped fingers, as if realization struck me. "Unless you canvassed the place first. You brought your cloak inside the store multiple times before going through with the heist. You watched from the corner of the offices as the managers entered the combination, which you memorized. Still, it doesn't explain how you entered the offices." I tapped the side of my head, pondering. "Vanek, any ideas?"

"Any rogue worth his thieving salt would need to have expertise with lock picks, right?"

"Thieves tools," I said, correcting the detective.

"My mistake. I've never played *Dungeons and Dragons*."

"Honestly, you're missing out. It's a good time. We have a monthly campaign. Would you want to join sometime? Fred runs it. Alina and Maya have joined. It's fun."

Vanek punched out his lower lip and rocked his head back and forth. "Maybe. I'll consider it."

"Sweet. We would love to have you." I shifted back to Will. "Anyway, motive. To fund your costume collection. It's expensive, especially for a guy whose only income is chore money from his grandma."

"I take care of her! She's sick, and she pays me for it. If I had a job, I wouldn't be able to stay home and help her."

I raised both hands in the air and stepped back. "Sorry. I'm sorry. Anyway, I'm done impersonating Sherlock Holmes. Any clarifying questions?"

"You don't have proof that I stole any of that money. You don't know it was me."

"William Derry, I tracked you to this Renaissance Fair and LARP activity. Even when invisible, a person still leaves tracks." I spared a quick glance at the sky, making sure my witty comment tracked. I thought it did.

"What tracks did I leave? Tell me, what proof do you have?"

"A red-bearded man, similar in size and appearance to one William Derry, entered every retail store multiple times in the days leading up to the robberies without being seen leaving the store those days. Not only that, but the same man was seen on camera leaving the retail stores the next day without having walked into the store that morning. Quite the conundrum."

"Doesn't make it me."

"Well, parking lots have cameras, too, believe it or not. So, we watched the CCTV footage of that red-bearded man of your size and appearance walk across the parking lot to his Toyota Avalon, which had a license plate number belonging to a Miriam Derry. Your grandmother." I threw up my arms in an exasperated shrug.

Vanek allowed me to take a breather. "Unfortunately, the recorded footage wasn't enough to charge you with a crime. It made you look suspicious, but we needed hard evidence." He revealed his other hand, the one still behind his back. In it, he held a search warrant. "Judge already signed this based on the video surveillance. So, would you care to unlock your vehicle for us, or shall we break a window?"

I didn't care to hang around and watch the ugly bits. "Before you proceed," I said, "I'm going to head back into the... into whatever that is in there. I owe Fred a few birthday beers and meat on a stick. Cheers, fellas."

I turned and power walked back into the LARP event.

The Half-Elf Rogue. Sunday, October 22nd. 1223hrs.

I NEED TO EXPLAIN the scale and scope of a LARP event, because it's truly impressive, even to someone like me, who finds the entire thing rather ridiculous.

Justin Jersey, the president of the LARP association in the Sacramento region, organized the event. Members pay a monthly or an annual fee, and those payments go directly toward the construction of the game. There's also a gate fee, determined entirely by any costs not met through yearly collection divided by expected players for the event. If too few people show, the annual fees increase; if too many people show, well, the annual fees decrease. All the money received always goes toward the games, which occur in waves.

Smaller, more budget-friendly events happen monthly. There's a loose story threading each event together, which culminates during their quarterly meetups.

Their annual event—the one Fred and I attended—is the conclusion of the year-long adventure. It's a three-day affair, usually running from Friday to Sunday. Everyone took part in the annual festival, usually held on fairgrounds for bigger events, ballrooms or community parks for smaller events.

The coordinators hired businesses to cater and work at the annual event. Food truck owners abandon their vehicles. They immerse themselves in the setting, performing as non-player characters and serving a single purpose of providing food and drink to the player characters, in exchange, of course, for coin.

The annual event is massive—hundreds of people gathering on dozens of acres.

On the first day, they have games. Archery, jousting, duels, wrestling, and pie-eating contests, amongst many others. While the contests happen, the nonparticipants wander the grounds, buying food, drinks, weapons, armor, potions, or any other supplies they wish to accrue for the battle games. It's not uncommon to find bards dancing and singing, playing a stringed instrument, while others craft.

Role-playing primarily happens on Saturday. Parties who have adventured all year receive their last missions. They solve riddles, square off against monsters, save someone in dire need of help, collect treasure, such as gold or enchanted weapons, and gather experience to purchase more skills for their characters.

The battle games occur on Sunday—capture the flag, hunger games, regicide, among others.

Fred and I purchased a single-day pass to the event, gaining admission to Sunday. We didn't need to immerse ourselves in the culture for the entire weekend, and since we didn't have a LARP adventuring party, we didn't care to join a random quest on Saturday.

The Sunday battle games seemed less committal and more fun.

I had left the fairgrounds to go to Will's car during a game of Regicide (each team crowns a king, who they then protect from the other team).

When I returned, the battle game had ended. The organizers scrambled to set up the next one.

I found Fred sitting at a wooden table with a chicken leg in one hand, a mug of ale in the other.

"My brave knight, may I have a seat?" I asked.

Fred tore off a chunk of meat. "Ah, I'm a barbarian. I know nothing of the chivalrous, hypocritical nature of knights." He spat on the ground. "I live freely, not bound by the laws of man, but the laws of nature."

"Okay," I said, forgoing my medieval accent. I sat across the table from him. "Did we win?"

"Ay." Fred tipped back his mug of ale, then he wiped his forearm across his mouth, erasing the foam skimmed across his upper lip. "Did you win?"

"Ay," I said.

"Do you hear that, my fellow heroes? Ghan the Gruesome and Captain Sack Jarrow have plucked the roots of evil and darkness from this world. Drink! Drink!"

A chorus of cheers erupted from those surrounding us.

Fred went bottom's up, slamming his tankard on the table when he finished.

"You should get Daphne here next year," I said.

"She'll never dress up. Believe me, I've tried plenty of times to convince that woman to do some private role-playing."

"That's not what I mean. Her food truck. She should apply to cater the event."

"Ah! Cheers! An amazing idea." Fred stood and stretched, his bulky muscles lengthening. "I need another ale." He plodded a dozen yards to a merchant tent, exchanged his gold coins (which would later convert into dollars) for two tankards of a domestic beer they relabeled as mead or ale for the event. He returned to the table. "I checked my phone to see if Daphne tried to contact me, and I had ten missed calls."

"From Daphne?"

"A potential client."

"Just from this morning?"

"He's calling about every twenty minutes, and he leaves a voicemail every time."

"About what?" I asked.

Fred shrugged, his broad shoulders lifting near his ears. "I only listened to one of them. He rambled a lot, you know? Sounded frantic, maybe scared. He mentioned something about a possession."

"Like... demonic?"

Fred shrugged again. "No idea. I'll call him back tomorrow and schedule an appointment, if you're interested in the case."

I reached out my hand. "You care if I listen to the voicemails?"

Fred removed his phone from his pocket and dropped it into my open palm. "Have at it. About seven minutes ago, they announced the next game starts in fifteen minutes. You're playing. That's not a question, either. It's hunger games—every person for themselves. I say we team up, you and me. Increase our chances at winning. Of course, one of us will have to take the fall at the end, but that's the sacrifice we'll make to split the treasure."

"What's the treasure?"

Fred grinned, a smile that went all the way to his eyes. "Knowing we overcame adversity and all the odds, that we bested every other combatant in the arena."

I rolled my eyes and played the first voicemail.

"Uh, hi. I'm Douglas Kosar. I... I need your help. Please." The message ended.

I played the next voicemail, time-stamped eighteen minutes after the first.

"It's Doug again. I'm trying to reach August Watson. There's something strange, unexplainable happening, and I need your help." Click. Message complete.

I listened to three more of the vague, clipped voicemails before jumping to the last one he left about twelve minutes ago.

"She's possessed. This house is possessed. We can't move out. We don't have the resources or the money. I don't know what else to do. Please, help me."

A horn cut through the din of conversation and stringed music and singing.

Fred popped to his feet and tipped back his tankard, polishing it off. "You ready?"

"I think I should call this Doug Kosar back."

"Nonsense," Fred said. "It's my birthday. You made me a promise, and I intend to make you keep it. Now, give me my phone, readopt your accent, and let's win this!"

Fred and I waded to the battlefield, an area of flatland come to life with props—boulders, trees, and small structures, like cabins or cottages. The participants gathered around a large perimeter. Throughout the map, or the setting, the organizers had hid a variety of weapons for us to find and use.

A disembodied voice boomed across the expanse of field. "Only one can survive!"

Another horn sounded, the pistol starting the race.

The rules were simple. It was an all-versus-all battle. Every ten minutes, the boundaries of the battlefield would shrink. Players couldn't roam beyond the current perimeter, otherwise they would experience instant death. When players entered combat, both possessing a weapon (armed combatants always defeated unarmed combatants) they settled their melee through a game of Roshambo. Loser had to leave the game.

Fred and I sprinted toward a lean-to built on the ground, leaning against two wooden posts. Another participant—a woman with blue markings across her face, wearing a twig-wreathed crown—reached the location simultaneously as us.

She stuck out a fist, then immediately pulled it back and retreated.

Fred guffawed with swelling pride. "She knew better than to fight against the both of us."

I shook my head and scrunched my face, confused why it mattered when settled through a game of chance.

"Alright," Fred said, ducking as he stepped beneath the sloped roof, "something good has to be in here. Captain Jarrow, keep an eye out for any threats. I'm going to dig around."

I thought of Douglas Kosar's voicemails while I surveyed the field for any impending danger. Why had he continued to leave short, clipped messages only to call back ten minutes later? Why not leave one continuous message with all the details?

"It doesn't make sense to ponder on it."

"What?" Fred asked, his voice a sharp bark.

"Nothing. Talking to myself."

"Nice. I like that you're staying in character. Keep it up."

It made no sense to dwell on Kosar's messages because of one simple truth he had stated. *We can't move out. We don't have the resources, the money.*

At the beginning of the year, I accepted a handful of cases for a minimal to no charge to build a reputation and gain exposure. After solving a few high-profile cases and stopping the theatrics of Daniel Quinn, my name had shot far beyond regional notoriety. Clients, during my sabbatical, called from every corner of America to have me look into their shadows and expose the monsters stalking them, and for quite a sum of cash, too.

My sudden surge in celebrity, along with my consulting job for Sacramento County Sheriff's Department, put me in a unique position. For the first time in my brief career, I could screen my clients. If they couldn't pay, I didn't have to play.

According to the voicemails, Douglas Kosar couldn't pay.

Yet, he seemed frantic and afraid.

Other paranormal investigators existed in Sacramento, but they perpetuated the idea of the supernatural; they fabricated evidence to create a reputation of ghost hunters. Contrary to them, I built my name on discrediting the paranormal, on taking off the mask and revealing the person behind the crimes.

If Kosar went to another paranormal investigator, they wouldn't help him. They would take the money he didn't have and complicate his fears and his problems.

A firm, spongy material pressed against my throat. I inhaled, realizing that someone had snuck up behind me.

"Fred?" I asked. "Did you backstab me?"

"Turn around," said a female voice trying on a bad southern accent. "No sudden movements and you'll live a few seconds longer. You'll even survive this encounter."

"You had one job," Fred said. "Watch for threats while I find a weapon."

"Did you find one?" I asked, rotating a slow circle and facing the hulking man. He held a longsword.

Between us, wielding two daggers, one pointed at me, the other at Fred, stood a slender woman. She wore dark leather covered by a black cloak that shaded her eyes and a black balaclava that covered most of her face.

"Drop your weapon," the woman said.

"You'll kill us both if I do," Fred said.

"I'll kill him if you don't. If you put the sword on the ground, I'll sheath my daggers, and we'll fight with fists."

"A petite little girl like you, against me?" Fred jammed his thumb into his broad chest. "No."

"Unarmed versus unarmed equals a fair fight. Roshambo. If you refuse, I kill your unarmed friend, then you and I square off, armed-versus-armed. Roshambo. We do this either you two against me, or you against me. It's your choice."

I rolled my eyes, finding the entire situation beyond silly. Yet, I held my tongue and let the encounter play out.

"Okay." Fred squatted and placed the longsword on the ground, then he stood straight.

The woman chuckled, and I recognized her laugh. A sense of agitation, pride, and frustration mixed and burned within me.

"I could kill you both now," she said.

"Will you?" I asked.

She twirled her daggers and dropped them into the sheaths at her hips. "No, but it's worth you knowing that I could have defeated you right here and now. Instead, I will draw it out, and I'll defeat you through a game of wits."

"Is Roshambo a game of wits or chance?"

"Wits when you use your head."

Fred pointed at the cloaked woman. "She's not wrong about that. Well, let's have a meeting of the minds."

"How does this work?" I asked.

"We all three go at once," Fred said. "If one of us defeats her, we both live, she dies. If one of us ties and one of us loses against her, well, one of us dies and the other remains to continue the fight."

"If we choose the same symbol, and she beats us, we both die?"

"Yes."

"This is the most ridiculous thing I've ever done," I said.

"Buying a Jack Sparrow costume was the most ridiculous thing you've ever done," the woman said.

"Are you ready?" Fred asked, shouting his question and punching out his fist to count rock, paper, scissors.

The woman formed two fists, one for Fred, one for me.

I also made a fist, adding a little oomph into my strikes, too. I didn't want to lose to the young woman, not after realizing who she actually was. So, I took the Roshambo battle extremely seriously.

"Row," Fred said, though we all chorused together to finish the rhythmic chant.

I instinctively went to rock.

Fred went with scissors.

The woman, who needed to lose to only one of us, also threw rock.

"What's that mean?" I asked, still uncertain of the rules.

"I'm dead." Fred grabbed his stomach as if a dagger had punched into his gut. He staggered back a few steps and dropped onto his butt. Gurgling noises bubbled up from his throat. "Please," he gasped, choking and coughing, "Sack Jarrow, my dearest friend, tell me wife that... that." He closed his eyes and poked out his tongue, speaking no more.

"We tied, so we're alive," the woman said.

"Not for long," I said. "Ro."

Again, we finished in chorus.

I finished with my hand flat, showing paper and slightly quivering, exposing my nerves.

She threw scissors.

"I'm dead?" I asked.

Alina threw back her hood and pulled down her balaclava. She beamed with joy, her eyes dancing with amusement. She wore a pair of elf ears over her own. "I knew Fred would pick scissors."

"What?" Fred said, reanimating to life. "How could you know?"

"Whenever we play at the office, you always go with scissors on the first round." Alina looked at me and winked. "Also, I figured you would either go with rock or scissors in the first round. So, I went rock, which would defeat you both in one fell swoop, or at least eliminate one of you."

"How did you know I wouldn't pick paper?"

"Same reason you didn't in the second round."

"Which is?"

"It's too risky."

"That makes no sense," I said. "It's a game of matched probabilities. Equal chance."

"No, she's right," Fred said.

"She's not right."

"She is."

Thankfully, before he could dive into a nonsensical explanation that I would pay little to no attention to, another character sprinted toward the lean-to, wielding a flail.

"I have a battle to win," Alina said, throwing her hood back over her head and drawing her foam daggers.

Fred and I exited the battlefield, our postures stooped. We returned to the wooden table after he ordered another beer and a plate of onion rings, and we sat on the same bench and watched the game progress, watched as Alina mowed her way through the contest, defeating one player after another.

Neither of us were even remotely shocked when the half-elf rogue was crowned victorious.

Holly Hanson. Monday, October 23rd. 1433hrs.

Strong hands wrapped around Alina's waist and pinched at her, and a loud voice shouted, "Boo!"

She squirmed from the uncomfortable, slightly ticklish grip, her heart rate a tick faster than baseline.

Rhett stood tall and gangly, his hair too long, frizzy, and unkempt. But he wore a disarming smile and possessed an air of easy-going confidence. When Alina returned to campus and quit the independent study program, he had re-enrolled as a senior, hoping to graduate.

They stood in the high school hallway, lockers lining the walls. Students flowed past them, heading to their next class before the bell chimed.

Alina and Rhett had a study hall, though, and the teacher, Mrs. Yang, didn't take attendance. She understood it was the last period of the school day for a class filled with juniors and seniors. As long as they were eighteen or went through the proper channels to sign out of school early, Mrs. Yang didn't ask questions.

Alina rarely skipped, preferring to use the library's resources to finish her assignments and work on research tasks for August or Maya.

"I thought you were going to get a haircut," Alina said, adjusting her backpack over her shoulders and heading off toward the study hall library.

Rhett ran his hand through his tangly mess of hair and padded after Alina. "Why don't you just ask me to chop off my arm while I'm at it?"

Alina rolled her eyes. "Can you not comb it at least?"

"Can you not wear tight cut-off jeans and a rolled up flannel shirt only making use of one button?"

"If you get a haircut, I'll wear whatever you want me to."

Rhett frowned and shook his head. "I'm sorry, sugar. It's not worth it to me."

"Well, what about a little shampoo and conditioner? You smell like a wet dog."

"I do wash my hair."

"With what? Body soap?"

"It's a 3-1 soap. Speaking of 3-1 soaps and crazy hair, how did your LARP tournament go yesterday?"

Alina snickered, thinking of how she had snuck up on August and Fred and dismantled them. "I only played in the hunger games game."

"You won?"

"Come on. Do you have to ask?"

"Just being polite." Rhett jogged a few steps forward, grabbed the library door, and opened it for Alina. "My lady, my champion, my queen in daisy dukes, after you."

The usually quiet space buzzed with excitement. Two-dozen students crowded together, speaking over each other, staring at their phones.

Mrs. Yang stood off to the side a few feet, staring at her phone's screen, her mouth agape as her eyes scanned behind her glasses.

Rhett whistled at the scene. "I haven't seen people this excited since the crowd waiting for me when I returned from the Minotaur's island. You know how many autographs I signed that day? You know how many book and movie deals I turned down? Some bigwig director said they didn't know who to play me, though, because no one in Hollywood is this good looking."

Alina ignored Rhett and circled around the crowd of students and approached Mrs. Yang—a forty-something, slender, athletic history teacher. She would occasionally join in on pickup basketball games in the school's gymnasium and embarrass the boys on the varsity team.

"Hey, Mrs. Yang," Alina said. "What's going on?"

The woman had a soft, inviting demeanor and a warm face. When she shifted her attention from the screen to Alina, though, a strange distance—a chill—emanated from her. For a second, Alina thought the woman might snap at her, turn her away.

"It's Ronald Greene," Mrs. Yang said, her tone sad.

Ronald, or Ronnie, Greene, a senior and golf star for Pleasant Valley High School, was one of those kids everyone loved to know. He cared for other students and teachers. He was respectful, thoughtful, funny, intelligent, and kind. No one, no matter if they belonged to the jocks, nerds, goths, preps, or any social clique in between, ever had a bad word to say about Ronnie.

Alina liked him fine, though she hardly knew him, but she thought he was too perfect—no notable flaws, no record of wrong, nothing that made him relatable or human.

"What about him?" Alina asked, glancing at the huddle of students.

Rhett had slipped into the mass, shoved his way forward and peered over someone's shoulder at their phone.

"He went missing over the weekend," Mrs. Yang said.

Alina sucked in a breath, held it deep in her core, and released it slowly through a whispered question. "How did he go missing?"

Mrs. Yang touched a loose strand of hair cutting across her vision, but she did nothing with it—she didn't tuck it behind her ear or fold it against the rest of her put up hair. She twisted it between her thumb and index finger before releasing it, allowing it to dangle over her face, sharp and skinny as a stiletto.

"I'm not sure," she said after a moment. "Apparently, according to this," Mrs. Yang handed Alina her phone, "it happened Saturday night."

The screen showed a *Sacramento Bee* article, written by a reporter Alina had never heard of: Audrey Peterson.

In effect, it said Ronald Benson Greene told his Mother he had a date on Saturday night—dinner and a movie in the IMAX theater. No further information provided details about where they ate, what movie they watched, or who he went on a date with. Ronnie didn't come home Saturday night, nor did he return Sunday morning. When his phone stopped ringing and went straight to voicemail, his parents contacted the Sacramento Police Department.

"I've read it a dozen times," Mrs. Yang said. "It makes no sense to me."

"What do you mean?"

"Ronnie has a vast network of friends and contacts. Yet, they don't have any idea where he went to dinner, what movie he saw, or who he went out with? Surely someone would have stepped forward by now, someone Ronnie confided in?"

Alina handed Mrs. Yang her phone back, saying nothing. Her thoughts sprinted through her mind.

"That's not the strangest part, though."

Alina's eyes focused on her study hall teacher.

Mrs. Yang tapped the phone's screen a few times, then she handed it back to Alina. She had pulled up another article, written by Jonah Daniels, the editor of *Here & Now*.

Alina read it, re-read it. When she finished her third read through, she offered Mrs. Yang the phone and stared distantly out the window at the sunny afternoon and the parking lot. The library, the students, the din of worried and speculative conversation melded together and formed a static background noise. Alina had fallen into herself, into the article written by Jonah Daniels, Maya's old boss, the editor of a tabloid reporting the supernatural as natural occurrences and as truth.

"You don't believe this, do you?" Alina asked, returning to the present, to the library, to the students who had dispersed and returned to their lives like the last five minutes hadn't happened.

"I don't know." Mrs. Yang hugged herself and shook her head. "I knew Grace, though. My first year as a teacher, she was in my American History class."

A firm hand squeezed Alina's waist, and warm breath fumed against her cheek. "I'm going to eat your brains." Rhett made chomping noises, grating his teeth against her ear and face.

Alina jumped, startled, and shooed him away, like swatting a pesky wasp. "What's wrong with you?"

Rhett sputtered in a high-pitched, forced laugh. "You're usually not jumpy. What's going on with you today?"

"What's wrong with you? Ronnie has gone missing, and you're messing around."

Rhett threw up his arms and scrunched his face. "What? Seriously? What do you want me to do, sit around and mope until he's found? It sucks. Hopefully, it's not tragic. But you expect me to act like a sad boy until we know what happened to him?"

"I expect you not to read terrible news one second, then turn around and act like a goof the next."

"First you want me to look civilized, now you want me to act civilized. If I didn't know any better, Ms. Moore, I might think you're trying to change me, which means you don't like me for me." He stuck out his lower lip in a classic pout.

"Did you see the *Here & Now* article?"

"I don't read fiction, remember? I barely read news headlines. Why? Did the crazy writers over there have a hot, crazy take about what happened to Ronnie? Was it aliens? I've told you over and again, aliens are into probing human butts." He glanced at Mrs. Yang and covered his mouth. "I'm sorry for talking about butts. I didn't see you there."

Mrs. Yang offered a slight, dismissive nod and walked to her desk.

"What's the word, bird?" Rhett asked, bouncing from foot to foot. "What did our hyper-reliable tabloid say about Ronnie?"

"An anonymous caller contacted the Sacramento Police. They said Ronnie went on a date with Holly Hanson."

"You're kidding me? Good for him. Wait." Rhett lifted his chin and scratched beneath it. "Is Holly Hanson the cheerleader whose thong always peeks out the top of her pants? When it's not showing, it's a pretty reliable sign she's not wearing any panties at all?"

Alina blinked hard for a few seconds, not sure what to say.

"Nope. I'm sorry. That's Jamie Davis."

"Those names aren't remotely similar."

"Who's Holly Hanson, then?" Rhett snapped his fingers. "Oh! She's that super smart chick going to Harvard next year, with the..." Rhett cupped his hands over his chest, pulling them away to signify size. "But she always hides them in boy T-shirts or hoodies? She's, like, that girl who, at the ten-year reunion, will have a massive glow-up, and all the dudes will kick themselves for not taking their shot. You know? Like that one chick from that one movie."

"Thanks for narrowing down that one chick from that one movie. I know exactly who and what you're talking about."

"Really?"

"Unfortunately, I do."

"Remind me of the names?"

"No."

"That's messed up."

"Also, you're thinking of Wesley Lewis."

Rhett exhaled, vibrating air through his lips. "Yeah, you're right. Who names their daughter Wesley, anyway?"

"I like that name for a girl."

"You also like the name Lincoln for a girl. Anyway, who's the Holly girl?"

"Holly Hanson," Alina said. "She attended this high school ten years ago."

"What?" Rhett asked, leaning back and holding the vowel for too long. "Ronnie boy caught himself a cougar? That guy doesn't miss."

"Can I, please, just talk without you interrupting?"

Rhett ran a hand across his lips, zipping them closed.

"Thank you," Alina said, exhaling a gust of frustration. "Holly Hanson died her junior year of high school, while here at school."

Rhett raised his hand and chewed on his lips.

"What?" Alina asked.

"Can I talk?"

"I just called on you."

"Where and how did she die? Only curious because I'm deathly afraid of ghosts, and if there's a ghost on campus, I'm going to reconsider my bid to graduate."

"I don't know those details. The article didn't say. I know she died on campus. The anonymous caller said Ronnie went out with Holly Hanson, a student at our school."

"Well, Alina, it was an absolute honor to know you. We had a good run. Um, we tried our best, and that's all anyone can do. But a high school diploma isn't worth attending a haunted high school. So, yeah. For the second time in my life, I'm dropping out."

"Don't be an idiot. The school isn't haunted."

Rhett glanced over his shoulder before leaning in and lowering his voice so only Alina could hear him. "Either Ronnie courted a ghost, or he lost his mind and thought he saw a ghost."

"You just said the *Here & Now* is fiction."

"What do you think, then?"

Alina kicked her toes against the floor and thought. "I'm not sure what to think, but I don't believe in ghosts."

"Yet, after a romantic date with a dead girl, Ronnie has gone missing."

"Supposedly," Alina said. "Obviously, the police didn't consider the anonymous call important enough to mention in their press conference. They don't have any leads, which makes me think they immediately discredited the idea of Ronnie dating a ghost. Also, Jonah Daniels has a moral compass that doesn't point north. He could have made up the entire story about the anonymous caller to capitalize on a trending tragedy in our area."

Rhett crossed his arms and looked Alina square in the eyes. "We're going full Scooby-Doo, aren't we? We're investigating this disappearance?"

"Yup."

Rhett cleared his throat. "I went into this study hall nervous about asking you to the Halloween dance. Turns out, that was the least of my concerns."

Alina snickered, though her demeanor brightened. She gently punched Rhett on his shoulder. "You're an idiot. You were going to ask me to the dance? I thought you hate dancing, and the idea of school dances, and Halloween?"

"Yes, to all of that. But I like you as much, probably more, than I hate all that other stuff combined."

Alina stepped forward and rose on tiptoes. She kissed Rhett on the side of his mouth. "I would love to go to the dance with you, but only under one condition."

Rhett aggressively shook his head. "Nope. I know your condition. I know what you're going to require. My answer is no. I like you a lot, and I enjoy being your boyfriend, but I have my lines. I will not, under any circumstances, wear a costume."

Alina aired out a knowing giggle. "I'm going as Freddy Krueger."

"A slutty Freddy Krueger?"

"You're going as Jason Voorhees."

"I don't know who that person is, but I'm not doing it."

Alina popped up on her toes and quickly kissed him again. "I can't wait! Now that we have that settled, we have other matters to attend. The game is afoot."

"Ah," Rhett said with a cheap smile, "Fred, right?"

"What?"

"That's what Fred from *Scooby-Doo* says all the time. The game is a foot. What does that even mean? How can a game be a foot?"

"Not like feet, you moron. Afoot."

"That's what I said."

"Afoot, one word. It means, like, happening or beginning to happen. The game is in progress."

"Why doesn't Fred just say, like, game on, or something?"

"Oh, my God. I'm going to murder you. Fred doesn't say it."

"Then why did you say he did?"

"I didn't say that, you said it." Alina bit back a scream and wheeled around. "I'm done with this, and I'm going to look into Ronnie's disappearance now."

"Ah. You're going afoot, looking into Ronnie's disappearance."

Alina ignored him as she walked away. She couldn't help but shed a warm smile.

Free of Charge. Monday, October 23rd. 1448hrs.

"I STILL CAN'T BELIEVE we lost to Alina," Fred said. He sat across the office, behind his reception desk. The top of his head just breeched the high counter. A chip bag crumpled, followed by aggressive mastication. "We're two grown men. You don't think, realistically, we could defeat a puny girl? It's ridiculous."

I sat at my desk and read through the updated report on William Derry, the Invisible Thief, as the headlines dubbed him—a rather generous and ego-stroking name for a criminal, especially considering we noticed and caught him.

"Are you listening to me?" Fred asked.

"Not really."

"You don't care?"

"About what?"

"The realism of the game? It makes no sense."

"We took part in a LARP event. None of it made any sense."

"She weighs, what, a buck-fifteen at most. I'm in a cutting phase, and I'm Slim Jim compared to what I usually weigh, and I'm still at two-fifty. You're how much? A buck-eighty, -ninety? Add that up. We're two grown, physically fit, muscular, handsome men. She's a single, tiny human being who can't curl twenty pounds. You're expecting me to accept we lost in a two-on-one fight against her?"

I looked up from my computer and stared at the top of Fred's head. "I saw someone throw rainbow-colored sand at a group of five people, and they all pretended like they fell victim to the paralyzing effects of a spell."

"That's magic!" Fred said, bolting to his feet and staring at me. "Magic. It's believable."

I frowned and cocked my head to the side.

"A little girl defeating two grown men in hand-to-hand combat isn't believable."

"We're really stretching how we define believable, aren't we?" I asked. "Do you know what's not believable? That I'm having this conversation with you."

"It just makes no sense," Fred said, collapsing back into his chair. He continued speaking, but quietly, mumbling beneath his breath, probably blaming me for the defeat. It was my job to keep an eye out for any threats, yet, somehow, Alina had surprised us.

Before Fred could build more momentum and continue with his complaints, a knock sounded on the office door.

A second later, the door slivered open, and the head of a forty-something year-old man poked through. He had brown hair freckled with gray and heavy, tired eyes sitting within a pale, fleshy, sickly looking face.

"Come in." I stood and stepped toward him.

"Are you August Watson?" he asked, his voice like sandpaper scraping against stone.

"I am. May I help you?"

"I'm Doug Kosar. I left you a few voicemails about my house..." he trailed off, which didn't surprise me.

Most of my clients, when they first presented their plights to me, stuttered and stammered, as if they didn't believe or refused to believe, refused to speak aloud, that a paranormal entity harassed them.

"I think my house is haunted," he said, dropping his gaze to the floor. "Worse, I believe that whatever demon has cursed my home has also possessed my stepdaughter. My wife and I, we're desperate." He lifted his eyes and looked at me, though I could sense his embarrassment and hesitancy. "We need help, and no one can help."

I glanced at Fred, who stood again. He shrugged. I tightened my lips and nodded.

"Have a seat," I said, gesturing to the client chairs I had set before my desk. "Would you like something to drink? We have water or coffee."

"No, but thank you." Doug shuffled forward and stiffly sat, his back pinned to the backrest, his arms at a ninety-degree angle atop the armrest.

"Doug." I found my chair and dropped into it, rolled it forward, and planted my elbows on my desk. "I don't want to waste your time, so I'm going to speak the hard truth up front. You're here because you've heard of me, you've heard of Tempest Michaels, or you're aware of the Blue Moon Investigative franchise." I paused and licked my lips. "Blue Moon has taken on and solved more than a handful of high-end, complicated cases. Because of that, we've earned a reputation, and we've become quite desirable. I have the luxury to pick which cases I investigate. Interest, of course, is a priority, as is compensation."

Doug looked at his lap and nodded.

"In your voicemails, you stated you don't have the finances to stay in a hotel. That concerns me."

He swallowed and nodded, but he didn't say a word.

"What do you do for a living?" I asked, hoping to break the tension that pulled him tight.

"I'm a general contractor. That's why I bought the house. It was on the market for dirt cheap. It needed some work, and I figured I could make the updates myself, save some money."

"But the house, haunted, prevented you from making the updates?"

"No, nothing like that. I made them. We moved in—my wife, step-daughter, dog, and me. It was after we moved in that... God, it sounds so silly to say out loud in a public space."

"It's a safe space," I said. "A space where I encourage you to share anything and everything, because the more information I have, the better equipped I am."

Doug sighed, not out of relief, either; more like someone sighing as they resign themselves to do something they would rather not. "Only after we moved in did we realize it was haunted, possessed by some malevolent entity. I never believed in anything like that. Hell, I still have a hard time accepting it. But there's no other explanation."

"You've sought help?"

"We had a priest bless and cleanse the home before we moved in. We contacted demonologists. Nothing has worked."

I rubbed the back of my neck. "What do you want me to do?"

"Find out what's going on. Give us an answer. You investigate the paranormal, right? You stop monsters from hurting people. Well, I want you to do that. I want you to protect my family."

"Move out of the house," I said. "That's how you protect your family."

"What about Emily?" Doug's voice rose. "She's possessed. She's sick. Moving won't fix her."

"It might help her."

"Where will we go?"

"I don't know."

"You can't help us, can you? You're like all the others. A charlatan. A fraud. You exploit other people's fears and grief for personal gain."

I clicked my tongue and considered his outburst. "Doug, my concern is twofold. My primary reason for hesitancy is commercial. Can you pay me for my time?"

He chuckled, more of a disbelieving, flabbergasted laugh than one bearing any root in amusement.

"My second concern rests squarely on the idea that the paranormal doesn't exist. Have you brought your daughter to a mental-health professional, someone who has experience and authority in situations like these? Move out of the house, build separation, find your daughter someone to speak to."

Doug roared to his feet, planting his hands on the desk, leaning forward and glaring at me. "I came here based on your reputation, that you care for your clients, that you care to help them."

"Doug, I'm afraid this case will waste both our times. I'm trying to help you the best I can."

"Then help me. Hear me. Listen to me."

I inhaled, allowing the air to burn in my lungs for a second before exhaling. "Okay. I'll listen. Tell me your story, beginning to end. If you change my mind, I'll investigate... free, too."

"You're serious?"

I nodded. "The floor belongs to you, Mr. Kosar."

Doug slowly returned to the chair. He shifted his head and stared out the window overlooking the side alley. "We've been there eighteen days. On the first night..."

Day One. Friday, October 6th. 1151hrs.

Doug climbed onto the front porch and stepped far enough into the house to close the door. Kathleen accompanied Father Hartke, guiding him from room to room as he blessed the home.

"Amen," she said. Doug could hear her emphatically agreeing with the priest's prayers from the other side of the house. "Thanks be to God!"

As the priest and his wife climbed the stairs to the second floor, Doug stepped outside for fresh air. Religion was a large and difficult pill for him to swallow. His mother had raised him in a fierce Baptist church, and organized religion played a discordant tune in every facet of childhood—including his mother's untimely death.

Marianne prayed fervently and constantly. Doug's dad had jumped ship for a younger woman who hadn't birthed him four children, but Marianne took the abandonment in stride, believing her God would provide. Her God had provided her with an aggressive form of cancer five years later. She and her four children, ranging from the ages of six to sixteen—Doug being the oldest—resorted to prayer.

Prayer resulted in Marianne Kosar dying six months after her diagnosis. Doug prayed their father would come back and take them in, but the man was a ghost, present only in haunting Doug's soul.

The experience of witnessing his mother, frail and pale and withering, on her knees more hours out of the day than any other position and begging God to heal her had jaded Doug.

If anyone deserved an answered prayer, God should have listened and answered Marianne's prayers. Yet, he had ignored her pleas, if he had heard them at all. His loud, demanding absence had driven Doug from the church, and he hadn't returned for over twenty years.

"You okay?" Emily sat in her wheelchair off the side of the front porch, petting Frank's hulking head. "You look lost."

"I'm fine," Doug said. "I just... I don't believe in any of that stuff." He nodded at the house which boxed in Father Hartke and Kathleen. "You're not going with them?" Doug leaned against one of the two porch columns supporting the overhang.

"I don't believe any of that stuff either."

Doug smirked and nodded with excitement. He and Emily hadn't connected, hadn't spent too much time together in the eighteen months he and Kathleen had been husband and wife. Doug carried the blame. He had made little to no effort with his stepdaughter, spending most of his free time pursuing jobs to jumpstart his floundering business.

"We'd probably screw up whatever blessing they're intending to incur," Emily said.

"You and your mom go to church every Sunday. I assumed you both believed."

Emily scoffed and rolled her eyes. "It's more like she drags me to church every Sunday. I tell her it's all a dumb fairytale, but I'm thinking that's the wrong approach now."

"Why's that?"

"I'm just convincing her she needs to keep taking me so I find God, or God finds me, or however it works."

Doug chuckled and glanced at the wheelchair ramp he had installed. "What do you think of that? You get up it okay?"

Before Emily could answer, Frank released a deep, protective bark, burst from his prone position, and bolted around the corner of the house.

"Frank!" Emily called, rolling her chair through the gravel and ruts with a concerted effort.

Frank continued barking—aggressive, cornered barking.

Doug hopped off the front porch and hustled around the corner of the house, leaving Emily stuck in the driveway behind him.

Frank barked incessantly at the side of the house, jumping against the exterior wall, standing on hind legs, slobbering against the newly installed windows.

Frank was Emily's dog and only friend or companion—apart from Kathleen's constant doting. Doug mostly avoided the Rottweiler, and he didn't feel confident approaching the one hundred-twenty pound, frenzied animal.

Instead, he kept a safe distance and called the dog's name, keeping his voice low and calm. "Frank. Frank, it's all good. It's Kathy and a friend in there. It's okay."

The Rottweiler growled, a menacing sound deep within its chest.

"Just Kathy and the priest in there."

"He's been a little on edge since we've moved here," Emily said. She wheeled up beside Doug, rolling easier on the level lawn than the uneven gravel. "He's never barked in his life, never really even growled. You've heard him these past few nights, though, right? He's barking at shadows."

Doug had noticed the dog seemed more on edge than usual. He chalked it up to the big canine sleeping outdoors rather than inside their apartment, to jumping at every cricket serenade and hoot of an owl. Besides, Frank didn't really bark but whimper a high-pitched, almost cry. It was different, at least, from the aggressive barking he'd just performed.

"I Googled it." Emily worked her way over to Frank, surrendered to the effort about halfway to him, and called the dog over.

Frank obeyed after a second of hesitation.

"Googled what?" Doug asked.

"Why he's barking."

"Nerves?"

"Exactly. He's probably developed an anxiety from the move, from living in this strange environment. Also, you're making him sleep outside. He's never slept outside a day in his life."

"Just until we're in the house and out of the RV," Doug said.

Emily nodded her agreement. "I know, I know. It's just... it's probably contributing to his behavior. Mom doesn't help, either."

Doug chuckled without having to ask for an explanation.

Emily gave one anyway, as if she spoke to vent rather than explain. "She's gotten worse with me since we've moved. I know you're working all day and most of the night in the house, getting it ready for us, so I'm not sure you've noticed, but she's not hovering. She's leeching onto me like a parasite. I'm surprised she left me out here alone right now."

Doug grunted, an acknowledging sound letting Emily know he had heard her.

"Anyway," the teenager said, shaking her head as if shaking away the thought, "The few articles I read said the dog, once acclimated to a new place, should settle down again."

"Are you nervous being here?" Doug asked, looking at the windows on the side of the house where Frank had shared his displeasure.

He thought of the face he had seen in the attic window.

"I mean, yeah. I've never lived anywhere but in that apartment. Well, I guess I lived in a house with my dad before he died, but I don't remember any of it. Mom and I moved out before I turned one; we moved into the apartment. Not long after we moved in, Mom brought Frank home. So, we've known nothing but that apartment." She smiled, but it looked sad and longing.

"I can see why this is scary," Doug said. "We're in the country, with nothing around, living in an RV beside an old home. If I'm being honest, I'm a little nervous myself."

"You are?"

"Yeah. We're taking a giant risk to live here, especially financially. To fail could really hurt us."

"How so?"

Doug gave a half-hearted shrug. "You can't tell your mom I'm telling you any of this. She would kill me."

"My lips are sealed." Emily ran her fingers across her mouth, zipping her lips.

Doug sighed and glanced at the blue October sky. "Well, we spent every dollar we had to purchase and upgrade this place—to make it a home for our family. If something goes wrong, we won't have anywhere to go. That's scary. That's really scary."

"What could go wrong?"

"A lot of things. It's an old house, you know? Maybe we're here a year before the copper pipes crap out and we have to remove and replace them. There are several things that can go wrong. I patched up the roof, but I doubt it'll prevent a windstorm from tearing it all apart again. So, I'm scared."

"What about work?"

Doug licked his lips and wiped his palms on his jeans. He hadn't shared the entire truth with Kathleen about his work. What could he tell his stepdaughter?

"What about it?" he asked.

"Can't you save some money, put it away in a rainy-day fund?"

If only it were that easy.

"I could, sure. But there's not much in the way of saving right now. We have the mortgage, all our insurances, food, gas, your medical bills." He stopped and looked at his stepdaughter with regret, hating that he had accidentally blamed their financial burden on her. He placed a hand on her shoulder. "I didn't mean it like that. I'm sorry. These are all things I would gladly pay twice as much for. All I'm saying is the house, the upgrades, the move… it's all additional expenses on a bank account already overdrawn."

"What about your books?"

Doug chuckled, tickled with amusement. "My books?"

"I've heard you tell mom you want to write true crime stories about the recent events that happened in Sacramento. The Vampire and Golem and Minotaur. That's a great idea."

Doug nodded. "Sure. Except, that will take time and money, too. I can't Google information for a book like that. It requires travel expenses, interviewing the people involved, speaking to detectives."

He knew what he was doing. Whining. Making excuses. And he hated himself for it, for appearing so cowardly in front of his stepdaughter. But no one had asked him how he felt about moving into the house, and his feelings, once tapped, now gushed outward without resistance. Living there was a dream come true, but it walked the thin line of being a nightmare, too.

"What do you think made him upset?" Emily asked.

"Who?"

"Frank."

Doug glanced at the dog, who lay on the ground at Emily's feet, calm now that his owner had arrived. "He probably saw your mom and the priest walk by the window, mistook them for strangers. Strange place, as you said. It's easy to feel vulnerable."

He ambled to the stack of boxes Kathleen had placed outside the RV, grabbed one, and headed back to the front door.

"You going to lend a hand?" Doug called over his shoulder. "I put a ramp there for a reason, you know?"

"Yeah, yeah, yeah. What about the gravel, though? You going to do something about that?"

Day Two. Saturday, October 7th. 0331hrs.

Doug jolted awake as a surge of primal energy shot through him. Darkness inked the master bedroom. Moonlight struggled to bleed through the dual windows behind the nightstands. Outside, contrasted to the afternoon before, heavy, rain-soaked clouds blotted out the moon and stars.

Had sky-shattering thunder drawn him from his sleep?

Doug waited in the dark for a flash of lightning to confirm the source of his sudden arousal. Beside him, Kathleen quietly snored, unperturbed by whatever had startled him awake.

Had he snapped awake after a bad dream? Possibly, but Doug didn't have any recollection, not even the fading, crinkling, half-baked images of a dissipating nightmare. Sweat didn't bead on his skin or soak the sheets, as it often did after he escaped a night terror, and he didn't exist in a state of panic and shock.

If not a bad dream or thunder, what had awakened him?

Not feeling the desperate urge to urinate, Doug eliminated any intrinsic, natural triggers. Something external, outside his body and mind, had brought him to consciousness.

Doug held his breath and listened as thoughts of the face in the attic window tormented him. After a minute of silence, he swept his feet out of the bed and touched the cold hardwood running across his bedroom floor.

With a slow, deliberate gait, he snuck through the door and into the hallway, following the sightless corridor into the kitchen. He wore nothing but his boxers, and he shivered from the deep chill permeating throughout the house.

Doug flicked the switch on the wall, and light exploded through the deep darkness, temporarily blinding him. He blinked a few times, allowing his sight to adjust. As it did, a heavy pressure settled on his chest, making it difficult to breathe.

The kitchen lay in a state of complete bedlam.

The food, which Kathleen had organized into the refrigerator and the pantry after Father Hartke finished blessing and cleansing the home, lay upturned, spilled, spread in puddles and piles across the tile floor. Dishes, which Kathleen had left in their boxes, deciding to organize them in cupboards the next day, lay in a thousand pieces.

Doug's favorite coffee mug (it bore the inscription, Size Matters, and had an image of an eight-inch ruler measuring vertically) lay beside his and Kathleen's wedding china, the entire collection shattered beyond repair. The wine and alcohol bottles, the milk and juice containers, the soda and beer cans lay empty, their contents dumped amongst the rubble on the ground.

He stood in the doorway, stupefied, rooted in place as his body adjusted to the sudden waking, his eyes adjusted to the sudden light, his mind adjusted to the unexplainable disaster before him.

Someone vandalized his kitchen. At least it explained what had drawn him from his sleep in a near-panic. He could strike that mystery off his ever-growing list of concerns.

Doug navigated around the mess to the sink. The water streamed from the faucet, steaming and scalding hot. Doug switched it off and padded to the refrigerator, closing the door and shutting the freezer drawer.

A few beer cans lay on their sides and trickled fizzy foam across the countertops. He picked up a half-empty can, cracked the pull tab, and drank what remained, hoping the alcohol would clear the sleep from his mind and help him swallow what had happened in the kitchen.

A series of shuddering chills racked his naked body. He walked to the upturned trashcan, righted it, and threw away the empty beer can. Then he moved into the hallway to check the thermometer.

Off

Doug turned the heat on and thought of Kathleen and Emily. If someone had broken into their home, why ransack the kitchen?

Would they have ulterior motives?

Frank barked, loud and rupturing.

A dark fear gripped him like writhing, powerful tentacles, wrapped around his throat, his chest, his legs. He stood cemented for a moment before launching down the hallway to the stairwell, terror propelling him.

Emily, despite Kathleen's abject objections to the idea, claimed her room upstairs. Doug had spent two days installing the electric lift to assist her up the steps—yet another expense they couldn't afford.

When he reached the top of the stairwell, he romped through the hallway and burst through his stepdaughter's door.

She screamed.

Doug flicked on the light.

For a moment, nothing but confusion existed—disorientation as light chased out the darkness, murkiness of the situation, of what Doug would discover, of who had entered Emily's room.

When nerves and the dust of the mental skirmish settled, Doug exhaled.

Emily sat up in her bed. She wore a mask of pure panic and helplessness. "What's going on?" she asked, her voice swallowed by sobs and Frank's ceaseless barking.

Doug drifted into her room and sat on the edge of her bed. He pulled her into him and hugged her as he stared out the window into the darkness. He fostered doubt and concern, and when he spoke, he spoke more to himself than to her. "It's okay. We're okay."

The dog stopped barking, though it continued to growl at the door as it lay on the foot of Emily's bed.

"What happened?" Emily asked. "I heard glass breaking—like a lot of glass. I didn't know what to do, not that I could do anything but lay here and scream and hope you or mom heard me and came up here to help me."

Doug shushed her, like calming a fussy baby. "I'm here now. It's okay." He held her as she cried. When her sobs subsided, he pulled away. "Did anyone come up here?"

"Like, who?"

"Anyone."

"I don't think so."

"I'm going to check every room and closet in this house, okay?"

"Please, don't leave me here alone."

"Of course not. I'll—"

"Emily!" Kathleen thundered across the room to her daughter's bed, nearly tackling the young woman. She grabbed Emily's face, squeezing her cheeks. "Are you okay? What happened? Was it Doug? Did he hurt you?"

Doug slowly removed himself from the bed and shuffled away until his back touched the window's cool pane of glass.

Had his wife insinuated he had—no, that he could—cause harm to Emily, that he was capable of such an act?

"What?" Emily asked.

"Did he hurt you?"

"No."

Kathleen glared at her husband with venom and dark, malevolent hatred. "Get out of her room! Now! Leave!"

"Mom, he did nothing but check on me."

"Get out!" Kathleen's high-pitched wail triggered Frank, and the dog broke into a frenzied bark once more.

Doug, too shocked and overwhelmed to respond, exited the room, closing the door behind him.

In a daze, a listless stupor, he moseyed around the upstairs, checking for any signs of further disturbance and searching for a hiding intruder.

When he cleared the second story, he continued his investigation downstairs.

There was no other destruction apart from the kitchen. Every single window, apart from his master bedroom, in the downstairs portion of the home was open, though, as were the back and front doors.

Doug went window to window, closing and locking each one, then he returned to the kitchen and cleaned the mess.

Eventually, morning sunlight wrapped around the storm clouds, illuminating the edges, turning them a darker gray against the bruised purples and blues. Doug hopped into his work truck and drove to town. He bought coffee and bagels before returning to the house.

When he stepped into the kitchen, Emily and Kathleen still hadn't come downstairs. Doug sat at the dining room table alone, eating his bagel and sipping his coffee in heavy silence.

Above him, the chandelier caught traces of the morning sunlight. The diamonds threw reflections and refractions around the room. It all felt surreal. The strange, dark beauty of the morning contrasted with the kaleidoscope of diamond light.

Doug focused his drifting thoughts.

What had happened last night?

The foremost concern, the one that haunted him most, was the doors and windows left wide open. Doug had locked everything before going to bed. He made sure of it. Kathleen had a tiresome streak of paranoia, a fearful and worrisome nature, and Doug knew, had made a habit, to double-check the security of the house.

Yet, there weren't any signs of a break-in.

Again, he thought of the face in the window from five weeks prior, of the noise in the attic, of its absolute emptiness.

How would someone have snuck into the home? Why would they have snuck into the home?

Doug came up with four solutions as he finished his coffee.

Kathleen, already upset with their move, worked to sabotage the experience. She woke up, opened all the windows and doors after turning off the thermostat, and wreaked havoc on the kitchen. When she finished her rampage, she crawled back in bed, quiet as a mouse, and feigned sleep.

Doug struggled to buy that theory. He woke because of the disruption in the kitchen, from dishes shattering against the walls and floor.

Second, someone squatted in their house. That person was upset now that the Kosar family moved in. On their tour of the house, Doug had seen a man's face, though the man had somehow escaped discovery that day.

That possibility seemed as farfetched as Kathleen orchestrating the affair, though. If someone secretly squatted here, Doug would have found proof during his remodel. Apart from the furniture and a few knick knacks left by the previous owners, nothing suggested someone squatted in the home.

Third, the previous owners or someone who knew them had a key to the house. For whatever reason, they wished to sabotage the Kosars' move-in experience.

Doug didn't spend too much time on that theory. He would run to the hardware store, buy new locks, and install them on every door. Easy fix.

Fourth, and most absurd, some spirit or entity lived in the home. The Kosars had disrupted its existence, making it upset.

He dismissed that as quickly as it popped into his mind. The residual fear and absurdity from last night, mixed with Kathleen's paranoia and the need to have a priest bless and purify the house, messed with Doug's mind. Ghosts or spirits didn't exist. Period.

Where did that leave him?

Each possibility felt less and less likely.

Doug, after consideration, was more confused than before.

"Hey," Kathleen said. She stood in the dining room doorway, her arms crossed over her chest

"I bought you coffee and breakfast."

"Thank you." She leaned against the wall. "Can I sit with you?"

"Of course."

Kathleen spared a broken smile before moving to the table and taking a seat. She cupped her coffee with both palms and stared out the picture window. "I'm sorry for what happened."

Doug blinked and nodded, not wanting to accept her apology, not caring to forgive her. She had assumed he, her husband, was doing something inappropriate with her daughter. That spoke marriage-altering volumes about how she thought of him, about the trust she had in him.

"I was afraid," she said. "I woke up cold and alone."

"How did you sleep through it?" Doug asked, a touch of accusation in his voice.

"I had my earbuds in because I kept imagining footsteps upstairs. At one point, I went up to check. Emily was sleeping, not that she could walk around, but... I don't know. I put my earbuds in and listened to a podcast to drown out the strange noises of a new home."

Doug still wanted to blame her, if not to have an answer and someone to blame. "How did you wake up, then?"

"What do you mean?"

"You ran into Emily's room, but you had your earbuds in. How did you wake up?"

She shook her head as if she didn't know the answer. "I think I woke up when you left the room. You weren't in bed, so I called your name. You didn't answer. I went into the kitchen and saw the mess, but not you. Doug, my body felt like God was squeezing the life out of me. The mess in the kitchen, all the open doors, and the cold. It was our first night in the house. I was afraid." Tears bled from her red-rimmed eyes. "When I ran up the stairs, when I saw you in her room, my fear made me think the worst."

"That I ransacked the kitchen, opened every window in the house, and went upstairs to mess around with your daughter?"

"I know it makes no sense. Nothing made sense, though. I was afraid."

"Where's Emily now?"

"Sleeping. She needed rest after what happened."

"Nothing happened."

"The kitchen? Someone broke into this place while we slept."

"This place is our home."

"No one wants to live here but you."

"Emily likes it."

"Emily doesn't know what she likes. She's sick, and she's scared, and she just doesn't know."

Doug wedged his tongue between his front teeth and gums, shielding himself from saying something hurtful.

"I'm sorry," Kathleen said after a second.

"For what?" Doug asked. "Are you sorry for destroying the kitchen?"

"What do you mean? You think I did that?"

"I don't know. I'm not sure what you're sorry for."

"Doug, why are you being like this?"

"Kathy, why are you apologizing? I want you to admit what you did wrong, how you hurt me, and possibly hurt your daughter."

"I would never hurt my daughter! My sole purpose in life is to protect her. You don't know what we've been through."

"You're right. I don't, because you won't open up to me. You won't share that part of your life."

"It has nothing to do with you."

"It has everything to do with me," Doug said. "I'm your husband. I need to know how to best love and support you. How can I do that if I don't know you?"

"You don't know me?"

"No," he said.

"Why did you marry me, then?"

Doug shook his head and looked directly at his wife. "Honestly, at this moment, I don't know. I can't answer you."

"That's awesome." Kathleen shrugged and stared out the window. "Great. Well, I'm going to get ready for the day. Maybe you can spend some time thinking about why you married me. Or, if it's easier for you, think of all the reasons you want to divorce me."

"Kathy," Doug said as she stood and hurried to the hallway. "I don't want a divorce." She disappeared around the corner, so he raised his voice. "I just want you to let me in!"

She didn't reply.

Doug dropped his head back and stared at the intricately carved custom ceiling, at the diamond-laced chandelier throwing speckles of sunlight across the room.

He spent the rest of the day replacing the locks on every door, installing televisions in various rooms, and unpacking boxes.

Kathleen avoided him.

Emily remained in her room the entire day, sleeping.

Day Three. Sunday, October 8th. 2137hrs.

Kathleen screamed, her voice bordering on icy terror.

Doug organized the new dishes and silverware he purchased earlier that day into the cupboards. He abandoned his task and sprinted to the living room, finding his wife rigid, one hand over her mouth, the other pointing at the dark panes of the window. Doug grabbed her and pulled her into him, his eyes never leaving his reflection in the glass.

"What happened?"

"I saw someone." Kathleen spoke in clipped, gasping breaths. "They were staring at me."

Doug stepped toward the front door. "Wait here."

"Don't leave me alone." Kathleen grabbed his forearm and squeezed, her fingernails digging into his skin.

"I have to go after him."

"Stay with me." Tears streaked down her face. "Please."

As much as he wanted to comfort her, he couldn't stand in the living room and hold his wife. He had to investigate the latest disturbance. If someone harassed his family, he had to deal with it.

Doug pulled his arm free of her grasp. "Go upstairs with Emily. Lock yourself in her room. When you're up there, call the police."

At the mention of her daughter, Kathleen's face changed from slack terror to hard resolve. "Okay."

"Don't leave her room until I knock." Doug turned and hurried out the front door, around the corner of the house, and to the living room window.

When he didn't notice anyone, he paced to the RV, stationed a few yards from the house. He walked around it, making sure no one hid behind the vehicle, before opening the door and stepping inside. He flicked the light switch, but the lights didn't turn on.

Had Kathleen disconnected the RV from the generator?

They stored a flashlight in the RV's storage cabinet. Doug grabbed it and powered it on. A bright-blue beam cut through the darkness. He stepped through the enclosed space slowly, moving intentionally, holding his breath as he searched for any signs of an intruder.

Nothing.

No one.

Doug exited and made a careful lap around the house. It rained earlier that day, softening the ground. Using the flashlight, he searched for footprints in the damp soil. He spent extra time outside the living room window where Kathleen had noticed someone looking into their home.

Once more, Doug found nothing of significance.

As he reentered the house, toeing off his muddy boots, someone leaped at him.

Doug stumbled back and yelped. He tripped over his capsized boot and fell hard. The impact sent a sharp jolt of pain up his spine, clamping his teeth against his cheeks. Blood filled his mouth.

Kathleen stood over him, covering her jaw with both hands and bearing a wild, animalistic look in her eyes—a look of primal terror. "Doug," she said, her voice a whisper.

Emily wasn't with her. That meant one thing.

Something was seriously wrong.

"What happened?" Doug asked, climbing to his feet. "Where's Emily?"

Before Kathleen could elaborate, headlights poured across their driveway, leaking through windows. A police cruiser came to a slow stop, and a broad, bald deputy sheriff stepped out. He placed one hand on his unclipped holster. Before approaching the house, the man scanned the surrounding property.

"What about Emily?" Kathleen asked, grabbing Doug's hand and jerking him around to face her.

"What about her?"

"There's something... wrong with her."

Doug touched his wife's shoulder. "Go into her room. Be with her. I'll speak to the officer."

"I don't want to be alone with her." Kathleen whispered the sentence, as if ashamed at her admittance. The words thundered off of her lips, though.

She dedicated her life and purpose to her daughter.

Kathleen didn't have a career. Her career was caring for Emily. She didn't have friends, other than Emily. She didn't have hobbies other than worrying about Emily. Kathleen's entire existence, her identity, revolved around her daughter.

For her to say she feared being alone with Emily spoke incredible, terrifying volumes.

"Is she okay?" Doug asked.

"I don't know."

"Kathy, is she okay?" He asked the same question because he didn't—in his state of confusion and fear—know how to phrase what he meant.

"I don't know!"

An aggressive knock thudded against the door. "Police!"

Doug inhaled and bit his lip, mentally counting to ten alligators before opening the front door. "Good evening."

The officer presented a bored, if not annoyed, expression on his face. "Is everything alright here?"

"My wife," Doug glanced over his shoulder and gestured at Kathleen, "believes she saw a stranger outside our window. I walked around the house, but I didn't see anyone."

The officer's square jaw and predatory eyes tightened, shadowing his features with a look of annoyance and impatience. "Is anyone hurt?"

"No," Doug said. "Not yet, at least."

"Not yet?"

"Someone broke into the house last night and—"

"Was this reported?"

"No."

"Why?"

Doug licked his lips and shook his head. His hands suddenly seemed too cumbersome and in the way. He didn't know what to do with them, so he shoved them in his pockets. "There wasn't any proof of a break-in."

"Did they steal something?"

"No."

"I'm confused, sir," said the officer who never introduced himself, whose name tag Doug couldn't read given the shadows crossing over his badge.

"That's why we never reported it. No break-in. Nothing missing. Whoever did it vandalized the kitchen. They broke our plates and threw our food around."

"Did you leave a door unlocked?"

"I'm pretty diligent at locking up."

"Could you have forgotten?"

"It's unlikely," Doug said.

"Do you remember locking up?"

Doug cupped the back of his neck and squeezed. "No."

The officer glanced over his shoulder. "Your wife saw a stranger on your property earlier?"

"Yes."

"Where?"

"Out the living room window."

"Ma'am, I'm presuming you're the wife in question."

"Yes," Kathleen said.

"Can you describe the stranger?"

"It was dark, and I didn't see him too well."

"Him? He was a male."

"I don't know for certain."

"What do you know for certain? Do you think you could have seen a shadow? Maybe your reflection?"

Kathleen wrung her hands, one over the other. "I don't know... maybe."

"That doesn't explain what happened last night," Doug said.

The officer sniffled, clearing his sinuses. "Sir, I can't speak for what happened last night, but with no evidence of a break-in, you probably left the door not only unlocked, but open. I would venture to say an animal crept into the house—"

Doug interrupted the officer with a sharp, abrasive laugh. "An animal? That's genius. Why didn't I think of it? Why didn't I come up with the idea that a raccoon snuck into my home and threw plates and bowls and glassware against the wall, dumped food onto the floor, and, for the heck of it, opened every window before scurrying away to terrorize the next home?"

"Every window was open?" the officer asked, a hint of curiosity, supplemented with amusement, planted in his voice.

"And the doors." Doug instantly regretted his admission.

"Did you open them?"

Kathleen's beady eyes bore into her husband. Doug could feel her doubts and suspicions aligning with the officer. Did she entertain the idea of Doug opening the home, airing out the dusty, acrid stench, going to bed and forgetting to close everything? Did she think an animal had wandered in, overturned their kitchen, and had left?

"Sir, you just moved into this house, correct?" the officer asked.

"Yes," Doug said, his voice weak and defeated.

"Either a family of animals nested in there before you evicted them, and they're employing some revenge. Or, and probably more likely," the officer winked, "the house is haunted. Unfortunately, I can't arrest raccoons or ghosts. If, however, you see a living human on your property, please call. I believe you have my number." The officer turned and marched to his vehicle.

Doug closed the front door and stared at the floor. He felt deflated. More concerning, he felt afraid.

Not the unknowing fear of an adult—not knowing where the next dollar or next meal would come from; not knowing about the health of a parent or the safety of a child. Doug felt the innocent, imaginative fear of a child—the bogeyman hiding behind the closet door, beneath the bed, in the dark corner where the laundry was piled onto the chair. The fear of ghosts and monsters existing.

"We need to check on Emily." Kathleen spoke beneath her breath, as if she knew she had to do something but would rather do anything else.

Doug turned, shouldered past his wife, and headed to the stairwell.

Emily sat on her bed, legs folded to her chest, arms around her shins. She stared at the wall directly across from her and rocked back and forth, mumbling gibberish beneath her breath. She was naked. Bright-pink scratch marks lined her arms and legs and face.

Doug drifted into her room. The gravity anchoring him to life and reality weakened. He placed a hand on the bedside to steady himself, to climb back to solid ground. "Emily," he said, except nothing came out of his mouth beyond a gasp. The word stuck in his constricting throat, too big to utter, requiring too much effort and strength to push through his lips.

Emily's light-brown eyes shifted, fixing on him with an animalistic, predatory gaze. A grin curled at the corners of her mouth, and she cackled—high-pitched and maniacal.

"Have you come back to finish what you started last night?" she asked in a feral tone.

Doug exhaled. Suddenly, the weightlessness reversed. Gravity doubled, tripled, quadrupled. He plunged into the deepest, darkest, coldest depths of the ocean, the pressure crushing him into atoms.

Emily fell backward onto her bed, staring at the ceiling, howling with laughter. She raised her legs and bicycle kicked them gleefully. "I'm ready. I've been waiting for you."

Doug averted his eyes, though not before noticing the scratches crisscrossing over Emily's stomach, chest, and thighs. She had clawed over every inch of her body.

Kathleen stood in the doorway of Emily's room. All the color had drained from her face. She exuded, simultaneously, an incinerating and an icy chill, and she held him in her eyes with judgement and vengeance.

"No," Doug said, finding a shadow of his voice. "She's lying."

Emily howled with laughter.

Tears streaked down Kathleen's pale, slack-jawed face.

Doug shook his head with raw deniability before rushing past his wife and leaving the room, hurrying down the steps.

Frank barked and barked and barked from behind him.

The house ran a dizzying circle around Doug, spinning like a top, like a flicked coin, twisting and twirling, slowing and wobbling, falling and lying flat.

Doug curled into a ball, staring at the living room's custom-carved wall, sobbing with fear now twofold—the imaginative fear of a child and the unknown fear of an adult.

114

Day Four.
Monday,
October 9th.
0423hrs.

Doug stepped through swampland. The air was frigid, the mud icy. Strange noises chorused around him—sounds not of the world. A chittering, a scorpion skittering up a tree or time ticking, though amplified, clicked incessantly in the background. Something moaned, its voice muffled as if screaming into the muck.

Doug's footsteps sank into the wet ground up to his knees. He struggled to release his feet, and he failed. The swamp closed around him. The strange sounds boomed, growing louder and sharper, stretching ever-nearer to him.

He went to scream, but like his feet stuck in the swamp, his voice lodged in his throat.

A banshee screeched through the mists of the cloud-laden night, its voice hungry and angry.

The rest of the swamp went silent, which proved more distressing than the unnatural noises.

Doug, now frantic, pulled at his legs to rip them free, but the sludgy earth pulled back, dragging him downward. The cold depths tightened around his waist, his chest, his neck.

An all-encompassing darkness enveloped and suffocated him.

With a last-ditch effort, he exploded upward, breaking through the muck and gasping for air.

Sweat drenched his body and soaked his sheets. He sat upright in his bed, out of breath, his heart crashing sporadically. Doug held his chest, applying pressure, as if he could physically force his heart to calm down.

Two things warred for position in his groggy mind, both terrible.

What or who had screamed in such a horrifying fashion, loud and long enough to drag Doug to the surface from the depths of his muddy slumber?

How had Emily, who had minimal use of her legs, kicked so effortlessly as she lay on her back and cackled?

Doug turned to his wife, to see if his sudden waking had woken her. Kathleen's side of the bed was cold and vacant, the pillows and sheets undisturbed. After the incident in Emily's room, Kathleen had stayed in her daughter's room, probably to draw forth the false secrets and lies.

Why had Emily said such a terrible thing? Why would she accuse Doug of something blatantly fictional?

Another piercing shriek, this one definitely outside of his nightmare, pierced the corridors of the home.

Doug winced, but endured, pinpointing the source from upstairs.

He didn't want to investigate and meet whatever new terrible mystery awaited him. He would rather pull the blankets over his head until the sun cracked through the windows and chased away the darkness. He would rather pack a bag, climb into his truck, and drive until he fell off the face of the Earth, or the engine stopped working—whichever came first.

Instead, Doug kicked the sheets off and padded out of his room, up the dreaded stairs to the second floor.

He stood behind Emily's closed door, unsure of what to do. Should he knock? Should he slowly open the door and peek inside, make sure everyone was okay?

As he contemplated, a violent thudding knocked three times from another room. Doug whirled, his eyes darting in the darkness, scanning the shadows for movement. He crept forward, moving down the hallway at a cautious pace until he turned into the guest bedroom.

In front of the window, highlighted by the sickly rays of moonlight, stood a figure. The man stood six-feet tall and possessed the corrupted, rotted face of a skull—hollow, deep-set, black eyes, a hole for a nose, and a cadaverous grin.

Doug stepped into the room to confront the figure. The person (the entity) darted away from the window, stepping fully into the darkness.

The room had a ceiling fan connected to the same switch as the light fixture. To turn off the light without shutting off the fan, too, they pulled a string. Doug blitzed toward the beaded string dangling from the fixture and pulled. Light poured through the room.

Boxes from the move filled the room, along with drop cloths covering the inherited furniture—a bed frame and two nightstands.

The stranger wasn't in the room, though. Doug didn't see anyone apart from his reflection in the dark-glass window. It wasn't a big room, either, and it had nowhere to hide.

The figure with a skull for a face had vanished.

Doug ran his hands through his messy hair and stared out the window into the night.

"What are you doing here?" Kathleen asked. The sudden sound of her familiar voice went off like a shotgun blast in his paranoid mind.

He jumped and gasped. "Jesus, Kathy."

"Why are you up here?"

"I heard a scream. I came to check it out."

She crossed her arms and stared at him with pure, white-hot anger.

"Kathy, hear me on this. I did nothing inappropriate with Emily."

"You're insinuating my daughter lied to me?"

Doug nodded with great exaggeration, emphasizing his point and his need for her to believe him. "That's exactly what I'm saying."

"Why would she lie about something like that?"

"What about the scratches on her body? Did you ask her about those?"

"Don't change the subject."

"She was kicking her legs in the air."

"You were leering at her, weren't you? Lusting over her?"

"What? No. Kathy. Something isn't right. Think about it."

"I've thought about it a lot—since you disrupted our lives and moved us here. You're not right. That's the only thing wrong here. You. You can sleep in the RV, but I don't want you in the same house as my daughter, not until I figure out what's going on with you and her. Are we clear?"

"Kathy, that's unreasonable. There's something seriously wrong here, with this house. I saw someone, too—same as you. I saw them in here."

"Enough. You came up here for Emily, didn't you? Did you really think I would leave her room, though? That I would leave her alone?"

Doug sighed, frustrated and defeated. "Did you hear the screams? They came from up here. How did you not hear the screams?"

Kathleen hugged herself, and a hint of fear mixed with anger crept into her face. "Emily screamed. She had a nightmare. Do you know why?"

He knew what she would claim.

"She relived whatever awful experience you put her through." Kathleen pawed at her face, wiping away tears. "I think you should leave now."

Doug felt his fear morph into desperation, but he suppressed it, swallowed it back. He nodded at his wife. Without another word, he went downstairs and collected a few of his belongings.

He didn't go to the RV, though. For the rest of the night, Doug walked around the house. He watched for signs of an intruder, thinking how he could best protect his family against...

Against what? A ghost?

Doug felt himself sinking deeper into the muck of the swamp. The cold, thick mud grabbed hold of him and pulled him into its dark, overbearing depths.

First Intermission. Monday, October 23rd. 1456hrs.

I CLICKED THE END of a blue pen with my thumb, popping the tip in and out. "Hold on," I said, cutting off Doug Kosar's story. "I have a few questions."

Doug cleared his throat. An expression of concern flashed across his deflated face. "I loved... still love my wife, despite everything. Further, I love Emily like a daughter. I wouldn't ever imagine hurting her."

I set the pen on my desk, stood, stretched, and shuffled to the coffee station, where I poured myself a cup. It tasted cold and bitter, but it did the trick. "Would like some?" I asked, raising my mug in the direction of where Doug sat.

He shook his head and stared at his hands, which he twisted around in his lap.

"Daphne is calling," Fred said, lifting his cell phone high in the air. "Should I take it?"

"Outside," I said, returning to my desk chair. I waited for Fred to close the office door before returning my attention to Doug. "You saw an entity inside the house? It disappeared into thin air?"

"I know how it sounds, but there's no other explanation. The room it ran into has one door in and out of it, a closet, and a window."

"And the furniture with the drop cloths?"

Doug nodded. "The window was closed, the screen still attached to the outside. The closet was open and empty."

I made a note of the occurrence. "And Emily. You said she was kicking her feet. Have you ever seen her do something like that before?"

"No. She has a mild paralysis. She can reposition her posture with some effort, but she can't... she kick or move her legs like that."

"Like what?"

"Effortlessly," Doug said.

I drank more coffee and wiped my lips, and I considered the beginning of Doug's retelling of events. "You believe some entity haunts your home and possibly possesses your stepdaughter? I want to make sure we're on the same page so I can help you to the best of my abilities."

"Right now, yes. At first, no. I didn't know what to think. All my theories fell apart. I thought Kathy orchestrated everything, considering she never wanted to move from the apartment. Then I thought Victor Petrov had something to do with it."

"Who?" I asked.

Doug glanced at the ceiling and rubbing his scruffy cheek with his fingers, the pose of a man thinking hard. "A few months before I purchased the house..."

Day Five. Tuesday, October 10th. 1522hrs.

A FEW MONTHS BEFORE purchasing the house, Doug's construction business had come to a grinding halt. He, about two years ago, stepped away from a well-paying job that had no room for growth. Doug had grown bored there, and he thought he could do better on his own.

Initially, he had a few clients—people interested in building custom homes. They hired Doug as their contractor, and he built their houses. After that first wave, though, the well dried. His phone went quiet.

Instead of living out his dream of building, Doug resolved to work odd jobs, performing handyman tasks. However, even that had dwindled. He barely secured enough work to earn enough money to fill his truck with gas each week.

Doug chalked the lack of business to a floundering economy. Still, he couldn't make excuses. He had to make money. Desperation had pushed him into gambling, and gambling had depleted the last of his financial reserves.

To purchase the house, Doug had contacted a private investor—Victor Petrov. Victor had lent Doug money before to help him claw his way free of previous gambling debt. This time, though, Doug owed him a down payment, six months' worth of mortgage, and the added interest they had agreed on.

In short, Doug had borrowed money because he wasn't making money, and he currently had no revenue stream to pay Victor back.

While cooped up in the RV alone, Doug used the time to think, to wrap his head around his floundering, faltering life.

What was happening inside the home?

With space and distance from Kathleen, the answer slapped Doug across the face with resounding clarity. How had he not realized it before? Victor Petrov had sent one of his goons to harass and terrorize Doug until he paid back the first installment of what he owed.

Doug couldn't help but chuckle at the obviousness of the answer. He felt silly and embarrassed for thinking Kathleen had anything to do with the strange events unfolding inside the home. He felt even sillier for entertaining the idea that a ghost or spirit haunted the house.

With the message received, Doug could respond. He had to respond by garnering some cash to pay Petrov. How? With work stalled, how would Doug earn money?

"I could rob a bank," he said, muttering to himself. He meant it as a joke, but speaking the words into existence, giving them weight, provided the idea with a possibility.

Outside of criminality, Doug wondered how he could earn money.

Emily's question from a few days back clobbered him. *What about your books?*

Apart from Doug's dream of building big, beautiful custom homes, he wanted to write a series of true crime novels.

Doug's mind churned with an idea—an idea featuring the face in the window, the skull-faced figure he saw last night. What if, for the sake of entertainment, a malevolent spirit haunted his house?

The Wi-Fi to the house extended to the RV. Doug sat at the cramped kitchen table and opened his laptop. He stared at the screen for a handful of seconds, not sure how to begin his research.

After a minute, Doug stood and ambled to the refrigerator.

Yesterday, after the incident with Kathleen, Doug turned on the generator and drove to the grocery store to stock the fridge with lunch meat and beer.

He cracked open a can and finished half of it in a single gulp. After grabbing a second can to prevent having to get up again, Doug returned to the kitchen table. He typed his house's address into Google, curious to see what information would appear.

On the first page, nothing showed other than past real estate listings.

Doug finished his first beer and cracked open the second. He didn't know the name of any previous owners, and he didn't know the names of the people who rented the home a few years back. He also didn't know how to find the information through a Google search.

He had to get creative.

Something strange was happening inside his house, something Doug couldn't explain.

"And it happened before!"

Emily's words, once again, rang through his mind.

It's a murder home. That's why we snagged it for so cheap. A few years ago, a family lived in the home and experienced strange occurrences. At first, they chalked them up to an old house playing tricks, but they couldn't make that excuse for too long... not after a series of unexplainable events. They experienced things they couldn't explain.

Before their move-in day, a customer at the hardware store overheard Doug speaking to an employee about moving into the home. The customer had scraggly gray hair, a dirty beard, and ripped clothing. He didn't appear to be shopping, but browsing. The old man stank, too, like rotten fruit and sour breath.

"That home has a long, violent, dark history," he said, his voice a cloud of whiskey and smoke. "Some say it's the Amityville of Sacramento."

"Bob, come on now," the employee, a young woman built like a lumberjack, said. "We all know that's nothing but campfire talk to scare kids. How about you keep your nonsense to yourself?"

"It's haunted, Louie. You know it same as me."

"I know this isn't a library. Unless you're a paying customer, what's your reason for being here?"

"You know I don't mean no harm."

Not long after, Emily shared the home's tragic history with Kathleen. How much of what Emily said was truth versus fiction?

That's what Doug needed to research—the dark, shady history of the home. When he learned enough, added it to his experiences, he could create an outline or a working draft for a book. The modern-day *Amityville Horror*. It was a sure-fire plan to make money.

With a fire burning beneath him, Doug revised his Google search. He wanted to read rumors and theories, to interlace those stories with flecks of fact and truth. He focused his attention on Reddit threads and news articles.

The first search brought back results from the renters who died in the dining room three years ago.

The news reports shared a surface-level recounting of the harrowing event, but enough details for Doug to have a picture of what happened.

On New Year's Eve, the Rowley family sat for their last meal. Mother and father invited their son, daughter, and their spouses over for dinner.

No one could say with certainty who cooked the meal or poisoned the food. Most speculation circulated around the mother, Carolyn. She lived a quiet, secluded life (a lot of internet opinions believed she lived an oppressed life, one her husband controlled). Carolyn and her husband, George, held their marriage together with Scotch tape, hope, and patience.

According to internet forums, a malevolent entity, a demon, possessed Carolyn, forcing her to poison herself and her family.

The logic, they wrote, went back to the origins of the house.

From its construction in 1946, when the original owner and builder, Vernon Nowak, returned from Germany after World War Two, dark rumors circulated about the home. They claimed Vernon built the house, against recommendation and sound advice, on burial grounds. Some said Vernon performed satanic rituals within the home, summoning hellish entities. Others mentioned Vernon, broken and twisted from the war, became a serial killer, performing monstrous acts within the basement of the home.

Since the house didn't have a basement, though, it would make it difficult to perform violent murders down there. Still, one piece of truth lived within the threads.

Vernon Nowak was the original builder and owner.

Doug refocused his research, digging into Vernon. Another flood of Internet forums appeared, as did a sprinkling of news reports.

One headline from the *Sacramento Bee*, written in 1967—twenty years after the house's construction—said, FAMILY FOUND DEAD AROUND DINNER TABLE. WERE THEY POISONED?

Doug's heart dropped to the ground like molten lead. He couldn't think, and his vision blurred. He grabbed his beer and downed a generous amount, hoping it would clear his senses.

When he set the beverage down, Doug reread the headline. He skimmed through the article.

According to the writer, the Nowak family sat down to eat, and they never stood up again. As with the Rowley family, nearly forty-five years later, the medical report showed large amounts of cyanide in the victims' bodies. Though no one could confirm, most everyone believed the wife had mixed poison into the meal.

After the Nowaks, four families, including the Rowleys, lived in the house. Each family died unexpectedly at the dinner table after eating their last meal together.

It was always the mother who the public believed to have killed the family.

In each of the five incidents, the killer used cyanide.

Doug leaned back in the booth seat and stared out the screened window. He held his fourth beer, but he didn't imbibe. Instead, he allowed his swirling, chaotic thoughts to run their course and settle.

Was the house haunted, after all? Had all the violent, untimely deaths corrupted the home?

Had Vernon Nowak practiced satanic rituals, cursing the property?

Did Vernon's spirit remain? Did his wife's spirit remain, possessing the mothers of the new families, using them to poison and murder?

Had Doug and Kathleen seen ghosts, supernatural entities in the windows, in the upstairs room?

Did something otherworldly possess Emily?

Each question seemed more farfetched than the next, ludicrous and ridiculous. Then again, it all made perfect sense.

Where did that leave Doug?

Should he call Father Hartke? The priest had already purified the home. Had his prayers not taken? Should he purify the home again? Should he look for demons lurking within the shadows? Did priests do that?

Should Doug contact a paranormal investigator? Maybe a medium, or a demonologist, someone apart from the Christian church with knowledge and experience to ban the entities.

Doug chuckled, laughing at himself for considering the solutions running through his mind. Only one answer existed: use the information and rumors and his experience to write a book.

A knock outside the flimsy front door quieted his thoughts.

He cocked his head, a trickle of concern cutting through him. Had he heard a knock? It was silent now, deafeningly so. Had the spooky tales, stirred with his beer, gone to his head?

Another light knock grounded him back to reality.

"Doug," Kathleen said, her voice low and mournful.

Doug fumbled from his seat, nearly toppling over. The beers affected him more than he thought. He clambered to the door.

Kathleen stood at the bottom of the two metal steps, holding her right arm with her left hand, rubbing her biceps. She had swollen eyes and a puffy face. "Can I come in?"

Doug stepped aside and gestured for her to enter. "Do you want a beer?"

"No, thank you." Kathleen climbed into the RV and sat in the booth across from where Doug had his laptop positioned.

"Is everything okay?" Doug slid into his seat.

"I don't think so."

"Is it Emily?"

Kathleen rested her hands on the tabletop and moved them in circles around each other. "She's worse than yesterday."

Doug chewed on his cheeks for a second, not sure how to respond.

Yesterday, Emily accused him of unspeakable falsities. How did it get any worse? The articles slid through Doug's mind—the families around their dinner tables, their last meals, the cyanide. He thought of wives pouring the poison into the food. Of demons and dark entities possessing the women, forcing them to undertake the dark deeds.

"Doug?" Kathleen asked.

"Hm?"

"Are you okay?"

"Yeah."

Her gaze fixed on the four beer cans left in plain sight. "You've been drinking?"

"There's a lot on my mind." He sniffled. "Do you believe her? Do you believe I could do such a thing?"

Kathleen shook her head, her eyes still fixed on the table, on the beer cans. "Maybe I should have a beer, too."

Doug went to the refrigerator and grabbed two beers, one for him and one for her. He popped the tab and handed Kathleen her drink.

She sipped. "I don't know what to believe. Why would she lie to me about that?"

Doug cracked his beer and drank. His lips tingled from a slight buzz. "I wouldn't ever do anything so monstrous."

"I know, but I also thought my daughter wouldn't lie to me. I don't know what I know." She took another pull from her drink.

"What did she do today?"

Kathleen spoke in a slow, chopped pace. "She's refusing to use the bathroom."

Doug sipped from his beer and thought about what his wife said. "Like, she's holding it?"

Kathleen shook her head. A tear streaked down her waxen cheek.

"What do you mean?" he asked.

"She won't go in the bathroom. It's everywhere—her sheets, her walls, the floor. She's gotten sick a few times, and she just lowered her head and threw up on herself."

Doug grimaced and shivered.

"When I told her to shower, she refused," Kathleen said. "I had to leave her room to shower. I felt so gross, and I don't know how long I stood beneath cold water after the hot water ran out, but I didn't know what else to do but stand there—stand there or come to you." She lifted her eyes and looked at her husband. "She's saying things, too."

"What things?"

"That we're all going to die. One day, we'll all sit down to eat, and we won't stand up again."

Doug's mind pulled in all directions, creating a tension headache dead-center in his skull.

"I'm so scared." Kathleen tapped the butt of her can on the table. "I don't know what to do."

"She needs professional help," Doug said. He knew Kathleen wouldn't want to hear that advice, but he didn't care. The situation had escalated. Emily needed help from people qualified to help her.

"My father saw a professional, and look how that turned out. Look what happened to him. You think I can suffer losing my daughter, too?" Her face darkened instantaneously, as if someone flicked out the lights. "It's this house. It's your fault. Her behavior—no, her decline. It all started when we moved. I warned you, Doug. I pleaded with you. We were happy and comfortable. Now look at us. What is this?" Kathleen shot to her feet and fled to the door.

"Wait," Doug said, snatching his laptop off the table and standing. "I need you to see something. Please, just... just look." He opened the computer. The screen showed the story about Vernon Nowak building the home and of his family dying in a cyanide-related incident two decades later.

Kathleen immediately, without even reading the article, covered her mouth. "That's him," she said, her voice muffled behind her hands. "In the picture, that's him."

"Who?" Doug asked.

"The man I saw in the window."

Day Six. Wednesday, October 11th. 0911hrs.

Two deputy sheriffs stood on Doug's front porch. One of them looked like the human who inspired Chief Wiggum from The Simpsons. The other deputy had dark, swollen eyes, splotchy skin, an aura of agitation, and slumped shoulders. His body appeared much more lived in than the other, older officer.

Doug greeted them with a reluctant smile. "Come in, please." He stepped to the side. "Would you like any coffee? Water?"

"Coffee, please," the younger deputy said.

"Nothing for me."

Doug led the two men into the kitchen, sat them down at the table beneath the over-sized chandelier. The morning sun crashed through the window, providing a warm, natural light in the room.

Kathleen arrived a minute later, serving a pot of coffee, three mugs, and a carton of milk.

"Do you have sugar?" S. Cron, according to the younger man's name tag, asked.

"Of course." Kathleen quickly disappeared, returning with packs of sugar.

Without a word of gratitude, S. Cron prepared his coffee.

G. Ackerman, the older officer, the one who looked like the pudgy cartoon character, scratched the top of his hairless head. "An officer responded to a call three nights ago, if I'm not mistaken?"

Doug glanced at his wife and frowned. "Three or four."

"Sunday night," Kathleen said.

The officer grunted affirmatively. "What was the nature of the call?"

"I saw someone through the window. He stood in our yard and stared into the house."

"I see," Deputy G. Ackerman said.

Doug poured himself a cup of coffee. "The night before, Saturday night, we woke up to a noise and found our kitchen turned upside down. Also..." he trailed off, carefully choosing how to describe his encounter with the skull-faced figure who vanished into the shadows. "I saw someone upstairs wearing a mask. I chased after them, but they slipped away."

The younger officer, S. Cron, stared at the table. Doug thought the man had fallen asleep. Then he flinched, stirred his coffee, and brought the steaming mug to his thin lips.

"Do you have reason to believe someone would harass you?" Ackerman asked.

"Maybe we disrupted a squatter," Kathleen said. "The house was vacant for almost three years. If someone used it as a shelter, and we displaced them, maybe they're trying to scare us."

"Yes," Doug said.

"Yes?" Kathleen and Ackerman chorused, though they shared varying tones. Ackerman posed his question out of curiosity. Kathleen had a hint of confusion.

Doug ran his tongue over his teeth and glanced beyond the chandelier diamonds, which threw sunlight across the wedding-cake ceiling. "Yes," he repeated. "That's why I called you here."

Ackerman tilted his head, patiently waiting for Doug to continue.

Kathleen failed to model patience. "What do you mean, yes? Do you know someone who would hurt us? Doug, what haven't you told me?"

Doug kept his eyes on the ceiling, finding it easier to speak to an inanimate object than look his wife in her eyes. It took him a few seconds to muster the courage and build the words and unleash his tongue.

"I have... a gambling addiction. Over the past few years, I've accrued a considerable debt, and I went to a private financier for help to pay my bills and maintain my personal and business credit. I owe him a lot of money." Doug closed his eyes and pictured the skull-faced figure. He shifted the image, putting the newspaper photograph of Vernon Nowak in his mind.

No one said anything for a long time.

The cartoonish deputy side-eyed Kathleen. The younger, most likely hungover, deputy blinked, spurring himself into an interested state. Kathleen went slack jawed; she donned a mask of confusion, repulsion, anger, irritation—a kaleidoscope of negative emotions.

In her tense silence, Doug's mind raced. Kathleen had recognized Vernon Nowak from the picture, the long-dead, first-time owner of the home. She recognized him as the man she saw outside the window.

What did that mean? How did it connect to Doug's debt, if at all? Were all the incidents related or disconnected?

Doug only knew if their recent troubles had any ties to his secret life, he had to come clean for the safety of his family.

"How much?" Kathleen asked, her voice low.

"A little north of half a million dollars now."

"Now?"

"Now that we've purchased the house."

"You, not we. You bought this home. Apparently, you used someone else's money to buy this house. We don't even own this home?"

"Legally we do." When Kathleen said nothing in response, Doug cut in, using the brief silence as an opportunity to explain himself. "Listen, I quit gambling."

Kathleen chortled, disbelieving.

"I'm in a gambler's anonymous class, and I put myself on a self-exclusion list from casino gambling. I'm working on the problem."

"I don't know what to say." Kathleen stood. "We owe our entire lives to another person. They own us, Doug." She covered her lips and her eyes turned pink.

For a beat, Doug thought she might say more, but she turned and left the room.

Doug scraped his tongue across the bottom of his teeth.

Deputy Ackerman adjusted his position and cleared his throat. "Do you believe your financier has harassed you these past few nights?"

"I don't know. It's possible."

"Well, if you want us to look into it, Mr. Kosar, you'll have to provide a name."

"I know."

"Otherwise, why did you call us here? We're not marriage counselors, here to mediate you confessing your sins to your wife."

Doug thought of Emily and her strange behavior since moving into the home. Did his financier have something to do with that? He recalled how she hugged her legs, stretched them back out, and kicked them.

What was the actual nature of her illness? Doctors couldn't define it, couldn't locate the root cause.

Doug didn't really know Emily that well, had never asked her about her sickness. He saw her in a wheelchair. He was told she had mild paralysis, asthma, dizzy spells, fatigue, weakness, and a list of other ailments, but he knew little more than what Kathleen shared with him.

Could Emily have stretched her legs from an angled position to flat on the mattress? Could she have kicked them? Doug couldn't answer with any confidence. Maybe she had a mild paralysis, one that prevented her from walking, but not from making small, subtle movements. Maybe her recent erratic and repulsive behavior was a symptom of her root, undiagnosed disease.

Maybe the idea of a possession was so far out of the realm of conversation, he should lock himself in a mental health hospital for entertaining the idea.

Maybe his accumulated stress had driven him half-mad.

With all the crazy swirling around him the past week, Doug no longer knew what to believe. Ghosts? Demons? Greedy financiers?

"My wife saw Vernon Nowak," he said to the deputy sheriffs.

"Who?" Ackerman asked.

"The original owner and builder of this home. He died with his family, in this very room during dinner, almost sixty years back. That's whose face she saw in the window the other night. Vernon Nowak's. I pulled up his picture yesterday, showed it to her, and she immediately recognized him."

"What are you saying?" Ackerman asked.

"Just sharing all the information."

"You think a dead man, the same dead man who built this house and died here, has returned as... what? As a ghost? To do what? Haunt you?"

"I don't know." Doug thought through the dark, violent, repetitive history of the house—each successive family dying at the dinner table, poisoned.

What if Vernon Nowak's spirit had tormented all of them, had possessed them, had driven them mad and forced them to carry out the murderous acts?

"We need to know what we're doing here. Are you scared of the man you owe money to, or are you afraid of a ghost? We can help you with one of those, but only one."

Doug wouldn't give up the name, not unless he desired to join the other inhabitants of this home in death.

"There's just... there's been a lot of weird things happening here. I wanted to sit you down and plead my case, see if we could convince you to send a unit out this way more than once a month."

Ackerman sucked air through his teeth. "I don't have authority over where the other units patrol. I have the power to respond to the public's safety concerns. So, unless you're willing to provide me with more actionable information." The cartoonish deputy shrugged his rounded shoulders. "Well, I can't do anything."

"I'm sorry to waste your time," Doug said, though he didn't feel like he had wasted his time.

In fact, the conversation had prompted him with a few ideas.

Doug showed the deputies to the door, closed it, and turned around, jumping from fright.

"Kathleen," he said, grabbing his racing heart.

Again, she bore a defeated expression, one that forced her to set her anger aside in place of pure fear. "It's Emily."

"What about her?"

Without another word, Kathleen turned around and ran up the stairs.

Doug trailed after her. He hadn't entered Emily's room since the incident. The first thing he noticed after a couple of days' absence was the stench. It was nearly unbearable. Flies buzzed on the floor, bouncing from plate to plate filled with old, untouched food. Emily had a bucket beside her bed, with yet more flies swarming the top.

Emily laid on her bed, still naked. She wore a smile that seemed a permanent, unnatural fixture on her pale face. A gurgling, choppy cackling emanated from deep in her throat and through her teeth. Her face had sunk in on itself, had become a living depiction of the skull Doug had seen.

"She's been like this for ten minutes," Kathleen said. "Just smiling and laughing."

"Can you not put clothes on her?"

"She curses at me if I try, takes them off."

"The buckets?"

"She refuses to leave her bed to use the bathroom."

Emily continued to smile and cackle. Her face trembled from the effort of holding the expression.

"She hasn't eaten since we moved into the house," Kathleen said.

The young woman suddenly ceased her laughter. A terrible silence filled the terrible room for a terrible second, immediately followed by high-pitched barking.

"Woof! Woof! Woof!" Over and over with no intention of stopping.

Frank, who lay in the room's corner on a dog bed, lifted his head and joined—his deep barks juxtaposing Emily's yapping.

Doug became dizzy from the stimuli. He didn't know how to process what he saw, heard, smelled. He reached out and planted his hand on the dresser for support. "Has this happened before?"

"What?" Kathleen asked, annoyance playing through her voice.

"Whatever this is?"

"Never."

"Is it a symptom of her disease?" Doug asked, knowing full well no one knew the affliction Emily suffered.

"I don't know."

"We need to take her to a doctor."

Kathleen rolled her sleeve and showed her arm to Doug. Teeth marks imprinted into her skin. "I tried. I forced her by grabbing her. She bit me."

The barking continued, driving Doug nearly insane.

"I can't be in here," he said, backing out of the room. "I can't listen to that."

"We have to help her."

"How?"

"Kill me!" Emily screamed. "Kill me! That's how you help me!" As she yelled, she clawed her fingernails over her bare skin, tearing into herself.

"No," Emily said, responding to herself, her voice low and afraid—a different person speaking through the girl's body. "Don't kill her. Sacrifice to her by killing yourselves."

Barking mixed with cackling cascaded through the room.

"I'm going to live on the moon!" Emily yelled.

"In Hell," said a deep, demonic voice.

"Hell's moon! I'm going to plant a garden."

"And grow nothing but human skulls."

"I'll water the fleshy soil with blood."

Barking and cackling.

"The skulls will grow and blossom hearts!" Emily shrieked.

"Big, juicy hearts ripe for the plucking."

"No!" Another voice, this one bordering on normalcy, rubbing against Emily's usual tone. "Stop it! Stop it, stop it, stopitstopitstopit!" She covered her ears and convulsed. "Mommy, help me. Please, mommy, help! Momma. Momma, help me." Tears streaked down her crumpled face.

Her sobs shifted. They turned into wails, into cackles, into a single, high-pitched scream.

Kathleen stood rooted to the ground. Her hands dangled uselessly near her thighs; her head lolled to the side. She looked as if she might collapse into a boneless heap.

Emily, now speaking in the guttural, unnatural male voice, rose to her feet. She stood on her bed and jumped, using the mattress like a trampoline. "I'm the queen of Hell's moon. I'll live there all my days, and I'll drink the blood and eat the flesh of my dolls."

Her expression changed to that of a little girl. She giggled and clapped her hands, jumping up and down all the while. "You are my doll," she said, pointing at Doug. "And you are my doll," she said, pointing at Kathleen. "I can't wait to play with you forever and ever and ever, on Hell's moon."

Emily went limp and dropped into a bundle on the bed.

The room fell into a horrendous silence, broken only by the hiccuping cries of Kathleen.

Day Seven. Thursday, October 12th. 1356hrs.

KATHLEEN REFUSED TO LEAVE Emily alone at the house; she barely allowed herself time to escape her daughter's bedroom to accomplish daily tasks, like eating or brushing her teeth.

"I'm not taking her to a therapist," she whisper-yelled to Doug that morning. They stood in the hallway outside Emily's bedroom door, Kathleen's hand gripped around the door, not allowing it to fully close.

"What about a doctor?"

"A doctor will say what they always say, that they don't know. They'll want to run tests that will come back inclusive. It's a waste of everyone's time."

"She's sick, Kathy."

"She's possessed."

Doug sealed his lips and exhaled through his nostrils.

"Go to Father Hartke," she said.

With no other recourse, apart from kidnapping his stepdaughter and taking her to an expert, Doug obliged his wife. He climbed into his truck and drove to the cathedral. He asked around for Father Hartke's whereabouts, eventually finding himself standing at the priest's open door.

His office was a dusty, cluttered space filled with wooden furniture and old literature. The computer atop the desk seemed out of place, out of time, an anomaly to the rest of the room.

"Mr. Kosar," Father Hartke said from behind his desk with a beaming smile. "Please, come inside and sit." He gestured to a sofa set on the wall opposite the bookshelf. "Is this about the house?"

"Yes."

"I have blessed it, purified it with holy water and the name of Jesus Christ."

"It's more than that."

"What do you mean?"

Doug swallowed and cleared his throat, fighting through his reluctance and embarrassment. Even speaking to a man who believed in a floating space god, Doug had difficulty admitting a supernatural phenomenon at his house. "We believe a malevolent spirit haunts our house," Doug said after a handful of seconds. "We also suspect that the entity has... possessed our daughter, Emily."

Father Hartke pressed the tips of his fingers together and chewed on his upper lip. "That's a serious statement to make."

"I feel silly saying it," Doug said. "I just don't know how else to explain what's happening."

"And what's happening, exactly?"

Doug relayed the events of the past week. He included the strange occurrences and the dark history, ending with Emily's alarming behavior. He purposefully omitted his gambling addiction and debt. "I don't know what else to think. You should have heard the way she changed voices, the way she carried a conversation with herself. It's like there were two, three different people speaking from within her body."

"Has she seen a professional therapist, one who could rule out or diagnose a mental health disorder? For example, we often see schizophrenia mistaken for demon possession."

Doug stared out the window placed behind Father Hartke. It overlooked the cathedral's parking lot. "You think she's schizophrenic?"

"I'm not a professional, and I don't have the authority to say as much. I'm saying it's a serious matter to contact the church about a demon possession. Our interference, without Emily going through the proper checks, could worsen her condition. Not only that, for the church to get involved requires approval, which takes time. There are regulations and procedures around a demon possession and exorcism. We have to perform an assessment and a consultation. It's not a matter we take lightly."

"I understand." Doug felt himself deflate. "When do you think… how long would it be until you could perform the exorcism, if that's what's needed?"

"It depends on the psychological and medical reports. It depends on the bishop's response. There are a lot of factors to take into consideration."

"Would you know by the end of the week?"

"Mr. Kosar." Father Hartke closed his eyes and inhaled. "Send your stepdaughter to a mental health professional. Make an appointment with her pediatrician. Inform them of what's happening. That's my recommendation. Until you complete those steps, there's not much I, or the Catholic Church, can do, other than pray for Emily."

"Prayer? That's comforting." Doug rose from his chair. "Your prayers, I'm sure, will make all the difference."

"Mr. Kosar, we're balancing on an extremely fine edge. We can't abuse the power of the church, and we can't risk the mental or physical health of your daughter. Do you see the complication? A rushed exorcism, one performed without the confirmation of a demon possession, would cause infinitely more harm than good. I'm in Emily's corner, which is hopefully your corner. My advice to you is to check off all the steps before resorting to the drastic, complicated measures of an exorcism."

Doug chewed on his cheeks and nodded. A sense of helplessness roared through him. He feared how Kathleen would respond to Father Hartke's advice. Would she take drastic, impulsive measures? Would she listen to him?

Doug didn't have any money, thanks in part to his gambling debt and his lack of work opportunities. He couldn't protect his family. He couldn't secure his home. As the man of the household, as the one meant to provide and protect, he failed miserably. To compensate for his budding insecurity, Doug had swam against the current of his core beliefs. He had gone to the church and sought the help of a priest to exorcise a demon from his stepdaughter.

His eyes burned from tears that he refused to cry, and he sniffled. "Thank you for your time, Father."

"I will pray for you and your family. Pray for security, for the spirit of the Lord to settle over your home, to bless and purify any darkness or corruption."

"Sure. You do that." Doug didn't intend to sound disingenuous or rude, but his emotions clipped his speech.

When he sat in his truck, he rested his forehead against the steering wheel and sobbed.

154

Day Eight. Friday, October 13th. 1554hrs.

DOUG PARKED HIS TRUCK in the auto shop's small, graying parking lot. When he cut the engine, he remained in his seat, buckled and staring out the dusty, cracked windshield at a planter filled with dying shrubs and faded red bark.

A client—they had noticed Doug's business card pinned to the board in Starbucks—called earlier in the morning, needing simple home repairs. Though Doug formed his construction company to build custom homes, he pivoted out of financial need.

He responded to the call and arrived at the customer's house that day—an elderly woman and recent widow. While there, he fixed her leaky sink and mowed the front yard. When he finished, the woman handed Doug a fifty-dollar bill.

Before going home, Doug stopped to meet with his financier. His loan shark. He sat in his truck for a few minutes, generating a dose of confidence.

As a thick cloud blotted the sun, Doug stepped from the truck and crossed the parking lot. He opened the door and stepped inside the humid interior. It smelled of rubber, grease, and popcorn.

A middle-aged woman sat behind an ancient, boxy computer. She wore tacky earrings, smacked gum, and yelled into the phone. "Mama, that girl is playing stupid games. If she keeps it up, she's going to earn herself a stupid prize, too. I don't mess with that. I don't know why you're messing with it, either. Mm-hmm. Who? Tracy? Oh, God, please. I wish she would knock on my door."

Doug stood at the counter and presented a shy smile.

The woman lifted a ring-lined finger in the universal gesture of wait. "If Tracy knocked on my door, if she talked crazy to me like she talked crazy to you... well, Mama, you know I keep a gun in the drawer. No. Come on. Who's going to miss her? Her mama doesn't love her, and she ain't got no daddy... well, other than her daddy, you know? But her daddy won't miss her either. Probably thank me with a bouquet of roses."

"Excuse me," Doug said.

"Hold on, Mama." The woman lowered the phone and glared at Doug behind a curtain of fake eyelashes. "What?"

"I'm here to see Victor."

"He's not here to see you. Bye, bye, now." She wriggled her fingers in a half-hearted wave, raised her phone back to her ear, and continued her verbal tirade.

Doug didn't have Victor's number, otherwise he would have called and made an appointment. Desperate, he leaned over the counter, inching his face nearer to the woman's face caked in makeup. Her perfume was intense and floral, and, like everything else in the auto shop, cheap.

"Tell him it's Douglas Kosar."

"I don't care if you're George Washington. What? No, not you, Mama. This guy at the office, coming in here acting like he can speak to Victor. He name-dropped himself like he's someone special."

"Katya," a male voice said from across the room.

Victor Petrov leaned halfway out a door in the back corner of the office. He was a military man through and through—a tight-cropped haircut, a pressed suit, a rigid posture, and a hard, marble physique.

"What have I told you about your phone during working hours? There's a customer. Deal with him."

Without a goodbye, Katya abrasively ended the call, sighing and grunting. She tossed her phone beside the computer and stared at Doug with a look of simmering annoyance. "This man here wants to speak with you, Victor, but he doesn't have no appointment."

Victor tilted his square head and narrowed his eyes. "Doug, is that you?"

"It's me," Doug said.

"Why are you here?" Victor seemed less than happy to see him.

"We need to talk."

"You don't dictate the terms of our meetings and conversations."

"No, but you'll find this... interesting."

Victor glanced at his gold watch. "You have three minutes." He disappeared behind the door.

Doug joined him in the office. There wasn't a chair for clients, so Doug remained standing.

"Your time has already begun," Victor said.

Doug scratched his cheek. "It's about the house."

"The house I bought you?"

"Yeah."

"What about it?"

Doug licked his lips. "Have you sent someone out there to... scare me?"

Victor chuckled, though it sounded more irked than amused. "If I had sent someone to scare you, you wouldn't have walked into this shop."

The implication sent a phantom pain through Doug's knees.

"What happened?"

"There's been..." Doug trailed off, unable to say hauntings. "There's been disturbances since we've moved in."

"Disturbances?"

"Someone broke into the house and ransacked the kitchen. Kathleen saw a stranger outside our window. I saw someone upstairs who wore a mask."

"A mask?"

"A skull." Doug cleared his throat and nearly shared Emily's recent behavior, but cut himself off.

If Victor had nothing to do with the invasions, he wouldn't have a role in the possession. Why mention it? Why work the man with ghost stories, especially when Doug owed him so much money?

Doug saw no reason to make Victor doubt his grasp on reality.

Victor clicked his tongue for a few seconds. "I invested in you, Doug. In your vision. You convinced me of your artistic skill, and you convinced me you could turn your home into something incredible. Do you remember our deal?"

Doug nodded. He remembered clearly. It had been his idea. He would remodel the house, turn it into something special. Once he completed construction, had the place looking like a gemstone, he would reappraise. The house he bought for half of the market's value would exceed the market price of comparable homes. Doug would pull the equity and give it to Victor.

"If you're running into complications because you bit off more than you can chew, well... well, Doug, a kitchen upheaval will be the least of your concerns. We're clear on that point?"

"Yes."

"Good."

"I... I've had little traction with work, which is why my payments have suffered, and... I didn't know if you sent someone to check on me, to send a message."

"Doug, while we're together and amicable, let's flip to the same page, shall we? I don't send messages. If I'm displeased, you'll never know, because the dead know nothing." Victor crossed his arms over his broad chest. "Get your house in order. Your home is my investment, and I take my investments seriously."

"Of course."

"Good." Victor exhaled, uncrossed his arms, and sat. "Since work has stalled for you, how's the book coming along? Have you found more time to write?"

Doug stalled to answer.

Not only had Doug offered the house's equity, he agreed to give Victor a percentage of any royalties earned from the sales of his books. Victor had invested heavily in Doug's creativity and promises.

"I'm still conducting research," Doug said. "The audience will rip me apart if I don't have the facts straight."

"Well, I would hate to put a deadline on your creative process, but when do you expect to finish writing the first book?"

Doug glanced at his feet and shrugged. "I'm not sure." Uncertainty wouldn't fly with Victor Petrov, though. "Definitely before Halloween next year."

"Mr. Kosar, our three minutes have expired. I really hope you're able to continue with the remodeling of your home while balancing a career, a dream, and a family. It's in both our best interests." Victor stood and gestured to the door. "You can show yourself out?"

"Yes," Doug said.

"Oh, and Mr. Kosar. My generosity has been overflowing, my patience vast. Those attributes aren't limitless. If you wish for continued peace within our partnership, you're going to pay for it. I need ten thousand dollars by the end of the month."

An iciness spread throughout Doug's body, freezing him in place. "I don't have that kind of money."

"I'm confident you'll come up with it. Now, leave, and never contact me again without me first contacting you."

Somehow, Doug found the strength to swing open the door. In a mindless daze, he shuffled through the lobby and out to the parking lot. He climbed into his truck, where he sat and stared out the dusty, cracked windshield at a planter filled with dying shrubs and faded red bark.

Day Nine. Saturday, October 14th. 2027hrs.

Doug stood just inside Emily's bedroom door, averting his eyes from his stepdaughter.

Emily refused to wear any clothes. The day before, or maybe the day before that—time blurred in the madness—Kathleen had forced pants onto her daughter. Emily kicked and thrashed and screamed, "They burn my skin!" After a minute bordering on a perpetuity, Kathleen threw up her hands and gave up. Emily had remained naked since.

However, she had painted her body with the food Kathleen had left in her room, the food she refused to eat. Emily smeared the soup and yogurt and oatmeal over her pale skin, and she plastered salad and meat and bread against her body like stickers.

"Eat me!" Her voice was a smoke-wrecked, deep, cavernous growl. She licked mustard off her hand, a cat cleaning its paw. "Eat me!"

Doug shivered and contemplated the idea of leaving her room, the house, the town, the state, the country. He thought of disappearing, of abandoning everything and everyone for a new, anonymous start.

Instead, he focused on his breathing.

"I scheduled a doctor's appointment on Thursday." Kathleen fought to keep her voice soft and steady, though it trembled. "You're meeting with a therapist on Friday,"

"Maybe I'll just eat myself!" Emily shifted her voice to a high-pitched shriek. She shoved a fist between her teeth and chomped, biting until blood leaked down her wrist.

"Emily!" Panic leaked into Kathleen's voice, her posture, her actions. She lunged forward and pried out her daughter's hand. "Stop it. Emily, stop!"

The girl cackled, a disorienting, grating sound stuck between a hiccup, a hyena, and a witch. Then, abruptly, she stopped, falling terribly quiet. A second later, she spasmed. Her entire body shook and convulsed, as if suffering from an epileptic episode. Drool and spittle slashed around her face and across the room.

"Doug!" Kathleen screamed. "Help me!"

"Doug!" Emily mocked her mother's tone as she continued to convulse. "Help me!" She stopped spasming and resumed laughing.

Doug grabbed his ears, nearly ripped them off his head to experience a second of silence.

"Your step-father paid a visit to Father Hartke yesterday," Kathleen said.

"Your step-father paid a visit to Father Hartke yesterday." Emily mocked her mother, speaking in a fragmented sob.

"We think you're possessed."

"As Marshall Nix possessed you?" Emily cackled.

Kathleen covered her mouth with shock. She went stiff as a board.

"Wait," Emily said, "possessed isn't the right word. Marshall Nix stuffed you." She grimaced and stared at the ceiling, shaking her head. "There has to be a better word than stuffed, though, right? He filled you with his... spirit, as with the Holy Spirit of Jesus Christ and God our Father." Emily rolled onto her back and bicycle kicked her legs as she laughed maniacally. "Occupied! That's the word. Marshal Nix occupied you." Emily rolled into a seated position. "Maybe the Devil has occupied me."

Kathleen openly cried; tears burned down her face, and her shoulders quivered with each labored breath. "Stop it. You don't know what you're saying. An evil entity is speaking through you. It's using you." Kathleen folded her hands and dropped to her knees. "God, Heavenly Father, please, please, bless this room with your presence. Fill Emily, my daughter, with your Spirit."

"As Marshall Nix filled my mother with his spirit," Emily said.

Kathleen inhaled a shallow, rapid breath. "Heal her mind and her body."

"As Marshall Nix healed my mother's body."

"It wasn't like that! It wasn't like that, you stupid, weak-minded little whore! That's why this is happening. You welcomed evil to your heart and renounced God. You're a harlot. A Jezebel!" Kathleen stood and stared at her daughter before wheeling around and leaving the room, slamming the door behind her.

Doug remained rooted in place, finding his feet extremely interesting.

"I'm sorry, Dougie," Emily said. Her voice bordered on normal. "I'm sorry for making those accusations about you."

Doug lifted his gaze and stared at his stepdaughter. He had a thousand questions and a million thoughts, but zero ability to voice any of them but one.

"Who are you?" he asked.

It was a question that showed his hand. Despite his better judgment, Doug believed a demon or a malevolent entity possessed his step-daughter.

"I'm Emily Regan. Who do you think I am?"

Doug swallowed his fear and uncertainty.

"I'm Vernon Nowak," Emily said. Her voice drastically shifted to the smoke-stained growl.

"I'm Matilda Nowak." Her voice adopted the high-pitched, grating quality.

"I hope you enjoy your food." Emily's normal voice returned.

She shuffled through the three distinct and drastically different voices without skipping a word.

"Enjoy it while you can."

"While you can still eat."

"And taste."

"While you're still breathing."

"And alive."

"This house—"

"—is a tomb."

"It's where people go to rest... forever."

"We have nothing left to do but die."

"No, we have already died."

"We're on the moon, now. We're floating through space."

"We're drifting across darkness."

"Across nothing."

"We're suffocating."

"Screaming."

"But no one can hear our voices."

"We're waiting to die."

"Waiting for the pain to end."

"Waiting to die so the pain can end."

"Do you hear that?"

"The laughter."

"The joy."

"The mirth of dying."

"Of not being dead, but of dying."

"Slowly dying and laughing all the while."

Emily's myriad voices blended together into a single sound, and she devolved into a maniacal outburst of shrieking laughter.

Abject terror burst within Doug, burned away the roots holding him in place. He spun on his heels and stumbled out of Emily's room, closing the door behind him, staggering across the hallway and down the stairs.

The sounds of her cackling chased after him. Even after he ran outside, her laughter stuck in his head, tormenting his thoughts. Along with the laughter, Emily's words ensnared him—they possessed him with a jealous, violent fury.

Marshall Nix.

Who was Marshall Nix?

Day Ten. Sunday, October 15th. 0003hrs.

DOUG SET UP HIS laptop, brewed a pot of coffee, and planted himself at the dining room table. He didn't bother to look for Kathleen, to speak to her, to ask her about Marshall Nix.

What would it accomplish?

Kathleen had a tendency, from early in their relationship, to run and hide from complications or conflict.

Once, right after Doug proposed to her, they sat on the living room floor near the coffee table, picking at a cheeseboard. Emily had gone to bed for the night, allowing Doug and Kathleen much appreciated alone time. Doug asked his new fiancé about her late-husband, Emily's biological father. He knew nothing of the man, not even his name, and had never seen a photograph.

Kathleen curled her hands into fists, and her face flushed. "He doesn't concern you."

"I think he does," Doug said. "I mean, I've fallen in love with you, and with Emily. That means I care for you, every part of you, including your past. I want to know everything."

"That was a different me. It's not the woman you're marrying."

"And me, at fifteen, was a different boy than the Doug you're marrying. Still, that boy shaped who I am. He shaped the man you're going to marry. Doesn't that mean something?"

"Only who you are and will be matters."

Doug scrunched his face, debating whether he should pursue the argument. The wine decided. "What if I were a serial killer, but I renounced my ways? You wouldn't want to know that? That information wouldn't matter before marrying me?"

"I'm not getting into this," Kathleen said. She stood, snatched the second bottle of wine they opened minutes before, and disappeared into the bathroom.

Doug pattered after her, pleading with her to stop and talk to him.

Kathleen shut the bathroom door, locked it, and drew a bath. She sat in the tub for three hours. At one point, Doug feared she might have had too much to drink, passed out, and drowned.

Eventually, he knocked on the door.

"Go away!"

That's how it always went whenever they came across an issue Kathleen preferred not to tackle. They argued and disagreed, and she disappeared.

After Kathleen fled from Emily's room, Doug assumed she went to drown her concerns and worries in alcohol, to burn them away in scalding bath water. When the bath cooled and the wine emptied, she would climb into bed and slip away from whatever ailed her. She would rise the next day with short-term memory loss.

Doug, sitting at the dining room table and sipping coffee, had the night to himself. He planned to use the time to dive into his wife's past and research the name Emily had provided.

He typed Marshall Nix into Google.

Doug expected the search results to yield social media accounts—the man's Instagram or Facebook—or to reveal his place of employment. Instead, the hits on the first page showed a dedicated Wikipedia and Murderpedia page, a list of YouTube videos, and several news articles.

Doug's heart bolted, his chest tightened, and his stomach flipped in quick circles. The room lurched. He wasn't sure why he had a violent reaction, because he had read nothing, had learned nothing, had proven nothing.

Yet, deep down, he knew without a doubt who Marshall Nix was. Not just the keywords used in the Google result descriptions—thief, sexual abuser, cult leader, murderer. Doug knew the other hats Marshall Nix wore.

Father.

Husband.

With a deep breath, Doug clicked on the Wikipedia link. He hoped his fears and suspicions would prove false, would prove nothing more than conspiracy and paranoia.

Marshall Nix grew up in a Seventh Day Adventist Church, as had the infamous David Koresh. Much like the religions co-founder, Ellen G. White, Marshall Nix considered himself a prophet of God. When the Adventist leaders rejected his prophecies and claims, Nix separated from the religion and created a sect.

The Children of Eternity.

The Children of Eternity gave all their possessions to Nix, including money, property, and their bodies. He claimed he wasn't only a prophet, but the Spirit of God infused with man. He was the second coming of Jesus Christ. To receive the Spirit's blessing, his followers had to fully surrender to Nix—everything and all of them.

Once Nix deemed members of his congregation ready for eternity, he would cease serving them food. Food, a temporary source of sustenance and strength, was the last mortal bond to break before achieving eternal life with God. The Children of Eternity would starve themselves.

Over ninety-two people died, starved to death during Marshall Nix's six-year reign as the cult leader. Hundreds had their entire lives—their homes, wealth, and families—stripped from them; hundreds had their bodies abused, used by Marshall Nix for his perverse pleasure.

For five of the six years Nix led the cult, backing him, supporting him, carrying and birthing his child for him, stood a woman named Barbara Jones.

In the image on Wikipedia, she appeared much younger, and she had a different name. But Doug recognized her. He recognized the young girl standing between her and Nix.

Kathleen's name (Barbara Jones) had a hyperlink. Doug hesitated, not wanting to click on it. Suddenly, his dive into Marshall Nix felt like a severe breech of privacy, like he was a voyeur into his wife's private past.

I should exit these tabs, close the laptop, and go to bed with my wife, Doug thought. What did any of it matter? Kathleen's past didn't get him closer to helping Emily, to purging the house of whatever entity haunted it.

Still, the colored letters of Barbara Jones' name beckoned him, begged him to click the embedded link.

Doug couldn't resist.

Barbara Jones never legally married Marshall Nix, but they called themselves husband and wife. Investigators cleared Barbara of complicity with cult activities, despite her relationship with the leader.

Nix emotionally, mentally, and physically tormented and abused Barbara. He starved her, of course, and he limited her sleep, her access to natural light, clean water, and necessities to live. Every few days, he would visit her, provide her with some food, some water, some attention—he would give her exactly what she needed. He was her savior.

Psychologists likened Barbara's relationship with Nix to a form of Stockholm syndrome. She realized her life was better with Nix in it, because he broke her mind and reshaped it to realize that.

Once she found herself pregnant, Nix would threaten to take the baby from her if she didn't cooperate with him. So Barbara stood complicit by his side, silent and obedient until the day he died.

Thallium poisoning.

According to medical experts, his death occurred over ten months. Barbara faced no criminal charges, nor did anyone question her about the death of Marshall Nix.

When he died, so did his cult.

Doug leaned back in the dining room chair and thought of Vernon Nowak and his family, as well as the other inhabitants of the home. They had all died after sitting at the dining room table and eating a cyanide-laced meal.

Barbara (Kathleen) had murdered her husband—never proven, never legally suspected, but Doug knew the truth—with Thallium.

A chill sprinted down his spine, and he shivered. He was chilled, but also, he was physically cold.

Doug stood and walked to the living room. Once again, someone had opened the windows and the front door, allowing the late October night into the house. After closing them, he stood in the darkness pervading the entryway, wondering what to do next.

Day Eleven. Monday, October 23rd. 1511hrs.

"HOLD ON," I SAID, sliding my phone out of my front pocket.

It was the third time someone attempted to call me in the past fifteen minutes. If it bore any significance to work, the caller would call the agency. Fred would answer and take a message or forward the call to me. For my personal line to buzz meant a personal matter had arisen.

I glanced at the screen and saw my sister's name, Rachel Stallings. She was due on November 11. Any call, let alone multiple, successive calls from her, had me frantic.

With a forced grin splashed across my face, I stood. "I'm sorry, but I have to take this."

"Of course. I need to use the restroom anyway. Where can I find it?"

"Back corner." I pointed to the single bathroom door.

Alina complained nonstop that she had to share a toilet with two men who didn't know how to use a toilet brush. She also made a rule that Fred couldn't go number two in the office; he had to find another restroom in the building. Unfortunately for her, and for me, Fred found it hilarious to ignore Alina's rule.

I stepped outside the office door into the hallway. Sarah Herling's office was directly across the way. Two steps, I could walk into the client waiting area where Giovanni, her secretary, would greet me. A sharp pang pulled against my chest—a tugging feeling.

After my many dating debacles, I had taken a break from relationships along with accepting new cases. That didn't make me less lonely, though. With Maya traveling across America every other week—avoiding her loneliness, or so I believed—I didn't have anyone consistently in my life who I cared to date. I definitely didn't care to download a dating app to go out with a parade of women until I found someone halfway compatible with me.

But Sarah... we had hit it off. I found her attractive, both physically, mentally, and emotionally. We had even gone on a fake date once, and we both had a blast. Why hadn't I followed up? Why hadn't I pursued her with more interest?

The answer was simple. Maya.

My phone stopped vibrating in my hand. I silently cursed, annoyed with myself for having become lost in thought. Maybe I did need to go on a date, find some companionship outside of an ex-NFL player, a teenage girl, and a puppy that still, only occasionally, peed on the floor.

It would have to wait until after my meeting with Doug—until after I called Rachel back.

"You know I'm only two, three weeks from popping, right?" Rachel answered on the first ring. "What if I was in labor? What if I was in an accident, and I needed you, and you ignored my call because... because who knows what you're doing? What do you do these days now that you're not working?"

"LARP," I said.

"LARP?"

"Yeah."

"Like dress up as an elf and fight other people with fake weapons?"

"I dressed up as a pirate. Captain Sack Jarrow."

"You're fourteen again. Jobless and playing make believe." Rachel exhaled and snickered. I could almost visualize her shaking her head. "I kind of like it for you. Now you just need a girlfriend."

"You keep that up, I might have tell you that you're now reminding me of mom."

"I'm already looking like her. In twenty years, we'll be twins. I'm not sure how I feel about that."

"Jake told me he doesn't mind." Jake was my sister's husband.

"Now you're being gross," Rachel said, but the amusement in her tone told me she found me halfway funny.

A brief moment of silence settled between us. "I'm with a client," I said.

"You're working again?"

"Mostly through my contract with the Sheriff's Department, but... yeah. This is a private case through the agency."

"How's it feel to be back in the saddle?"

"Comfortable. I think I missed it."

"That's because you're a junkie. You're addicted to the mystery."

"Well, not to be curt, but to cut this conversation short, did you blow up my phone for a specific reason, or just to chat about nothing?"

"We never chat about nothing anymore. What's wrong with this?"

"Nothing," I said.

"Remember when we were kids, and we would pretend to be different characters, and we would have pretend conversations about those pretend characters' lives? Oh, God. Did we LARP? Please tell me we didn't LARP."

"You're a bigger nerd than Fred. Seriously, Rachel. I'm with a client. We need to wrap this up."

"My baby shower is this Saturday. I thought it might be fun for the men of my life to enjoy the afternoon to themselves. So, I scheduled a tee time for you, Jake, Dad, and Adam."

"A tee time?"

"For a round of golf."

"I thought Dad, Adam, and Jake golfed with Fred." I almost continued that thought, asking, *Why don't you ask him instead of me?* The old August would've gone through with the question. Not anymore. Now, I regretted having let slip my statement about Fred golfing with my dad, brother, and brother-in-law. So, I scrambled to recover. "Did I make it into the cool crowd finally?"

"Is that a yes?" I could hear Rachel's smile in her voice.

"It's a yes, but also, you couldn't have asked me through a text? You had to call a hundred time in five minutes?"

"You respond to text messages about as often as it snows in Sacramento."

"Next time leave a voicemail. Save your spam dialing for an emergency, like when you're in labor."

"7:08 Saturday morning at Haggin."

"It's in my calendar."

"Tell Fred we missed him Saturday night."

"I don't know what to know," I said, ending the call.

Sarah's door stood tall and terrifying three feet across the hallway. I considered stepping inside, asking Giovanni if she was free for a moment, and proposing a date. Butterflies danced in my stomach.

A knock rapped against the window I leaned against.

I turned and saw Fred framed in the glass, the blinds twisted open. "You have call on the line," he half-shouted through the glass. He could've taken one step to the side, opened the door, and relayed the information in a normal way. Instead, he chose to shout.

I didn't care to fall in the same trap. I opened the door and stepped into my office. "Who?"

"Vanek."

Doug had returned to the client chair set before my desk. "Tell him I'll call back in thirty minutes." Not waiting for Fred to protest, I paced to my desk and plopped into my chair. "I'm sorry about that."

"It's fine. It allowed me a chance to collect my thoughts."

"We left off with Emily's behavior declining. Did you see or consult a health professional? A doctor? A therapist? Anyone other than a priest?

"Kathleen did, yes."

"What did they say?"

Day Eleven. Monday, October 16th. O9OOhrs.

Kathleen flipped through a dated magazine as she waited in the doctor's office. Emily sat beside her in her wheelchair, staring at her phone. She wore clothes for the first time in over a week, and she had showered before stepping out of the house. By all actions and appearances, Emily had reverted to her normal, cheery, if not moody, self.

Not wanting to upset her daughter and inspire an outburst, Kathleen refrained from speaking to Emily. It wasn't easy, for she had a thousand questions and a thousand more concerns. Yet, fear reigned her in and prevented her from acting on impulse.

"Kosar, Emily," a joyful female called from across the waiting room.

A young woman with acne scars, frizzy hair, and a look of near-burnout touching her eyes stood in nurse's attire before an open door. She looked like someone who would rather do anything but what she was currently doing.

Kathleen stood and grabbed the handles of Emily's wheelchair and pushed her through the waiting room.

"Hello," the nurse said. "I'm Diana. Please, follow me."

Diana went through preparing Emily for the doctor. She weighed her, took her temperature, checked her blood pressure, and asked her a series of questions. Kathleen held her breath, waiting for Emily to snap. Cordially, though, and without incident, Emily answered.

Diana stood from the rolling stool and walked to the door. "Dr. Wong will be in shortly."

"Thank you," Kathleen said, exhaling for the first time since stepping into the doctor's office.

"Can I tell you a secret?" Emily asked after Diana closed the door, leaving Emily and Kathleen alone.

A bundle of nerves sat in Kathleen's throat. "What's that?"

Emily leaned forward from the paper-covered bed and whispered. "We're going to die. All of us. You and me and Doug."

"Stop it, Emily."

"I think you're going to kill us, just like you killed my father."

"Emily! I said to knock it off."

"Why did you kill him? Did you not love him?"

Kathleen bit her lip and stared at the wall covered in medical posters, and she struggled against tears.

"Did you not like the way he slept around with every woman in the cult? Or did you not like that he was a mass murderer who starved his followers to death?"

"They chose not to eat! He didn't force them to do anything."

"Why did you poison him?"

"I didn't."

Emily giggled, a horrific sound that bounced off the cluttered walls. "That's not what the internet says."

"That's what the police said. They never investigated me as a suspect. It doesn't matter what the internet trolls might think. I'm innocent."

"How long have you planned to kill Doug?"

Kathleen chomped down on her cheeks. A trickle of blood leaked into her mouth.

"Do you not love him? Is it because he has financially ruined our family?"

"That's enough."

"Don't you have my daddy's fortune stowed away?"

"Stop calling him that."

"Was he not my father?"

"He had nothing to do with you."

"Except that he donated his sperm to create me."

Kathleen rapidly breathed through her nose.

"You inherited his fortune, didn't you? You inherited all the money and land his followers deeded and donated to him? Why didn't the police confiscate the money? Do they know about it? Have you told Doug? Does he know you're flush with cash? Does he know you could free him of his debts?"

A gentle knock sounded on the door.

Kathleen wiped her eyes with the blade of her hand. "Come in," she said.

A small woman in her mid-forties entered the room, possessing an aura of carefree cheer. She had a disarming smile and bright eyes, and she moved like a fiery ball of energy. "Hello, hello, hello. I'm Dr. Wong. You are Emily?"

"Yes," Kathleen said.

"You're Emily?" Dr. Wong asked Kathleen.

"No."

"I'm confused." The doctor chuckled.

"We're all confused," Emily said. "I don't know who is who or what is what."

Dr. Wong snickered as she washed her hands. "Well, I know I'm not your regular pediatrician. Dr. Waddle is on vacation, as you're aware. She went to Bali, and I, for one, am envious." Dr. Wong dried her hands, sat on the rolling stool, and faced the computer. "Alright. What do we have here? Emily Regan Jones."

"That's what I'm told," Emily said.

"You have a history... wow. Wow! You have a medical history, don't you?"

"I'm a regular here."

Dr. Wong clicked her tongue as she skimmed the computer screen. "Asthma, confirmed. Muscle fatigue and weakness, reason unconfirmed. You've tested negative for Addison's disease, acidosis, diabetes, lupus... and the list goes on. Nothing confirmed, though you have a lot of symptoms." The doctor looked away from the computer and faced Emily. "So, what brings you into my office today?"

"Abnormal behavior," Kathleen said.

"Ah." Dr. Wong smiled. "The chronic and untreatable disease of teenager-itis. My professional, medical advice, give it time. Practice patience. It will, with a little luck, go away on its own."

Kathleen didn't find the doctor's humor funny. "Abnormal behavior as in, she defecates and urinates in her bed. She rubs her food all over her body. She refuses to shower, to brush her teeth, to dress herself for the day. I think she's lost ten pounds in a week because she won't eat. She's become violent, even to the point of biting me. And she talks to herself, saying crazy, illogical nonsense."

Dr. Wong's airy demeanor grew heavier and darker with each passing word. By the time Kathleen finished speaking, the doctor had crossed her arms over her chest and wore a frown.

"We moved into a new house about a week ago. That's when the behavior began. I don't know why—I don't know if it's related to an underlying disease or a mental breakdown or what. We have an appointment with a therapist tomorrow. I just..." Kathleen exhaled an airy laugh, as if embarrassed. "Short of a demon possession, I don't know what's going on with her."

"Apart from a mental disorder, personality changes from a medical condition usually involve only a few reasons," Dr. Wong said. "Dementia, which Emily is too young to experience, or cancer. Specifically, a brain tumor."

Kathleen swallowed her tongue, and the room caved in around her, crushing her. She couldn't breathe. She couldn't see or feel anything apart from a vibration, a deep-rooted buzzing that tormented her. "A brain tumor?"

"Has Emily had severe head trauma at any point in her life?"

"No."

Dr. Wong nodded and blinked too hard. "Drastic behavioral changes could also stem from a thyroid disease. I would recommend imaging of the brain and blood tests for thyroid functioning. If we can eliminate those early, we can explore other, less dangerous, causes. I think you're making a wise decision by taking her to a psychiatrist. If she's suffering from schizophrenia, bipolar disorder, or depression, they can help her."

Kathleen heard the doctor's words, but she didn't really comprehend them. The constant vibration ruled her mind. Besides, her baby couldn't have a brain tumor. That wasn't possible.

"Mrs. Jones," Dr. Wong said.

"Kosar," Kathleen said.

"Nix," Emily said, giggling.

The doctor frowned again—her fiery energy snuffed by Emily and Kathleen. "I'll refer you to a specialist, and I'll order blood tests. We'll move forward from there. In the meantime, don't miss your appointment with the psychiatrist tomorrow. That's the most important thing."

"Do you really think she can have a brain tumor?" Kathleen asked.

"I can't say for certain what's wrong with her, but I can say with confidence you are doing the right thing by jumping on this early." Dr. Wong faced Emily. "How do you feel right now?"

"Honestly, we skipped breakfast to get here on time." Emily burst into a fit of laughter before she reached the punchline line, so she had to sputter it out. "I'm starving to death."

Day Twelve. Tuesday, October 17th. 1022hrs.

EMILY SAT IN THE backseat with headphones cupped over her ears, her music blaring loud enough for Kathleen to hear it from the front seat. She fixed her eyes on the rearview mirror, adjusting it so it reflected her daughter.

Emily appeared cadaverous. A yellowish, waxen tint covered her pale skin, and her eyes sank into her shallow face. Despite her protestation of hunger at the doctor's office the day before, Emily refused to eat when Kathleen drove through Taco Bell. Kathleen ordered food, her daughter's usual order. Yet, when they arrived at the house, Emily smashed it into doughy tortilla balls and chucked them across her room.

Terrified and helpless, Kathleen pulled a chair into Emily's bedroom, where she sat all afternoon, where she slept all night. She hadn't spoken to Doug for over a day. Not that she had sought him out, but he hadn't come to her either. Instead, it almost felt like he avoided her.

Yesterday evening, when Kathleen slipped out of Emily's room to grab dinner, Doug exited the kitchen as she entered—as if avoiding her entirely.

Why, though? What reason would he have to avoid her? She should avoid (*leave—I should leave*) him. He's the one who lied about his finances and imprisoned their family in a house they couldn't pay for. He incited Emily's recent bout of unexplainable behavior. If they had not moved out of the apartment, the place where Emily and Kathleen had lived for nearly a decade, none of this would have happened.

Doug had insisted, though. When Kathleen posed a rebuttal, a counterargument about her concerns, he dismissed her, as if what she thought didn't matter to him.

Now look at them. Doug was silent and absent, scrambling to pull a few dollars together to repay his financier. Emily was sicker than ever before. And Kathleen had to pick up the broken pieces of their shattered lives.

As they sat in the psychiatrist's parking lot, Kathleen peered into the rearview mirror at her daughter. Emily bobbed her head in time to the excessively loud music and stared out the back passenger window.

A gut-wrenching feeling squeezed Kathleen, suffocated her. She had vowed, after leaving Marshall Nix, to protect her Emily from the dangerous, unpredictable world. When she married Doug, she had done so out of a sense of duty more than out of love. Doug represented a positive, constant father figure for Emily. He represented security. Stability. With him in their lives, Kathleen could focus on Emily, on keeping her safe.

Except, Doug had crumpled like water added to a paper man. He couldn't handle the pressure of a marriage, the responsibility of a father. He had steered their ship into the center of a storm, and he hadn't prepared for the possibility of a storm. Their lives sloshed and twirled and lurched around them, and all they could do was hold on and try not to fall overboard.

Kathleen helped her daughter into her wheelchair and pushed her into the psychiatry office.

Dr. Amy Riddle was an angular woman with sharp features, almost resembling a hawk. Despite her petite size, she was intimidating. She sat across the dark-toned office—dark leather chairs, a dark metal desk, dark wooden bookshelves—like a wolf stalking her prey. "Mrs. Kosar," Dr. Riddle said, "Emily. Good morning. I want to make this meeting's purpose clear. We're not here for a session, but to assess and discuss your concerns. So, why don't we do that first?"

"Okay," Kathleen said.

"What brings you here today?"

"I'm possessed by the evil spirit of Vernon Nowak, a man who killed his family over fifty years ago then killed himself. He has penetrated my body, and now he uses me like his puppet whenever he pleases."

Emily snickered, a great deal of sarcasm heaped into her voice. "That's what my mother and my step-father believe, anyway."

"What do you believe?" Dr. Riddle asked, her expression never changing, remaining tight and scrunched.

Emily shrugged dismissively. "I think I hate my life, especially my mother. I hate her so much, and I wish Vernon Nowak's spirit would possess my body and use me to kill her like he killed his family. That's what I think."

The words stung Kathleen like a swarm of hornets biting her—they physically hurt her enough that she cringed and flinched as Emily spoke.

"Why is that, Emily? Why do you hate your mother?"

"Because she has killed dozens of people."

A cryptic silence and an iciness filled the office. Kathleen shivered. Emily smirked.

Dr. Riddle never changed her stony expression. "She murdered dozens of people?"

"Poor choice of words," Emily said. "She's responsible for the deaths of dozens of people. She's responsible for so much evil, one might think the spirit of Vernon Nowak possessed her."

"Kathleen," Dr. Riddle said, shifting her sharp eyes, "how would you like to respond?"

Kathleen's mouth had gone completely dry. She licked her lips, circled her tongue around the inside of her mouth to wet it, to oil the hinges enough for her to talk. "We moved into a new house almost two weeks ago."

"Oh. My. God," Emily said, drawing out each vowel. "Blah. Blah. Blah. It's the same dumb story and excuse for everyone, isn't it? Why can't you accept responsibility for what you've done and continue to do? Why? Why not? Why can't you?"

"Emily, please, allow your mother to speak her thoughts."

Kathleen swallowed back a sob. "We moved into a new house and that's when she displayed odd, erratic behavior. She refuses to behave like a civilized person anymore."

"Civilized?" Dr. Riddle asked.

"She won't eat, dress, shower, brush her teeth, or comb her hair. She refuses to use a toilet, but uses her bed and rests in her filth. When we—my husband and I—speak to her, she grows upset and says outlandish things in different voices."

"It's because I'm possessed," Emily said. "Duh. There's a demon inside of me, and he feels so, so good."

"See what I mean? She's extremely crude and speaks in such a foul manner. She's harmed herself and me. The doctor said she could have a brain tumor. I'm sure you'll say something like schizophrenia. Emily's not wrong when she says Doug and I think she could suffer from a possession. That's the problem, though. We don't know what's wrong with her, and so we don't know how to help her, and it keeps getting worse. Every single day it gets so much worse." Tears formed and fell freely from her eyes.

Dr. Riddle held her tongue for a few seconds, shifting her stoic attention between mother and daughter. "Emily, would you care to respond to your mother?"

"Why? It won't matter. She'll only hear what she wants to hear, but she won't listen to me. She won't see me."

"Is that what this is? You're forcing your mother to look at you. Emily, looking and seeing are two vastly different things, despite what many think."

"You're taking my mom's side, then?"

"I'm not taking sides. I'm merely stating that if your behavior, as your mother described it, is a conscious decision, a ploy, for your mother to see you, it's the wrong tactic."

"What do you mean, I don't see you?" Kathleen asked, shifting to face her daughter. "What does that mean, considering my entire life revolves around you? All I do is see you and your needs, and I recognize them, and I meet them."

Emily threw back her head and bellowed laughter. "Wow. Really? You do everything you do for *me*? That's the joke of the century. Everything you do, all of it is for *you*, and you alone."

"I've sacrificed my entire life to take care of you."

"You're pathetic."

"Ladies," Dr. Riddle said in her sharp, lucid voice. "Please. I understand you're both feeling wronged. It's not my agenda to pick a side, to make one of you feel inferior to the other. It's my goal for you to hear each other and to see each other—to recognize and empathize with the perspective of the other person."

"What is wrong with my daughter?" Kathleen asked. "Why won't she eat? Why won't she bathe? This isn't a matter of... of understanding perspective. It's a matter of sanity, of life and death. She's not well."

"Kathleen, I'm an impartial observer, and I've only observed this single interaction. You've told me what you've observed at home, and I appreciate that, and it's noted. I have not observed it, though."

"You're calling me a liar? Why would I schedule this appointment with you just to make up stories?" Kathleen shook her head and mumbled beneath her breath, leaning over and collecting her purse off the floor. "This was useless and a waste of time. I should've stuck to the church."

"Wait," Emily said. "Mom, wait."

Kathleen half-sat, half-stood, hovering over her seat before lowering herself into the chair. "What?"

"The voice in my head is telling me to stay here, with the heathen. It's begging me not to go to the church. Please, don't make me step inside the church. I'll scream and scream and scream, and I'll thrash, and I'll rip out my hair, and shout curses. I don't want to go into the church.

Please, let's stay here with Satan's pawn." Emily's smile stretched into a clownish grin. "Just kidding. Let's have a chat with Father Hartke."

Kathleen, wide-eyed and slack-jawed, turned to Dr. Riddle, silently pleading with her to help.

The psychiatrist merely stared back, watching Emily with interest.

"Thanks, Doc, for nothing," Emily said. "I won't be coming back, but maybe give your card to my mom. She can use a lot of help up in the old attic. There are a lot of skeletons living in there." Before anyone had the chance to respond, Emily rolled herself out of the office.

"I'm so sorry," Kathleen said, red and burning with embarrassment. "You can email me the bill for this session." She stood and waded toward the door. "I'm so sorry."

As she stepped into the lobby, someone intercepted her, grabbed her wrist, and screamed, "Boo!"

Kathleen nearly fainted with fright, but anger replaced fear when she saw Emily standing before her, wearing a wide-set grin.

"That's how easy it would be, Mom. You wouldn't ever see it coming."

"See what coming?" Kathleen's voice was broken and muted, because she knew the answer without having to ask the question.

"Me coming. Me coming to kill you."

Day Thirteen. Wednesday, October 18th. 1800hrs.

KATHLEEN HAD COME HOME the day before, after seeing Dr. Riddle, and shared with Doug what happened. She also went back a day, telling him about the appointment with Dr. Wong.

"I don't know what to think. I don't know what to do. Doug, what do we do?" She stared catatonically out the living room window.

Doug paced back and forth behind the couch. Between them, filling their silence and the cold of the house, the fireplace burned wood, cracking and popping.

"Doug?"

"What?"

"What do we do?"

Doug had spent the past couple of days researching people who could help them. Father Hartke had all but said the Catholic Church couldn't help, and if they could, the process would take time. Anything learned from a doctor or psychiatrist would also take time—tests, observances, and an array of drugs and medications.

Doug couldn't wait. Neither could Kathleen. They needed an immediate fix, not only for Emily's sake, but for their future. If an evil spirit haunted their house and possessed their daughter, they needed to exorcise it. So, Doug had dedicated the last two days to finding that immediate fix.

He found Jack and Janet Perron, self-proclaimed demonologists with track records to prove their authority. On two other occasions, they had eradicated malevolent spirits from homes.

Kathleen accepted the idea without hesitation. In fact, Doug thought she looked relieved at the idea. Seeing color redden in her face for the first time in a week drew a chuckle from him.

"What's so funny?" she asked.

"Gallows humor."

"What do you mean?"

"Laughing in the face of death, that's all. What else can I do, you know?"

Kathleen, as if testing it out, laughed as well. Softly at first, but her amusement grew and became infectious. She and Doug leaned on each other and laughed like two people with nothing left to do but laugh.

"The craziest part about all of this," Doug said, wiping a tear from his cheek, "is you went to the doctors, and I went to the self-proclaimed demonologists." He took a deep breath. "It's just... it's crazy how fear will turn us around, drive us to seek answers beyond our scope and understanding."

Kathleen touched her husband's face and looked at him with doe eyes.

Doug wanted to lean forward and kiss her lips, but he pulled back an inch. Despite their warm moment, a cold, dark chasm existed between them. She had partnered with Marshall Nix, a cult leader responsible for nearly a hundred deaths. She had stood by his side.

A small voice in the back of Doug's head reminded him that Nix had manipulated and abused her, forced her to stand by his side. Kathleen had played no active role in the illicit activities. She only behaved in a way she deemed best to protect her daughter. And that wasn't a lie—that was her core.

Kathleen had always behaved in a way she deemed best to protect her daughter.

"What are you thinking about?" Kathleen asked, her hand grasping Doug around the back of his neck.

Doug took a second to gather his thoughts. She didn't know he had learned about the cult, and he wasn't sure if he wanted to share that knowledge yet. There was something deeply powerful about knowing something about someone without them being aware. It was like watching her through a one-way glass. Did he want to lose that edge?

Before he could decide, a knock sounded on the front door, startling them both.

Kathleen giggled, covering her heart. "I'm so skittish these days."

"Me, too." Doug walked to the front door and opened it.

A husband and a wife duo in their early sixties stood on the front porch. The husband, Jack Perron, had a neat gray beard trimmed to perfection and slicked-back hair with more black than gray in it. He wore a sharp suit and a gold crucifix hung over his tie. The wife, Janet Perron, had chestnut hair tied in a braid, and eyes that seemed to change color with every blink.

"Hi. Um, good evening. I'm Doug. And," he turned and reached back for Kathleen, "this is my wife, Kathy. Please, come inside. I have beer in the refrigerator and coffee in the pot, if you're thirsty."

Janet closed her eyes and muttered beneath her breath, raising her hands to her forehead, connecting all five of her fingertips. After a few seconds, her eyes snapped open, and she stumbled back a step. "I sense," she said, breathing hard, "a powerful, malignant presence within your home."

Doug licked his lips and glanced at his wife. She stared wide-eyed at the woman. "What does that mean?" Doug asked. "What do we do?"

"You said we can come in?" Jack asked, his tone level. "Let's start there."

Doug and Kathleen stepped aside, allowing Jack and Janet into their home, taking them into the kitchen.

"Dark energy feeds on negative emotions," Janet said. "Hate, anger, and fear fuel evil, provide it with power." She faced Doug. "You shared your experience with us. I'm aware of your fear, possibly your confusion. What of anger, though? What of hate? Have you felt a tension in your marriage?"

Doug stared at the floor, which must have served as enough of an answer.

"The longer you stay here," Janet said, "while fostering such harmful emotions, the stronger the entity becomes. The more violent, the hungrier to destroy and devour."

"You're saying we should leave?" Kathleen asked.

"That's impossible," Doug said. "We don't have anywhere to go."

"The entity is like a leech. It has attached itself to you. It feeds on your doubt and negativity. Even if you move, it'll follow you. To rid yourself of it, to banish it from this home and from your souls, you must poison it."

Again, the word, the action that recently haunted Doug. Poison.

"How?" Kathleen asked, ever too eager to learn how to destroy.

"With positive emotion," Janet said. "You must always fight darkness with light, negativity with positivity, hate with love. If you wish to sever your connection from this evil, you must employ laughter, empathy, patience, hope, and faith, even in the most dire of situations. It will test you. The more you fight it, the harder it will fight back."

"You can't expel it?" Doug asked.

Jack stepped forward to answer the question. "We can help by providing you with an advantage. We'll cleanse your home, fill it with a positive aura, and we'll pray for you. Ask the Lord to fill your hearts with His presence, with His love. In doing so, we won't exorcise the entity, but we'll weaken it. We'll create an opportunity for you to fight."

"What about my daughter?" Kathleen asked. "Is she possessed?"

"It's likely that she is," Janet said. "Darkness such as this prefers to attach itself to young women, usually those at the age of menarche. Though we may expel the entity from your home and from your souls, it will be much more difficult to exorcise it from your daughter."

"What do you mean?"

"A possession differs from a haunting. With a haunting, we can cleanse the home by burning sage, cleaning, and reorganizing the furniture. Often spirits haunt familiar locales. To change something is enough to rid yourself of the evil. Exuding positive emotions only strengthens your cause. A haunting is an external event. With a possession, the entity has seized control of a person's soul. It's internal."

"We've exorcised entities before," Jack said. "The first step is the most difficult. We have to identify and name the entity attached to your daughter. Only by using its true name can we compel it to leave, and even then, it will resist. It's a tricky process, one best performed by an acting and qualified member of the clergy."

"It'll take too long for the church to help us," Kathleen said.

"That's why we called you," Doug said. "We're desperate."

"Unfortunately, unlike the church, we're not a charity," Janet said. "We can help, but our services require compensation."

"Whatever the cost," Kathleen said. "Please, just help my daughter."

Doug grabbed his wife's hand. "Excuse us." He tugged on her arm and led her into the dining room. "Whatever the cost? We can't afford to stay in a hotel room. Whatever the cost isn't a realistic payment option."

Kathleen averted her gaze, staring at the chandelier. She whispered, the words barely leaping off her lips. "I can pay it."

"What?"

"I have money."

"What?" Doug asked, utterly confused. He cocked his head. His hands clenched, squeezing Kathleen's knuckles together. "What do you mean, you have money?"

"You're hurting me."

He hadn't realized the pressure he applied to her. Doug released her hand. "Kathy, what do you mean?"

She massaged her fingers and stared at the rain-drop diamonds on the chandelier. "I inherited some money, and I put it away in case... just in case, you know?"

"I don't know. I've busted my butt to provide for this family."

"You've gambled away all our finances."

Doug bit his lip. "You've had money this entire time? How much?"

"It doesn't matter."

"We could've used it to advertise my company. To pay back the debts I owe."

"The debts you owe, not me."

A crazy thought crashed into Doug, one borne from the anger of being blindsided. "It's his money, isn't it?"

"Whose money?

"Nix's. Well, not his. It's their money, the people you and he killed. They gave you everything, right? All their land and fortune. When Nix died, you inherited it all. How's that possible, Barbara?" Doug used her birth name like throwing a jab. "Why did the police not seize your assets?"

Kathleen lowered her gaze and stared at her husband, terror rich in her eyes.

"How do you live with yourself, knowing you possess all that fortune that belongs to the families of those you killed?"

Like a cobra striking, Kathleen reached out and slapped Doug across the face. "You know nothing." Without another word, she shoved past him and headed back into the kitchen. "I'll pay whatever you ask. But you have to help my daughter."

Doug remained standing in the dining room, his hand touching his stinging face. He stared out the picture window, collecting his thoughts.

As he calmed, a face—a skull—appeared behind the dark glass. It had hollow eyes and sunken cheeks and the permanent grin of death.

Day Fourteen. Thursday, October 19th. 0224hrs.

Jack and Janet worked deep into the night and early morning, cleansing and purifying the home from negative energy. Janet burned sage and moved through the house. Jack organized leather-bound books and used strange equipment to banish otherworldly creatures.

The demonologists moved at a painstaking pace. "Every detail has to be right," Jack said as the time rushed toward midnight. "We have to negate the pent-up negative energy pulsating within the house before battling it. It takes time."

When Janet completed her course of the house, burning sage in every corner of every room, she returned to the kitchen and removed candles from a canvas bag. She spoke a mantra beneath her breath as she lit seven white waxen candles with seven matchsticks. Once lit, she spread them around the house.

"One in the entryway, near the threshold of your home," she said. "One for each room—the master bedroom, the two bedrooms, the playroom, the living room, and the dining room. Places of congregation and fellowship. The candles represent divine light, that which expels the darkness of evil."

After she placed the candles, Jack secured a container of salt, and Janet reached for a vial of holy water. Once more, they went from room to room. Jack seasoning the home with salt, while Janet soaked the floors and walls with water. As they worked, they prayed aloud.

"It's going to work," Kathleen said during the madness.

Doug swiveled his jaw back and forth and shook his head. "If not, we're going to have quite the mess to clean up."

"That's what you're thinking about? We have to stay positive, remember? We have to believe."

"Like I believed in this marriage?"

"What does that mean?"

"You have a fortune you hid from me. Do you know how much I've stressed about finances?"

"Because you're a gambling addict, and you pissed away all your money?"

"Because you spend every dime I earn on some drug or trial or medical nonsense for your daughter." The words singed Doug's lips as they exploded out of his mouth. He immediately closed his eyes with regret. "I'm sorry. I didn't—"

"You meant it. But it's not my fault, and it's definitely not Emily's fault, that you can't manage your money."

Doug chewed on his cheeks, not knowing how to proceed. Anger, fear, and guilt all swirled together, forming a vortex of negative emotion—forming into doubt. He turned to Kathleen, sadness in his eyes. "What if it doesn't work? What do we do?"

Kathleen marched out of the kitchen.

Twenty minutes later, everyone congregated in Emily's room.

Janet and Jack prayed over the teenage girl. They asked her pointed, clarifying questions about the entity possessing her—mostly prying out the demon's name to use against it.

Emily spit at them. She cackled and screamed, answered crudely and nonsensically, changing the pitch of her voice.

Doug stood with his back against the bedroom door, his arms crossed. Kathleen stood beside him, though a distance spanning worlds and realms separated them. She had one arm over her chest, the other upright, so her hand covered her mouth.

After grueling, painstaking hours, Emily collapsed, her body as boneless as a rag doll as sleep overwhelmed her.

The Perrons packed up their tools, and Doug led them to the front door.

"We've recorded everything," Janet said, holding Doug's icy hands in hers. "We'll review our notes, share them with colleagues to hear their professional opinions, and then come up with a plan."

"A plan?" Kathleen asked. "I thought... did you not perform the exorcism already?"

"We prodded." Janet released Doug's hands. "In terms of war, we canvassed the battlefield to learn about our enemy. Hopefully, after further discussion and research, we can discern the name of the entity."

"When will that be?" Kathleen asked.

"We'll be in touch soon," Jack said. "But until we know more about this entity, we can't say for certain. There's nothing we can do until we've discerned its identity."

Janet drifted to Kathleen and grabbed her hands. "Remember, positive emotion will weaken evil. Laugh whenever you can. Express joy and love more than lament and hate. Disadvantage yourself to advantage your loved ones. Positivity will repel the entity."

Kathleen nodded her understanding, but concern masked her face. "You said that if the spirit feels threatened, it will fight back. What if it does? What if Emily becomes worse?"

"Contact a priest," Jack said.

Doug cleared his throat. "We already did."

"Contact a priest and ask him to pray over your family, even if it's from the cathedral."

"When we're confident we can do more, we'll return to continue with the process," Janet said. "Once we've identified a name, we'll go to work exorcising the demon."

"If you can't come up with a name?" Kathleen asked.

"We'll repeat tonight and speak with Emily again to learn more about its nature."

Jack grabbed the door handle and swung it open. "Also, to be clear, even if we have a name, we can't return until you've submitted the payment. I'll invoice you for tonight, as well as for the time we'll spend researching the entity."

An anger-fueled heat flushed through Doug at the mention of payment. He exhaled, though, keeping his cool and expelling himself of the negative emotion in an intentional practice to breed positivity.

"I'll send you the money as soon as I receive the invoice," Kathleen said.

"Remember to smile and laugh," Janet said, following her husband out the front door.

Doug, not having anything to say to his wife that would encourage positivity, went to bed.

He slept little, waking before 0700hrs. Kathleen snored beside him.

He slipped from bed and ambled into the kitchen, brewed a pot of coffee, and prepared breakfast.

Kathleen arrived in the kitchen a little before 0800hrs. She still wore her pajamas, but lacked makeup, and her hair stood in a ratted mess. Doug hesitantly wrapped an arm around her waist and pulled her tight against his body.

"You look amazing." He kissed her.

She kissed him back.

When they pulled away, they smiled at each other.

Janet's parting words haunted Doug's mind—remember to smile. He planned to do just that, even if it hurt or became uncomfortable. Doug intended to go over the top with positivity to save his family, his marriage, and the house.

He fixed a plate for Kathleen, poured her a cup of coffee, and placed the meal at the dining room table. They sat beside each other, playfully kicking one another's legs.

"Can I pray?" Kathleen asked.

Doug shrugged, pretending to contemplate the question. They had never prayed as a family or as husband and wife. Though Kathleen attended church most Sundays, Doug didn't care for her to bring religion into his life. Yet, at the breakfast table, after experiencing what they had experienced over the past two weeks, Doug welcomed the prayer.

"Please."

Kathleen grabbed her husband's hand. "God," she said. "Bless this food that my gracious, awesome husband prepared. Bless our home." She emphasized home, not saying this house or this place, but highlighting home. "Bless our family with your spirit. We pray these things in your wonderful and powerful name."

"Amen," said a quiet voice from the edge of the room.

Kathleen and Doug nearly jumped from their seats.

Emily sat in her wheelchair behind them.

"Is there enough food for me?"

Had God answered Kathleen's prayer? Had the Perron's cleansing techniques worked on Emily?

Doug was speechless at the sudden emergence of his stepdaughter, at her speaking calmly and asking for food.

What had happened? Was it their over-assertive display of positivity that beckoned her downstairs?

"Baby." Kathleen covered her mouth in shock.

"Of course there's food for you," Doug said, working a smile onto his bewildered expression. "Come to the table. I'll make your plate." He stood. "Are you hungry?"

"I'm starving." Emily wheeled her chair to the head of the table.

Doug hurried into the kitchen, as if haste might deter Emily from reverting and retreating to her room. He threw her plate together. "Do you want whipped cream on your pancakes?"

"And berries, please."

Doug put the finishing touches on her breakfast and delivered the meal. "Extra bacon, no eggs, and fluffy pancakes, just like you like it."

Emily chuckled, an innocent sound. "Thank you."

They sat around the old table, a picture of the perfect family. The three of them smiled and laughed. They conversed even after polishing off their plates and pushing them forward. The simple practice of stepping into pure love had momentarily erased Doug's concerns.

He forgot about his inability to find work, his debt, about the entity roaming within the home, about the Perrons and the priest, about Kathleen's ties to the cult. It all stepped into a shroud of mist, leaving Doug to enjoy the warm moment.

A moment that lasted beyond breakfast.

Emily offered to help clean the kitchen. Doug connected his phone to a speaker and turned on a classic rock station. The three of them washed, dried, and put away dishes, singing and dancing as they worked.

When they finished the chore—a task Doug never wanted to end—Emily wheeled her chair back a few feet. "It's a sunny day. Can we sit outside and..." she trailed off and shrugged, as if afraid to finish her question.

"We can do whatever you want," Kathleen said.

"I just wanted to sit outside and read and hangout." She glanced at Doug. "Do you have to work today?"

Emily's question, though innocent, brought a dark cloud over the room.

"Not today," he said.

"What do you think, then?" Emily asked. "Can we enjoy the weather?"

They did. Emily threw a tennis ball to Frank, who lumbered after it like an oversized seal. Kathleen watched, a proud, relieved smile carved into her face. Doug tinkered around the yard, pulling weeds and raking fallen leaves.

The day slipped away, hour by hour, little by little, moving toward the long, dark tomorrow far too fast.

Day Fifteen. Friday, October 20th. 2324hrs.

Doug worked outside beneath a canopy of construction lights. He seeded the soil he had leveled to grow his lawn, transplanting shrubs and trees from pots to holes he dug. Clouds blotted the late-night sky, dark and heavy, and an occasional pattering of rain sprinkled to the ground. The weather report foretold an incoming storm, one that would wash the Sacramento region for the better part of a week.

Despite the chilly night, moist air, and the cool breeze, Doug paused his toiling to wipe sweat from his brow. As he stared across the dark horizon, a piercing, glass-shattering scream ruptured from inside the house.

For a few seconds, he remained frozen as his mind processed the sudden screech. Then he burst across the yard, through the front door, up the stairs, and into Emily's bedroom.

After their picture-perfect day—the sunny break from the storm ravaging their lives—Emily fell into a near-catatonic state. She was, or Kathleen surmised, worn from the exerted energy of the day before. Emily had gone to bed early, had slept all morning into the early afternoon.

Cue the blood-curdling scream.

Kathleen beat Doug to her daughter's bedroom. Doug fell in behind her. His eyes prodded around the room; his heart crashed in his chest. He suspected the worst.

Emily sat in bed. She covered her mouth with both hands; her eyes were hooked wide open with fear.

Kathleen nearly tackled her daughter. "Baby, what happened? Are you okay?" She held Emily, brushing her knotted hair with her fingers.

Doug ran in the opposite direction as the bed, moving toward the closet, throwing open the door to check for threats.

What kind of threat? A ghost? A monster?

Nothing beyond clothes and shoes hid in the small, dark space.

Doug returned his attention to Emily and Kathleen. "What happened?"

"Frank." Emily gasped out the dog's name. Tears filled her eyes and slipped down her cheeks.

"What about Frank?"

"He's gone."

"Gone where?"

"I don't know!"

"Baby, what happened?" Kathleen asked, stroking her daughter's hair. "Can you tell me what happened?"

Doug cracked his knuckles, feeling helpless and not knowing what to do. He combed his fingers through his unkempt hair, which had grown more unruly by the day since moving into the house. "Where's Frank now?" He tried to keep his voice steady, but the question boomed off his lips.

"He took him," Emily said.

"Who took him?"

"The man without a face."

The entity with a skull for a head crossed Doug's mind. "Who?"

"Vernon Nowak," Emily said. "That is what he says his name is. Vernon Nowak."

"You've seen him before?" Doug asked. "You didn't tell us?"

"He… he sometimes comes into my room at night when I'm sleeping."

"What?" Kathleen said. "He does what? Doug, call the police."

Doug remained rooted in the middle of the room.

"I thought he was fake, like an extension of a dream, but he just came in here." Emily spoke fast. "Frank growled, but Vernon hit him."

"Hit him?" Doug asked, growing more confused with each passing word.

Frank weighed over a hundred-fifty pounds. Who would hit a dog that large?

What would hit a dog that large?

"Frank went quiet," Emily said. "Vernon picked him up and carried him away."

"Baby." Kathleen rested her face on Emily's shoulder.

Doug couldn't compute how someone (*something*) had carried Frank away fast enough to avoid getting seen by Doug or Kathleen. He was sure Emily screamed when Vernon hit Frank. Surely Doug responded quickly enough to climb stairs before anyone (*anything*) could carry off an enormous dog.

"Where did he go?" Doug asked.

"That way." Emily pointed at the wall behind her, at the spare bedroom.

Without hesitation, Doug rushed out of Emily's room and into the spare bedroom, not sure what he would do if he encountered Vernon. Unfortunately, he saw nothing apart from the boxes they hadn't unpacked and bedroom furniture covered in dusty drop cloths.

The entity had vanished again, and this time, with Frank as its prisoner.

Doug returned to Emily's bedroom, crestfallen and defeated.

"What do we do?" Kathleen asked, staring at her husband with crazed eyes. "We can't stay here. We can't risk whatever is haunting us to hurt my daughter."

Emily wore a pleased and knowing smirk.

Anger didn't boil within Doug, though. Fear did. A newborn fear spawned from personal revelation and newfound belief—a dark, evil entity haunted the house and possessed Emily. It had already hurt the girl by taking over her mind and body.

"We can't leave without Frank," Emily said. "We have to find him."

"Doug," Kathleen said.

"We don't have anywhere to go."

"Doug."

Doug grimaced and half-growled. Kathleen was right. They couldn't stay at the house another night. "We can sleep in the truck for the night. That's the best I can do without time to plan."

"What about the RV?"

Doug nodded for a second before switching to a quick shake. "Maybe... but we're on the property. Who's to say whatever is happening inside the house won't spill over? We can give it a shot, but I don't know."

"You can borrow more money."

He thought of Victor Petrov's response to Doug's house call. "I can't."

"Doug."

"Kathy, I can't. I'm too far in debt."

"I don't care about your debt. I want out of this house. Get us the money to move us somewhere else."

"Okay," Doug said, his voice becoming cool and calm.

"Okay?"

"Get us a hotel room."

"What?"

"You have money, right? An entire fortune that doesn't belong to you? Use it. Pay for us to leave this God-forsaken home, if that's what you really want."

"I can't," Kathleen said, lowering her gaze.

"You can't, or you won't?"

"I can't."

"Please enlighten me. Why can't you save your daughter in her time of need? You do nothing but dote on her all day, every day. But when it matters, you can't step up to the plate? Why is that?"

"It's in assets, not liquid cash. It's tied up in banks and stocks and properties. It'll take days, possibly weeks, to access it."

"What about a credit card?"

Kathleen slowly shook her head.

"What about the Perrrons? You offered to pay them for their services. How do you plan on doing that if your money is tied up?"

"I had small amount of cash put aside. A rainy-day fund."

"It seems like you have a hell of a lot of excused put aside. Do you want to help your daughter or not?"

"What do you think?" Kathleen asked, raising her voice.

Doug growled and rubbed the back of his head as he stared at his stepdaughter—a caricature of pain and fear. "Okay. Fine. We'll stay in the RV until you can liquidate some more money."

Emily's entire demeanor shifted. She cackled, throwing back her head and howling at the ceiling. "I don't think that's possible. I don't think that's a possibility, unless you wish to burn, burn, burn in Hell."

Kathleen separated from her daughter and scooted away, nearly tumbling off the edge of the bed.

"Burn, burn, burn, in Hell, Hell, Hell." Her maniacal shrieking calmed. In a deep, gravely voice, as if played by a recording, Emily asked, "We'll only escape this house through death."

Doug backed out of the room, ran across the hallway, and stepped into the playroom, which overlooked the RV-side of the house.

As he stared, the flames engulfing the RV and licking the storm-laced sky danced in his eyes.

Day Sixteen. Saturday, October 21st. O552hrs.

DOUG SPENT THE NIGHT outside with firefighters and law enforcement officers. Over the few hours of preliminary investigation and interviews, they hadn't identified the source of the fire.

He chewed on his cheeks and twisted his hands around each other. His thoughts ran rampant, spinning from the fire to the ghost to Victor Petrov. Had Emily, while in her bed, used demonic power to ignite the fire? How had she known the RV burned? How would Victor Petrov react to the catastrophic incident? Doug was also, per the usual, worried over money. He had declined an insurance policy for the RV, as he couldn't afford the payment. How would he replace it? Where would they stay?

Where did that leave him?

A few days ago, Doug had put the RV for sale on Facebook Marketplace, Craigslist, and the local paper. He received a few interested messages, too. Now, burned to the ground, he had no hopes of selling the RV to recoup some money.

The charcoaled RV also prevented them from leaving the house unless the three of them desired to sleep in his truck. It could work. They could set a mattress over the truck bed, pack a bundle of blankets, and sleep beneath the stars.

Except for the dark clouds and the impending storm.

Doug needed to buy a day or two, enough time to borrow more money to pay for a hotel room.

What horrors awaited them in the meantime? Would they survive another night in the haunted house?

That's how Doug thought of it now. A haunted house.

Beneath the cloud-soaked sky, he swallowed back mind-shattering laughter. How much longer could he keep everything inside before he detonated?

Haunted. How else did he explain everything that had happened over the past two weeks? Emily's erratic behavior, the entity appearing and disappearing at will, the upturned kitchen? None of it made any sense, unless processed in the light of the supernatural.

Which pitted Doug deeper in his financial hole. He owned a haunted house, which meant he had to make the best of it, which ultimately meant he couldn't run away. He had to stand and fight.

How did he fight back, though?

The Perrons wouldn't return until they conducted research. Doug choked back another laugh—a speculative outburst. How did they perform research on an unseen entity? They didn't. They wrote an invoice, which included the time they spent preparing for the exorcism. But they could have written any arbitrary number. How would Doug or Kathleen refute it?

Then there was the Catholic Church. Father Hartke could help at no financial costs. It seemed his help would come after an investigation on their end—a process Doug didn't have time to wait on.

The Kosars needed immediate saving.

A tall, bulky female officer approached Doug in the early morning dark. She interviewed him about the fire, noting his responses. She referenced the deputy sheriffs who visited the home over the past couple of weeks, asking about why Doug had contacted them. "Does it relate to the fire?"

Doug answered the questions in a basic, nonchalant manner. How would she, or any other officer, stop a ghost or a demon or whatever haunted the home? Why waste her time? Why waste his time by spewing nonsense about the supernatural?

"Do you think someone is harassing you?" she asked.

Doug thought of Victor Petrov. He had asked Victor that same question. *Have you sent someone to scare me?* Petrov objected to the idea, convincingly, too. Doug doubted Petrov sent his men to harass him, even as the RV burned.

"No," Doug said, staring at the blackened remains of the RV.

"You don't have an insurance policy on the vehicle?"

"No."

"What do you think happened?"

"I don't know."

"Did you or your wife leave the stove on by accident?"

"No."

He hadn't entered the RV since the night he stayed there, and he hadn't bothered with any propane-related mechanisms during the time. Kathleen, at least to his knowledge, hadn't entered the RV since they moved into the home.

"So, what are you saying?" the officer asked.

"I'm not saying anything."

"Are you saying the RV randomly caught fire?"

"I don't know."

He knew, though, or he believed he knew.

Emily, through her possession, had somehow, from her bed, ignited a flame that devoured the RV. She was showing off her newfound power. It was a show of dominance. If she wanted, she could burn the entire house down. She could kill Doug or Kathleen without resistance.

Yet, Doug couldn't say that to the officer. A *demon has possessed my stepdaughter, and she lit the fire from her bed, using her mind, like the kid from that Stephen King novel.*

At the thought of the ridiculous explanation, Doug swallowed a laugh bordering on the maniacal level of Emily's cackling.

"Well, we'll coordinate with the fire department. They'll investigate the origin of the fire. If they suspect any criminal activity, we'll let you know."

"How long will it take?"

The woman shrugged her broad shoulders. "A few days, maybe a week. It just depends." She reached into her shirt pocket and removed a card. "If you remember anything, or think of something useful, anything at all, please call me."

Doug accepted the card. The name—which he had missed when she introduced herself—read Linda Kelly. She turned and walked away, but not toward her cruiser with flashing lights. Toward his house, where two other officers spoke with Emily and Kathleen.

Doug pattered after Linda, heading toward his wife and stepdaughter. As he reached them, the uniformed officers broke away and congregated a few yards off. Doug grabbed Kathleen's shoulders and pulled her to face him.

"What did you say?"

"The truth."

"That," he lowered my voice, "Emily did this."

"We don't know that. We don't know what happened. That's what I told them." She shimmied away from Doug's grasp to create space between them. "That's not entirely true, though. I know exactly what happened."

"What?"

"You happened, Doug, and you bought this place, despite me begging you not to. You're responsible for all that's happened. For Emily's..." Kathleen trailed off, never to finish the sentence.

Doug knew what she meant to say; he could guess between one of two responses. Emily's possession, or Emily's mental decline. Either way, Kathleen blamed Doug for everything.

Suddenly, the day where their problems had drifted away on the lazy breeze seemed so far, so very far away.

The police and firefighter presence didn't vanish, but slowly dwindled throughout the morning and day. Late into the evening, the last investigator clocked off and left their property, leaving the Kosars alone.

Emily joined Doug and Kathleen at the dinner table. For a bright second, Doug believed everything had returned to normal—that their night would march forward as the day before had gone. Emily had joined them for dinner, after all. She sat before her plate, brandishing an innocent, if not shy, smile.

"Kathy," Doug said, "could you pray?"

Kathleen reached forward and grabbed her fork, and she dug into her meal without a word to Doug.

Taking the hint, Doug reached for his fork and circled the spaghetti around the prongs.

Emily shoved her fingers deep into her throat, forcing herself to gag until she vomited skinny tendrils of bile onto her dinner plate. "Excuse me," she said with a sloppy grin. "Where are my manners?" She grabbed a handful of noodles and shoved them into her mouth, smearing the red sauce around her face so it looked like a bloody mask.

Kathleen's features blanched.

Doug stared at his stepdaughter in disgust and wonder.

Emily stood from her wheelchair, her palms planted on the table for support. She smiled widely, and half-chewed spaghetti noodles oozed from her mouth. "One, two, three, four, five," she said, chanting in a voice two octaves lower than her normal tone. "Once I caused my family to die. Six, seven, eight, nine, ten. I would love to do it again." Her right hand shot upward, and she uppercut herself in the chin.

Kathleen gasped.

Doug jumped to his feet.

Blood mixed with the tomato-based spaghetti sauce leaked from Emily's mouth. She poked out her tongue for a second—a teasing motion—before slapping herself across the face. A red welt formed on her cheek.

"Stop it," Kathleen said.

"She's going to die," Emily said, now in a high-pitched tone. "You're all going to die. One by one. Terrible, violent deaths."

A plate flew from the kitchen into and across the dining room. It shattered against the wall. Another dish, a glass cup, smacked against Doug's arm and broke when it landed on the ground.

He looked into the kitchen, but saw nothing or no one.

Emily staggered forward on weak, under-used legs, walking like a zombie to the nearest wall. She placed her hands on the ornate custom trim, holding herself upright. She reared back her head and slammed it against the plaster, leaving behind a blood stamp.

Kathleen's trance broke. She burst from her seat and sprinted around the table to grab her daughter. Doug joined her. He helped drag Emily away from the wall.

The girl thrashed and screamed. "I'll kill you all! I'll kill you all!" Emily went slack in Doug's arms, slinking to the ground in a boneless heap.

She giggled beneath her breath for a few seconds. "Do you know the Muffin Man?" Emily asked, her voice normal again.

"The Muffin Man?" she asked, her voice lowering to a demonic growl.

"The Muffin Man. He lives on Murder Lane." She fell into a fit of cacophonous screams and giggles.

Kathleen met Doug's eyes, her face a picture of horror. "What do we do?"

"You take the fork, you shove it in your eye," Emily said. "You pry it out, and you eat it until you die." Half-held by Kathleen, Emily made a claw with her hand. She dragged her fingers across her face. "Mommy, make me stop. I'm hurting me. I'm hurting me so, so good. Mommy, please." She giggled.

"Doug, what do we do?" Kathleen screamed.

Doug couldn't remember how to move, let alone what to think or how to act. He hovered over his wife and stepdaughter, speechless and motionless with fear and confusion.

"If you don't save me, Daddy," Emily said, "I'll swallow my tongue. Is that what you want? For me to swallow my tongue?"

"Stop talking like that!" Kathleen screamed. "Stop it!"

"God," Doug said, reacting on autopilot and a sense of survival. He dove into an instinct natural to all humans throughout all of time. He battled the unknown and the unexplainable with prayer. "Help us. Help Emily fight whatever is holding her hostage. Please, God. I swear to you, I will do anything. Please, just help us. Save us. Save Emily. Please." His prayer devolved into a pleading, begging chant.

Yet, it worked.

Emily's chittering silenced. Her thrashing stilled. Her bugged eyes closed. She went limp, as if catatonic.

Doug hoisted her into his arms and carried her up the stairs into her bed, where he laid her down. When he turned to leave her room, Kathleen stood behind him.

They stared at each other for a moment, but neither said a word. A million thoughts ran through his mind. Should he stay in the room with Kathleen and Emily, protect them from another potential outburst? Should he speak to his wife, apologize to her, offer her comfort?

After a few seconds of saying or doing nothing, Doug slipped past Kathleen and went downstairs to clean the dining room.

Day Seventeen. Sunday, October 22nd. 2357hrs.

DOUG SPENT THE DAY on his phone. He called Victor for money, the Catholic Church to send someone to his house, and the Perrons to convince them to expedite their research. He reached out to people who posted their construction needs online, who offered to pay next to nothing to have a tree limb removed or a hole in their wall patched. Doug slotted as many house calls into his calendar as possible, using his general contractor's license to perform handyman tasks.

Doug booked a solid day's worth of work, which would earn him a decent amount of cash, which would transfer directly into Victor Petrov's pocket.

Even after Victor returned his call, and Doug reported the latest incidents, the man drew a hard line. "Live with your demons and whatever is haunting you until you've paid me my money. You can play Scooby-Doo after you've bought out your debt."

The threat played a death toll through Doug's mind. Without access to cash, Doug couldn't pay for a hotel room. To save his family, he had to repay his debts or convince someone to cleanse their house for free. Both paths felt daunting and near impossible.

Besides, what waited at the end for him? What if he orchestrated Emily's exorcism and purified the house, driving away the evil spirits? Would Kathleen, after all that had happened, stay with him? Would she ask for a divorce? Did Doug want to stay with her, especially after learning about her cult ties and hidden fortune?

It seemed like a monumental problem hiding behind the colossal one standing directly before them.

Doug reflected on the day, on his phone calls, on his thoughts as he took a steaming shower. He rested his head against the tile wall and watched the water drizzle down the drain.

What if I steal a page from Vernon Nowak's book? What if I make dinner, poison my family, and solve all my problems at once?

The thought, which abhorred him, also enticed him. Had the evil presence within his home latched onto his soul as well? Had it possessed him?

Doug shoved the dark thoughts away, scouring his mind for a more practical, less violent answer.

Like a steel blade cutting through his spine, the frigid water cut through Doug as the temperature plunged, stealing his breath for a second. He gasped and frantically played with the faucet knobs, adjusting the temperature. The water didn't warm, though. He turned off the water and grabbed a towel, quickly dried himself and dressed.

He glanced at his phone. It was nearly midnight.

What time had he stepped into the shower? How long had he stood beneath the steaming stream? Had he depleted all the hot water?

Doug padded barefoot into the kitchen to grab a beer. A hot pain rushed up his foot. He hopped backward into the hallway and grabbed his heel. A wetness painted across his hand. Hopping forward on one leg, he flicked on the light, not caring if it woke Kathleen.

Blood covered his foot and his fingers. A glass shard stuck into the pad of Doug's heel. He grimaced as he removed the wedge, hissed as it slid from his skin and clattered on the messy floor.

Broken dishes, once again, littered the kitchen. With the lights now on, Doug waded to the pantry cabinet, where they kept the first-aid kit. He avoided the broken plates and glasses. Once he secured the kit, he cleaned the wound and applied bandages.

With the bleeding staunched, Doug dared to assess the damage to his kitchen.

Contents of open drawers lay upturned and spilled over the kitchen floor. Cabinet doors lay askew on hinges, the plates and pots and spices and oils scraped onto the ground. Bags and containers were open, the flour and sugar and cereal and pasta and chips dumped throughout the kitchen. Bottles and cans and cartons from the fridge lay empty and dumped out. The windows were shattered to smithereens. Blue fire burned on the stovetop.

The dining room lay in a similar state of disarray. Windows shattered. The table overturned. Chairs snapped in half. The diamond-laced chandelier strings pulled apart, so they hung like decorative streamers.

The chaos continued into the living room. Above the fireplace, where the television had hung (it now lay broken on the hearth) was a spray painted message: LEAVE OR DIE. The warning, written in bold red, dripping letters, repeated itself over across the entire living room. On the walls, the ceiling, the floor, and drop cloths covering the furniture.

Kathleen screamed from the master bedroom.

Ignoring the pain in his foot, Doug hobbled through the hallway and into their room, flicking on the light.

Kathleen sat up in bed. She pointed at the ceiling. Doug followed her finger. Four dolls hung from the blades of the ceiling fan, all dressed and designed to appear like Doug, Kathleen, Emily, and Frank. They spun in lazy circles.

"What's going on?" Kathleen asked. "I heard you yell, and I woke up and saw this. What is it?" She hopped out of bed. "Is Emily okay?" She moved toward the door, then froze, her eyes wide, her lips slightly parted.

Doug turned. A shock of fear jolted through his body, forcing him nearer to his wife.

In the doorway stood the skull-faced entity. It stared at Doug and Kathleen, its head slightly cocked, as if amused. It pointed at them.

"Go away!" Kathleen screamed. "Leave us alone!"

As if it took orders from her, the figure side-stepped, disappearing into the hallway.

Doug, spurred into action, scampered toward the door and peered outward. The entity had vanished. He limped back to the kitchen, the dining room, the living room, searching for the skull-faced demon, finding nothing but the utter destruction of his house.

From upstairs, a door slammed.

Doug rushed outside to his work truck, grabbed a sledgehammer, dashed back into the home, and up the stairs to Emily's room. He threw open her door.

Kathleen already stood a few feet inside, trembling and swaying like a young tree caught in a heavy wind.

Emily clung to the wall like a spider, her feet and hands stuffed into holes she had punched or kicked into the plaster. She clicked her tongue, like a rabid insect clinking its fangs together.

The door leading into her room slammed behind Doug.

He whipped around, raising the sledgehammer, but he saw nothing. He shifted his gaze to Emily, uncertain of what to do, where to go, how to proceed. Should he grab Emily, drag her into bed? Should he chase after the entity harassing them?

From somewhere on the other side of the door, more glass shattered.

"Take care of Emily," Doug said, throwing Emily's door open and jumping into the hallway with his sledgehammer ready to swing.

Slowly, sliding his feet along the hardwood floor, Doug moved through the hallway to the Jack and Jill bathroom. He toed the slightly askew door open and stepped inside.

The mirror had a spiderweb crack rippling outward from the center. Someone (or something) had painted in red over the shattered glass, LEAVE OR DIE.

Doug stepped to the shower stall, threw open the plastic curtain, and staggered backward. His bare feet stomped through the splintered glass that had fallen on the tile floor. The pain didn't compute, though.

Inside the bathtub lay the maggot-ridden corpse of a squirrel, as well as three snakes that slithered around the gory remains.

Doug, limping, walking gingerly, leaving bloody footprints in his wake, shuffled to the spare bedroom. He panted, breathing rapidly through his mouth. The sledgehammer trembled in his shaking hands as he shouldered open the door.

The room appeared intact, apart from the heap of unpacked boxes and the furniture covered in dusty drop cloths.

Doug turned to pad across the hallway and check the playroom. As his head swiveled around, he saw a silhouette. Before he could react, he stood eye to eye with the skull-faced entity.

Doug flinched and stumbled back two steps.

"Leave!" it screamed in an unnatural, demonic growl.

Doug yelled and lunged forward and arched the sledgehammer through the air.

The figure dipped to the side, dodging the frantic blow. It slipped into the playroom.

Doug took chase, slamming into the large room, ready to strike again.

Nothing but the inherited furniture covered in drop cloths occupied the room. Doug went from table to armoire to bookshelf to couch. He peeked behind the bulky furniture in desperate hopes of locating the skull-faced entity.

He found another broken window. The midnight October wind slipped into the house and wrapped around Doug, sending a sharp chill down his spine. He kicked himself into action, though, knowing he couldn't stand around frozen with fear.

Doug backtracked, returning to Emily's room. His feet bled, but adrenaline muted the pain.

Kathleen remained a statue where he had left her.

Emily remained a spider in her web, waiting patiently for a fly to entrap itself.

Doug hadn't noticed before, probably deaf from shock, but he now heard Emily singing another nursery rhyme.

"The itsy, bitsy spider crawled up the water spout. Down came the blood and washed her family out."

"Get down from there," Doug said, his voice a gruff whisper. He cleared his throat and tried again, shouting his command. "Get down, Emily!"

"Come and make me." She turned her head over her bare shoulder and licked her lips as she glanced at Doug.

"Why is this happening?" Kathleen asked.

The bedroom lights cut out, pitching the room in substantial, thick darkness. After a few seconds, they turned back on. Then, like a child learning about the effects of a light switch, they went off and on, off and on, over and over and over.

Below them, on the first level, a deep moaning climbed up the stairs and floated into Emily's room. It sounded like a foghorn lost in the storm out at sea. When it ended, a cacophonous chuckle took its place, like rapid machine gun firing.

"He's going to kill me and you. Death for everyone." Emily threw back her head and roared with laughter, releasing her grip on the wall and falling backward. She landed on her bed, where she kicked her feet and threw her arms and tossed her head back and forth, all while chanting, "He's going to kill me and you. Death for everyone. He's going to kill me and you. Death for everyone."

Doug dropped the sledgehammer and dashed to the bed. He grabbed his stepdaughter, fighting against her writhing limbs, and he lifted her. "We're leaving," he said, turning to Kathleen.

"Where?"

"I don't know, but we're leaving right now."

"I'm not dressed." Kathleen spoke as if from the other side of the world, or from another plane of existence. Her voice had a distant listlessness; her eyes glazed. "I'm not packed, either."

"We'll get you new clothes." Doug limped to the door.

"How?" Kathleen grabbed her husband as he passed her. "How? You're broke, remember? You can't afford a hotel room. Where will we go? How will we purchase new clothes?"

"You'll figure it out," Doug said. "*You* have the money. I'm sure you'll figure it out."

Kathleen leaned over and lifted the discarded sledgehammer. "I should bash your head into the wall! I shouldn't have married you, you leech. You vampire. Look where you brought us!"

Emily screeched with glee as Doug held her. "Kill him. Smash his brains. Bathe in his blood." Her fingernails burrowed into Doug's back, digging across his skin.

"We'll stay at the church. Father Hartke said they have a place we can stay in case of emergency," Doug said. "It's protected, too, the church. We'll be safe there."

Kathleen seemed to calm at the idea.

Doug lied through his teeth, though. Father Hartke never had offered safe lodging. But Doug needed to diffuse the situation and get Kathleen on board with him. They needed to escape the house before it swallowed their family whole.

"We have to leave," Doug said.

Kathleen slowly lowered the sledgehammer, allowing it to thud against the ground. She stared wide-eyed at her husband.

Emily verbalized an impressive string of profanities, flopping back and forth like a fish in Doug's arms.

"They can help her. The priests at the church. It's our best bet." Doug sank his bloody heels into the lie.

"Okay," Kathleen said. "Alright."

Not wasting another second, Doug turned and flew down the stairs. As he moved through the hallway, past the dining room, a pendulum swing caught his attention. He slowed, noticing the chandelier swaying back and forth in exaggerated arcs.

A few seconds later, Kathleen caught up to him. As she did, the screws and bolts holding the light fixture snapped. The chandelier crashed to the ground, breaking into innumerable pieces.

Kathleen screamed.

Doug groaned, as if shot in the stomach. The strength left his body, and he nearly dropped Emily, who maniacally laughed at the scene.

"Leave!" a voice boomed from the stairwell. The entity with the skull face stood halfway up the steps—the dark inhabitant of their home. Without hesitation, without offering a fight, Doug lumbered out the front door, across the driveway, and into his truck.

Day Eighteen. Monday, October 23rd. 0011hrs.

For a heart-wrenching second, after loading Emily into the backseat and climbing behind the wheel, Doug feared his truck wouldn't start. Panic surged through his veins as he imagined the dark entity sabotaging their means of escape. Had the dark entity cut wires? Drained the gas? Slashed the tires? The possibilities swirled in his mind, amplifying his anxiety.

Doug's thumb hovered over the power button, hesitating to press it. What if the truck didn't start? What would they do? Where could they possibly go to escape the clutches of the malevolent force haunting their lives? Every second felt like an eternity as doubt and fear consumed him.

"Doug!" Kathleen's voice cut through the air, filled with determination and desperation. She reached across the front seat, flicked her husband's hand away, and punched the button.

The truck purred into life. The headlights bathed the house, revealing the skull-faced entity standing on the porch, a haunting image etched into their minds.

With a surge of adrenaline, Doug kicked up gravel as he burned out of the driveway, leaving their cursed home behind. His hands gripped the steering wheel tightly, knuckles turning white as he sped toward the cathedral. It was their last hope, a beacon in the night where perhaps someone would be awake, respond to their distress, open the doors, and offer them refuge from the encroaching terror.

The minutes stretched on like torturous hours as Doug raced through the night. The road seemed to stretch out endlessly, each passing second heightening his sense of urgency. He glanced back at Emily in the backseat, the nonsensical words spilling from her mouth like a demented chant. He couldn't make sense of her ramblings, but they added to the overwhelming dread that gripped his heart.

For the second time in hours, for the second time in years, Doug prayed Father Hartke or another priest would answer their call.

Why not pray?

Doug believed an evil presence, a demon or a ghost, haunted his house. If he could believe that, could he not believe in the benevolent entities, too? In the Holy Ghost and angels?

He didn't utter his prayers aloud. He fervently, though silently, pleaded with God, imploring Him to spare their family.

In the truck's backseat, Emily continued the verbal barrage. Doug tuned out most of what she said, but he caught pieces of her unending monologue.

"When birds burrow in the ground and fish crawl on four legs and snakes fly, then rainbows will appear like sunshine and the wind will gust like hot, steamy breath. One, two, three. A, B, C. You see me, and I see a tree. A tree to tie a rope. A rope to tie around my throat. A branch to hang and dangle. A happy death while I strangle."

Kathleen, overcome with anguish and fear, buried her face in her hands and sobbed. Her cries echoed through the truck, mingling with Emily's disturbing monologue. Doug could hear the insults directed at him, but it all felt distant, like a haunting background noise. His mind was consumed by the pressing need for help, for salvation from the nightmare they found themselves in.

Finally, the cathedral loomed before them, a sanctuary in the darkness.

Doug parked the truck right at the sidewalk, his breath coming in ragged gasps as he rushed out before Kathleen could question him. He reached the front door, his fists pounding on them with desperation born of sheer terror. His voice echoed through the silent night, hollering for someone, anyone, to answer his plea for help.

Desperation gnawed at his soul, pushing him to take out his phone and dial Father Hartke's number repeatedly. Each unanswered call deepened his despair, until finally, on the fourth attempt, a groggy voice answered.

"Hello."

Relief flooded through Doug, mingling with a renewed surge of urgency as he poured out their nightmarish situation to the disoriented priest.

Hartke remained quiet for a time, as if piecing together the late-night call. The priest's silence stretched on, testing Doug's already frayed nerves. Finally, Hartke asked, "Where are you now?"

"The church," Doug said with a mix of relief and anxiety.

A few seconds of rustling and grunting elapsed. "Allow me to dress. I stay in the presbytery next to the cathedral." Hartke provided Doug with directions. "I'll meet you out front."

"Can we stay with you tonight?"

A few minutes later, carrying Emily, with Kathleen trailing him, Doug arrived at the presbytery. Father Hartke waited, spotlighted by the full, unobstructed moon. He hustled in their direction and placed a comforting hand on Kathleen's arm. "Please," he said, "follow me." Hartke led them into the presbytery. "Lay her here." He gestured to a couch older than Jesus.

Doug assumed he meant Emily. He lowered his stepdaughter, lying her on the couch. She rolled her eyes to the back of her head, so only the whites showed, and she blew spit bubbles.

Kathleen stood still at the edge of the room, an added piece of furniture.

Doug backed away from the couch and fixed his attention on Hartke. He shoved his hands in his pockets, removed them, twisted them around each other. "We don't have money. We don't have anywhere to sleep."

The priest nodded with a calm, understanding motion. "I can offer you a place to rest tonight, but I can't provide temporary lodging beyond tonight."

Doug licked his lips and sniffled. "Father, I... we need protection. Spiritual protection. Please."

The priest didn't hesitate. He kneeled on the rug beside the couch and placed a hand on Emily's arm.

She recoiled at his touch and hissed at him.

"Emily," he said, his voice like the ocean.

Her voice adopted a low, menacing growl. "Emily is gone."

"Who are you?"

"I am Aeshma."

Hartke recoiled, moving his hand away from Emily's arm as if burned. He grasped the crucifix around his neck and transitioned into prayer.

Doug padded to Kathleen and wrapped his arms around her waist. She didn't move, though he half-expected her to shove him away. She remained still as a statue, standing and staring at her daughter in a state of frozen shock.

"I'll make this better," Doug said. "I promise I'll make everything better." He kissed her damp, sweaty forehead and stared out the window into the night.

As Hartke prayed, Doug thought of a way to fulfil his promise to make things better. How could he cleanse his home of the darkness living within it? How did he cobble together enough money to pay Victor and rent a place for his family to stay?

The solutions were dark as the night, murky and impossible to detect.

Doug felt trapped in a labyrinth of despair, desperately searching for an exit that seemed just out of reach.

The world had turned against him, and he found himself sinking deeper into the abyss, with no clear path of escape in sight.

The Next Step. Monday, October 23rd. 1527hrs.

I RAN MY HAND over the coarse stubble on my neck. Doug's narrative hung heavy in the air, leaving me grasping for words, for comprehension. How does one respond to such a chilling tale?

A pregnant silence settled in the office, the weight of the story stifling any potential response. I shifted my gaze towards Fred, who stood tall behind the reception counter, his head swaying from side to side. It was a not-so-subtle gesture, a silent plea, to dismiss the case and abandon Douglas Kosar.

I rose from my chair, walked to the coffee counter against the back wall, and poured myself another cup. The liquid had been sitting there all day, its warmth cooled to a bitter taste. Yet, it held the one element I needed above all else—caffeine.

"Can you help me?" Doug's voice quivered as he rolled his hands together.

"Do you truly believe that your house is haunted by the spirit of its original builder and owner?" I asked, attempting to wrap my mind around the inconceivable. "That this entity, or perhaps another soul that perished within those walls, has taken possession of your daughter?"

"Stepdaughter."

"Sorry."

"I don't know what else to believe."

I shuffled towards my desk but refrained from sitting. Instead, I veered sideways, bypassing Alina's desk, and came to a halt before the window overlooking the desolate alleyway. "I'm no demonologist like... what were their names again?"

"The Perrons."

"I'm not like them, Mr. Kosar."

"Doug, please."

"Nor am I a priest. I can't purge your home of negative energies or perform exorcisms on your stepdaughter," I explained, my voice tinged with a sense of resignation. "I am an investigator, someone who delves into the mysteries of the unexplainable and offers logical explanations. In my experience, ghosts, spirits, and demons—the whole supernatural shebang—don't exist. The real monsters are always human, wearing a mask of deceit. A mask resembling a grinning skull, perhaps." I cleared my throat, turning away from the window to face Doug. "If you genuinely believe your home is haunted and your stepdaughter is possessed, I'm sorry, but I can't provide any help."

Doug nodded, his eyes reddening, moist with unshed tears. "I don't care if you believe in ghosts or not. I need help, and you're my last hope. Please."

"I'm not a charity," I said. "I don't work for free, Mr. Kosar."

He struggled to suppress his desperate sobs, but his efforts were in vain. After a moment of regaining his composure, Doug stood up. "I apologize for wasting your time."

I lowered my gaze, staring at my worn-out boots.

When I established my investigative agency, I fervently hoped to uncover proof of the supernatural. With every fiber of my being, I yearned to unveil the existence of an unseen realm—specifically, to prove the existence of ghosts. I longed to cross over to the other side, to communicate with spirits, to apologize for any role I played in their demise. I would have taken on countless cases for free if it meant I could seize that opportunity.

But in recent months, I had undergone a transformation, a process of growth and self-reflection. The existential urge to explore every paranormal call no longer consumed me.

Yet, I hadn't ever encountered a genuine ghostly case before, especially one of this magnitude. One teeming with all the implications and insinuations of a genuine haunting and possession.

The question loomed large. Would I forsake my roots, the very passion that propelled me into this profession because someone couldn't afford my services? I now had a contract with the Sacramento Sheriff's Department, a lucrative one at that. I didn't need Doug's money.

I couldn't turn him away. I couldn't say no.

"Doug." His name popped from my lips before I had the chance to stop it.

He was halfway across the office when he halted, casting a glance back at me over his shoulder.

Fred groaned, collapsing into his chair and disappearing behind the reception counter. He knew the decision I had reached.

"I just moved into a new house a few months ago. My father is a contractor, but his expertise seems to have skipped a generation. I'm not exactly the handiest person," I admitted. "I'll consider this case for a trade."

"Anything. I'll do anything," Doug responded eagerly, turning fully towards me, his eyes wide with anticipation.

"Are you familiar with electronic installations, like setting up a home theater or surround sound systems?"

"I can handle it," he affirmed.

"Then install a home theater for me, and I'll look into your case."

"It's a deal. God, yes. It's a deal."

"Doug."

"Yeah?"

"If you're right, and this case somehow and someway lands in the realm of the supernatural." I shrugged and frowned. "I can't do anything about that—I can't exorcise or purify. However, I'll vouch for you to any paranormal experts or to the church, or to anyone who can help."

"Thank you. Thank you so much," Doug said, his voice tinged with gratitude.

I bit my lip, scraping my teeth against my upper lip. "If I discover anything, I'll contact you. That's the next step, alright? Unearthing the truth through thorough investigation."

"Just, please, hurry."

"How's Emily doing today?"

"Not well. And once Victor finds out that I've left the house, he won't be pleased. I'm terrified, August. I know you're sticking your neck out for me, and I don't want to burden you further, but please... please, hurry."

"I'll do what I can. In the meantime, stay with your wife and step-daughter. Even if they don't want you physically present, be available to them."

"Thank you. Thank you so much," he said, his voice filled with relief.

I returned to my desk and exhaled.

"I don't do haunted houses, boss," Fred said as Doug closed the door behind him. "And I sure as hell don't do demon possessions." He tore open a bag of Skittles, pouring them into his mouth. "Demon possession is my worst nightmare."

"You say that about everything."

"This time, I mean it."

I opened my laptop and started from the beginning, typing in Vernon Nowak.

Hooky. Tuesday, October 24th. 0911hrs.

Rhett shot Alina a wary look, his eyes narrowing as he closed his locker with a resounding thud. The high school hallway, awash with frenzied students, became a swirling vortex of chaos. Lockers banged shut, echoing like ominous thunder, while the cacophony of adolescent banter filled the air.

Alina, her arms crossed defiantly, offered Rhett an unnerving smile—a grin that hinted at hidden motives and dangerous secrets. Her lips stretched wider, contorting into an exaggerated expression that oozed malevolence.

"I don't like the way you're looking at me right now," Rhett said.

"You don't like my face?" she taunted, her voice dripping with a sinister playfulness.

Rhett's gaze remained fixed on her, suspicion etching lines on his brow. "Not when it looks like that."

"It always looks like this," Alina said.

"Mischievous, like you're up to no good?"

Alina's smile grew wider, a malicious gleam glinting in her eyes. "That's my natural face. I'm always up to no good."

"Seriously, you're creeping me out. Why are you smiling like that?"

"Because I'm happy," Alina said, stretching her forced smile wider across her face.

"Well, I don't like your happy face."

"I have a plan. We're going to play hooky today."

"Okay," he said, succumbing to the magnetic pull of Alina's wickedness. "I like the sound of that plan."

"To investigate Holly Hanson," she said, her words carrying the weight of ominous secrets.

Rhett's eyes narrowed, his voice laced with caution. "Who?"

Alina rolled her eyes. "Are you kidding me? We had a conversation about Holly Hanson yesterday."

"This is the exact reason I test so poorly. I swear, all the weed I smoked in my early teens really messed with my head. You shouldn't believe what people tell you. Marijuana doesn't improve cognitive functioning. That's a fallacy. A lie. It's propaganda created by the media."

"No one said smoking weed improves cognitive functioning, especially for a teenager."

"Really?" Rhett planted a hand on his hip and offered a speculative look.

"Really."

"What about all the people who say it enhances focus and concentration? All these brainiacs at fancy colleges smoke to help them study. You're telling me that doesn't improve someone's smarts?"

"No, it doesn't make you smart. Focus isn't intelligence." Alina raised her hands and shooed away the conversation like fanning a foul stench. "It doesn't matter. We're playing hooky to look further into Holly Hanson, the dead girl responsible for Ronnie Greene's disappearance."

"Oh, her? The ghost chick?" Rhett's eyes bulged like saucers, his face contorted into an exaggerated expression of terror as he stepped backward. "No. Nope. Chalk me up as a scaredy-cat, but I'm not on that Scooby-Doo vibe."

"Would you do it for a Scooby snack?" Alina asked with a coy grin.

"Hilarious, but no. Not even for a Scooby snack."

"Rhett, you're going to allow your girlfriend to wander into danger without you there to protect her."

"I don't allow or disallow my girlfriend to do anything. She does that all on her own, because she's her own individual person. I can strongly advise her not to do something, which I'm doing right now. Will you listen? No. Why? Because you're an independent, often idiotic individual."

"You have such a romantic way with words."

"It's a curse, honestly. I can't speak a sentence without sounding like Romeo."

"Fine." Alina crossed her arms. "I'll go alone, then."

"Okay."

"Alright."

"Sweet."

"Awesome."

Rhett's foot tapped anxiously, his gaze darting back and forth, his voice laced with hesitation. "You can't make me go," Rhett said. "I'm a strong, independent individual capable of independent thought without your influence."

Ten minutes later, Rhett drove his truck with Alina in the passenger seat. He gnawed on his cheeks, refusing to speak to Alina. She didn't mind the temporary silence. In fact, she used it to update Rhett on her discoveries from the night before.

"Holly Hanson died ten years ago at the school. Though the details of the incident vary, the cause of death remained a constant between the different testimonies and forums I read." Alina paused and looked out the passenger window, stalling to retell what she learned. It was horrific, bordering on cartoonishly violent—or something from a campy horror movie. "Hacked with a sword."

"What?" Rhett asked, taking his eyes off the road to look at Alina. He curled his lip in disgust. "What does that mean?"

"A cutlass," Alina said. "Someone took a cutlass and sliced Holly Hanson to ribbons."

"What's a cutlass?"

"Like a pirate sword. It has the hand guard, the curved blade. After the murderer killed her—"

"The pirate."

"Not a time for jokes," Alina said.

"Sorry."

"Anyway, they rolled her body into a gym mat and stashed it in the storage closet. That happened on a Friday. The wrestling team found her body on Monday when they brought the mats out of storage for practice."

Rhett's face contorted in a mix of horror and revulsion.

"That's not the creepiest part," Alina said.

"Well, save the creepiest part for yourself. I don't want to hear it."

Alina ignored him. "I was reading a 4chan board about the incident. An anonymous poster, someone who claimed to have attended high school with Holly, said there was a secret game happening on campus. Apparently, an anonymous curator contacted a couple of students, challenging them to perform a list of tasks that grew increasingly violent. The students would take pictures and send them to the anonymous person as proof. Then they would receive their next task. Holly died as a sacrifice to the game."

Rhett scrunched his nose and squinted his eyes. After a second, he said, "I'm uncommonly handsome. I've had grown women compare me to a young Mick Jagger, but better looking."

"No one has ever said that to you."

"You don't know that. Anyway, that's not the point."

"What's the point?"

"No one has ever complimented me for my brains. So, my beautiful flower, you're going to have to elaborate if you want me on the same page as you."

Alina gathered her thoughts, organizing the information she had garnered while staying up all night and pounding a pot of coffee—a poor habit courtesy of her mentor, August Watson.

Speaking of August...

Alina pried her phone from her pocket and glanced at the screen. He had sent her a text message earlier, but she had been so focused on convincing Rhett to skip school, she forgot to read it.

Alina tapped on the unread text. In typical August fashion, he typed as little as possible, sharing as little as possible, which left Alina uninspired to take action on his request.

Call me when you can.

"Earth to Alina," Rhett said, backhanding Alina's leg with a light tap. "You cognizant?"

"Cognizant?"

"Yeah, cognizant. You don't know what that means?"

"I know what it means. I'm shocked you know what it means."

"First, you don't have to be mean about it. Second, I downloaded this learning app which offers vocabulary building exercises. Cognizant was the word of the day today."

"A learning app?"

"Well, I mean—and don't let this go to your head—you're super smart. I haven't met anyone as intelligent as you, and it makes me feel, occasionally, like I'm a dummy. Eventually, you'll figure it out, too... that I'm a dummy, because you're super smart and that's what you do. You figure stuff out. And when you figure out I'm a dummy, well, I mean, a handsome face can only take a guy so far with a girl like you."

"If it makes you feel better, I've always known you were a dummy. It was one of the very first things I figured out about you."

"Really? You mean that?"

"With all my heart," Alina said, placing both her palms over her chest.

Rhett glanced at Alina, his face a sarcastic puddle of gratitude. "You love me for who I am? That makes me the luckiest fella in the entire world."

"Take a left at the light," Alina said.

Rhett clicked on the blinker and merged into the turn lane. "Anyway, the game. What's that about?"

"Apparently, ten years ago, an underground game," she put the word *game* in finger quotes, "became a local sensation. I emphasize the game, because, well, it was like the game in the *Saw* movies. Not everyone wanted to play."

"I've never seen the *Saw* movies."

"Seriously? Do you live under a rock?"

"People call me Patrick."

Alina nodded. "That makes sense."

"What makes sense?" It took Rhett a second, but realization dawned on his face. "You had me feeling confident a second ago, but now you're comparing me to Patrick from *SpongeBob*?"

"You compared yourself to him."

"As a joke to me living under a rock, because I hate horror movies."

"Take it back. You don't hate horror movies."

"I'll never take it back. They're scary, and I don't like to feel scared. It's that simple."

Alina rolled her eyes playfully, letting out an exasperated sigh tinged with a hint of amusement. "Alright, well, ten years ago, there was this secret game. A certain individual who wore a creepy mask that looked like a psychotic doll—"

"Like Chucky?"

"I'm going to kill you," Alina said, chuckling beneath her breath. "Did you just reference a horror movie after saying you don't watch horror movies?"

"Everyone knows *Chucky*."

"Everyone knows *Saw*."

Rhett scrunched his face and shook his head. "It doesn't ring a bell."

Alina grabbed her hair, wanting to pull it out. "Anyway, the creepy doll-faced figure would contact random teenagers. It would provide a task to the teenager, threatening the kid if they failed to perform the task, or if they told anyone about it."

"Threatening how?"

"I don't know. The details were vague. This theory was a rumor, never substantiated or proven, but considered a hoax."

"What were the tasks?" Rhett asked.

"Again, conjecture, but the person who posted on the 4chan board said one of the later tasks was to kill someone with a cutlass—or that's what he was told by the person who murdered Holly Hanson."

"They caught the man?"

"The woman, yes. She's currently serving a life sentence in Folsom Prison."

"Does time keep dragging on for her?"

"What?" Alina furrowed her brow, her expression a mix of perplexity and bewilderment.

"Seriously? You're harassing me about some lame horror movie, but you don't know Johnny Cash's *Folsom Prison Blues*? We have a huge relational gap between us, don't we?"

Alina blinked a few times, not sure how to respond. In the end, she ignored him and continued with her recounting of information. "The game was called The Mama Bird Challenge. Apparently and horrifically, it has resurfaced. Mama Bird has appeared to a few teenagers, demanding them to perform a series of challenges, otherwise suffer consequences for their disobedience."

"What consequences?" Rhett asked.

"I'm not sure. However, I think Ronnie Greene's disappearance has something to do with the game."

"I don't like the tone you said that in. It implied more than just finding out what happened to Ronnie."

"We have to find Ronnie before he's hurt or worse, and we have to learn who Mama Bird is before she manipulates another teenager into hurting themselves or someone else."

"Honestly, that's a lot," Rhett said. "I mean, and hear me out, we've—as in you and I—have already taken down a psychotic murderer dressing up as a Minotaur. Doesn't that seem like enough? Like, haven't we contributed enough to society to take a break from lunatics who prey on teenagers? I don't really care to find myself hunted again. It wasn't fun the first time around. I doubt it will be fun the second time."

"It's not about fun." Alina glanced at Rhett, her shoulders slumping. "It's about saving lives and helping those who need our help. What good are we if we sit around and do nothing?"

"We're safe."

Alina's patience wore thin, her voice sharp and edged with irritation. "Did anyone who ever accomplished anything do it by feeling safe? Or did they take a risk? Did they put themselves in harm's way to better the world?" She grabbed the passenger door handle. "You know what? Don't answer that. I don't want to know how you respond to the question. Turn there." She pointed into an empty stall along the city sidewalk.

"Why are we at the IMAX theater?"

"It's where Ronnie supposedly went with Holly Hanson. We're going to interview the staff, see if they know anything. After that, we need to get an appointment with Grace Volkman."

"Who?"

"The girl who murdered Holly Hanson."

The Wrong Girl. Tuesday, October 24th. 1003hrs.

THE IMAX THEATRE STOOD like a tower, its sleek glass facade reflecting the surrounding city. Rhett jogged past Alina and opened the door, holding it for her.

"Thank you, Sir," she said, offering a slight bow.

As she stepped into the theatre, a strong aroma of popcorn and butter crashed into her. A deep-rooted craving to watch a horror movie with a big bag of popcorn, a box of candy, and an iced-coffee overwhelmed her. Instinctively, she looked for a screen with movie showtimes. Movies, specifically horror movies, were her Heaven on Earth.

Alina brushed away the urge, fighting through the tempting scent of popcorn. They didn't have time to watch a movie. Still, it wouldn't hurt to plant a seed. She interlaced her fingers into his hand and leaned her head on his shoulder. "If you ever want to spoil me, take me to see a scary movie. Oh, and buy me all the concessions you can afford."

Rhett's permanent grin faded for a moment as he pondered the proposition Alina threw his way. "Well, considering popcorn at the movies cost about the same as a college education or a brand-new house, I'm thinking the only snack I can buy is a bag of Skittles from the gas station. Now, we'll have to sneak them in, but I've perfected the art of muling candy into a movie."

Alina tilted her head, feigning interest. "I didn't know you were a bad boy."

Rhett pushed air through his pursed lips. "You think that's bad? Baby, don't get me started on my two-for-ones."

"Two-for-ones?"

"I pay for one movie ticket. When the movie ends, I sneak into another movie without paying. It's a big crime, and big crime often comes with big time. But I've survived this long without getting caught."

"You're a criminal mastermind."

Alina scanned the lobby for a manager, spotted a red-headed, plump, middle-aged man. He was the only employee visible on the floor. She approached him with purposeful confidence.

"Excuse me, sir."

"Hello," he said in a lazy drawl—not a southern one, either, but something undetermined.

"I'm investigating the disappearance of Ronald Greene. According to my sources, he and his date came to this theatre Saturday night. Did you, or do you know of anyone here, who worked the Saturday night shift?"

The man had buggy eyes that nearly popped out of his head. His tongue poked out of his mouth, lolling out and covering his upper lip. "This Saturday?"

"Yes," Alina said.

"Like, this weekend?"

Alina furrowed her brow, a flicker of confusion crossing her face.

Rhett snapped his fingers, a loud, abrasive sound that cracked through the empty theater. "Wait, you meant this upcoming Saturday? Do you think she asked about a missing kid who went on a date this upcoming weekend?"

"Is that what she means?"

"Not at all."

"You mean last weekend?"

"Yes," Alina said.

"And not last weekend, as in two weekends ago," Rhett said. "Last weekend as in two days ago."

"This past Saturday?" the man asked.

"This past Saturday, yes," Alina said.

"I wasn't working."

"Do you know someone who was?"

"Probably Gianni."

"Is Gianni here right now?"

"He's the manager."

"Is he here?" Rhett asked.

"Yeah."

"May we speak to him?" Alina asked.

The odd man looked over his shoulder at a closed door across the lobby. "I can ask him."

"We would very much appreciate that," Alina said. "Thank you."

The man turned and hobbled to the door. He gently knocked on it with an open palm.

A couple of seconds later, it opened, revealing a tall, skinny man, the opposite of the short, portly man in every way. "Murray, can I help you?"

"These people would like to talk to you, Sir."

Gianni, without having to rise on tiptoe or lift his chin a fraction of an inch, peered over Murray's thick, tangly red hair. He wore a scowl—one that appeared carved into his face after dealing with years and years of disappointment. "Can I help you?"

Alina closed the distance between them and worked a smile onto her face. "Hi, I'm Alina. This is my friend, Rhett."

"Friend?" Rhett asked, taken aback. "That's all I am to you?"

"We're investigating the disappearance of Ronald Greene. He supposedly went on a date at this theatre Saturday night."

"This Saturday?" Gianni asked.

"Not this upcoming Saturday," Rhett said.

Gianni narrowed his eyes and scowled at Rhett. "Obviously."

"You would think."

"Anyway," Alina said, righting the ship, "did you work Saturday night?"

"I did."

Alina fished in her back pocket and removed two folded pieces of paper. She separated them, straightened one out, and handed it to Gianni. Murray leaned forward to look at the image, as well.

It showed a picture of Holly Hanson before her gruesome death ten years prior. She was pretty, with squirrel-brown hair, an innocent smile, and a charming countenance.

"Did you see her Saturday night?" Alina asked.

Gianni took a moment to study the image, eventually shaking his head. "I'm sorry, but I rarely mingle with customers unless there's a complaint or an incident."

"Could I speak to your box office staff who worked that night? Or do you have security footage we could look at?"

"You can speak to my staff. Jeff worked until closing on Saturday, and Amy worked the concession. They're both here right now. I'll have them look at the picture to see if they recognize the girl. If not, I'm sorry, but there's nothing else I can do."

"I appreciate your cooperation," Alina said. "When you show them the picture, could you also show them this?" She unfolded the second piece of paper, which showed a picture of Ronnie Greene. "It's the boy she was with. Maybe they would recognize him, if not her."

Gianni nodded, sparing a glance at the printout.

Murray leaned in, looking at the second image. He gasped and covered his too-small mouth. "I saw him." He pointed at Ronnie. "I saw that man. He has the same hair as me. I told him so. I said you have the same hair as me." The man chuckled and shook his head, lost for a second in the memory.

"You saw him Saturday night?" Alina asked, confused.

"Yeah."

"You said you didn't work that night," Rhett said, verbalizing Alina's confusion.

"I didn't work, but I saw a movie."

"I could punch a cement wall," Rhett said.

"Was he with this girl?" Alina pointed at the image of Holly Hanson.

"Not her."

Alina's heart raced in her chest.

"We saw the same movie," Murray said. "I liked it... well, it was okay. I wouldn't suggest it to anyone. The editing was choppy and disorienting. Their use of the green screen was jarring. But the acting was pretty good, albeit some stiff dialogue."

"What? He's like a cinema genius?" Rhett asked, glancing at Alina.

"Murray," she said, hoping to keep him on track.

The man went rigid, his shoulders pinching back. "How did you know my name?"

"Gianni said it."

He exhaled, and his posture relaxed. "Oh. You scared me for a second."

"I didn't mean to."

"It's okay. I just… I thought you were a psychic or something. They terrify me. I don't want to know the date or manner of my death. Please, please don't tell me."

"I won't. I just want you to tell me who he," Alina tapped on Ronnie's face, "was with on Saturday night."

"A girl."

"What did she look like? Did you hear him say her name, like I heard Gianni say your name?"

Murray, with everyone's eyes and attention drilling into him, shifted his gaze to the dirty floor. He leaned over and picked up a discarded paper ticket. "I missed this last night," he said, turning to Gianni. "I'm sorry."

"It's okay." The manager reached out a long, slender hand. "Here. I'll throw it away. If you can answer the…" Gianni trailed off, slightly cocked his head. "Who did you say you were again?"

"I'm Alina Moore, and I'm a part-time investigator for the Blue Moon Investigative Agency here in Sacramento. This is my associate, Rhett Jensen."

"Associate?" Rhett threw up his arms. "I went from friend to associate? Why don't we tell them the truth? Hmm? Why keep lying to them about who I really am? Mr. Manager," Rhett squared up to Gianni with an exaggerated show of bravado, "I'm not her associate, nor am

I her friend—well, okay, I'm her friend. But I'm a special friend. I'm her boyfriend."

"We technically haven't labeled it," Alina said.

"What?" Rhett placed both hands over his chest and fluttered back a step, as if shot through the heart. "We haven't labeled it? We agreed not to date anyone else. I turned down Mary Jane Parker the other day."

"That's a made-up name."

"You don't know that."

"No one by that name goes to our school."

Rhett shrugged, nonplussed, as if he didn't care. "I talk to people outside of school."

"It's literally the name of Mary Jane Watson if she married Peter Parker." Alina flexed her hands, annoyed with herself for falling into Rhett's antics and allowing him to distract her from the investigation. "That's beside the point."

"You're right." Rhett clapped his hands and smiled. "We're exclusive, meaning I'm her boyfriend and she's my girlfriend."

"No." Alina grimaced, cutting herself off from falling further down the rabbit hole. "That's also beside the point." Alina turned to Gianni. "We're investigating the disappearance of Ronald Greene, because, according to our sources, he was last seen with a woman dead for ten years now."

"Blue Moon specializes in paranormal investigation," Rhett said, placing a hand on Alina's shoulder. "I don't think you mentioned that tidbit of important information, so I thought I might share to clear up any confusion."

Alina had a strong temptation to turn and scream—just scream at the top of her lungs—into Rhett's face. She swallowed her frustration, drew a smile across her face, and returned her attention to Gianni. "We're not here with any authority. We're investigating a case."

"Shouldn't you be at school?" Gianni asked.

"You would think so," Alina said. "But we have back-to-back study halls before lunch. Unfortunately, our afternoons are packed with classes. So, we're on a time budget here." It was a lie, but not one Gianni could prove or disprove unless he made a few calls.

"Well, Murray is also on a time budget," Gianni said with a chill in his voice that didn't exist seconds before. "I'm going to throw this ticket away. When I return, Murray needs to get back to work."

"That's fair," Alina said, not wasting time before regarding Murray. "Who did you see with Ronald? With him." She pointed at the printed out picture.

"He was a with a girl, but not with that other girl."

"Did you hear him use her name?"

Murray nodded.

Alina forgot to breathe. "What?"

"I don't remember it. I heard him call her, though. She walked ahead, and he called her to come back."

Instead of dwelling on the shocking fact that Murray had heard but forgotten the girl's name, Alina switched her line of questioning, sparing a quick glance at Gianni, who dragged his feet to the furthest trash bin away.

"What did she look like?"

"Really pretty, like you." Murray covered his mouth and shook his head back and forth. His cheeks turned bright red. "I'm sorry. I didn't mean it like that."

The comment, coming from a middle-aged man and directed toward a sixteen-year-old girl, made Alina squirm inside her skin. From beside her, she could feel Rhett's cheery, aloof demeanor shift to something sharp and focused.

"Can you describe her physical appearance?" Alina asked.

Murray shook his head, still covering his mouth.

"Murray, please. It's important to the case." She inhaled and pushed past her pride and the creep-induced goosebumps covering her arms. "I appreciate your compliment. I do. What about me reminds you of her? Is it my skin color? My hair? My build?"

The pudgy man turned away and looked at the concession stand, breathing through light sobs. "It was her eyes." He choked out the words.

"Her eyes?" Alina asked. "We had the same eyes, like the same color?"

"You both have sadness in them."

Hands clapped together in a brisk, biting sound. Gianni stepped into the picture. "Murray, it's time you go back to work."

Without a word, the skittish man scurried away.

"I hope he provided you with useful information, but take anything he says with a grain of salt," Gianni said. "He suffered a head injury a few years back, and it's affected him and... well, yeah. He's not the same man."

"What do you mean?" Rhett asked. "Did you know him before the accident?"

"I went to college with his sister. He's a little older than me, though. Had a career and all that. I didn't know him too well, but I met him a time or two before the incident."

"Is he dangerous?" Alina asked, the question flying off her lips before she could reel it back in. She still felt a sense of discomfort after his comment.

"Murray?" Gianni shook his head. "The man wouldn't hurt a fly. Anyway, believe it or not, I work a little around here, and I need to get back to it. I hope we helped."

"You did," Alina said. "Thank you for your time." She nodded and turned away, thinking of Murray and what he had said.

It was her eyes. You both have sadness in them.

283

The Walkthrough. Tuesday, October 24th. 1004hrs.

I STOOD ON THE Kosar gravel driveway, shuffling around in a circle to take in the entire property. Rain sprinkled around me. According to Fred, it wouldn't rain any more than a light pattering until later this week.

Doug Kosar provided me with the address to his haunted house, along with the location of his spare keys. I asked if I could scope his property and walk through his home to get a feel for the layout and match his retelling of events to his real life house.

The remains of the burned-down RV stood like a charcoaled skeleton in the side yard.

My feet crunched gravel as I moseyed up the driveway to the wheelchair ramp.

"It's creepy," Fred said, padding behind me.

"It's a house. What's creepy about it?"

"Just being here and seeing the carnage Mr. Kosar mentioned. It's, like, one thing to hear about it, but it's different to see it in color. I imagined it was so much worse. Darker, you know? Scarier, like a cartoon haunted house. Instead, it's all so... gritty and real and tangible, like it can be anyone's home. It's creepy."

Reality versus imagination or expectation was sometimes a brutal truth. Though the property appeared neglected, the house seemed like any other old country home—sunburnt, weathered, covered in dust and cobwebs and abandoned wasp nests. It needed a facelift, sure, but nothing separated it from the next house. That simple realization had an eerie note to it.

Any typical home could house monsters.

I ascended the ramp to the front porch, wrapped my hand around the doorknob, and twisted. It unlatched and swung open without resistance. No key needed.

Doug and his family had fled from the home in a panic, and despite him having shared the spare key's hiding spot, I figured they might have forgotten to lock the door in their swift retreat.

"I don't like that," Fred said. "The haunted house is welcoming us inside. That's not for me."

I glanced over my shoulder. "If we survive this walkthrough, I'll buy you lunch today. Anything you want."

"You'll buy me lunch every Tuesday for a month."

"Deal." I returned my attention to the foyer, lit only by the morning sunlight splashing through the windows. "If we survive."

"Why would you say something like that?"

Without warning, I whirled around and grabbed Fred's arm, shouting, "Boo!"

He exhaled a high-pitched noise somewhere between a gasp and a scream, and he flinched, jumping away from me. After a second, when he realized no danger existed, a dark cloud covered his face. "That's not funny."

I was about rolling on the ground with laughter. "What was that sound you made?"

"I didn't make a sound."

"You whimpered."

"I don't whimper. I didn't make a sound."

I calmed myself and reached out to pat Fred's shoulder. "You okay?"

He wriggled away from me. "Don't touch me."

I shrugged, lifting my hands near my ears and grinning like a madman, turning and entering the house.

The first thing I noticed was the chill resting in the air. The cold didn't surprise me, though, not with every visible window being shattered.

I drifted into the living room first, to the nearest window. The broken glass lay outside the house, tangled with the weeds. "See this," I said, pointing it out to Fred.

"What? The broken window?"

"Glass outside of the house. Someone broke the windows from inside. Question is, who?"

"Or what? Maybe the evil force exploded, like something from a movie, causing all the windows to shatter outward."

"Sure, maybe," I said, not buying that explanation for a second. "Or maybe we need to separate ourselves from Doug's version of the story. He's an unreliable narrator. He's seeing the incident from his limited perspective influenced by fear and uncertainty."

Fred rapped his knuckles on the window frame. "You think one of them is the ghost?"

I nodded in acknowledgement. "It seems more likely than a ghost being the ghost."

"Who, then?"

"Kathleen hated living in the house, right? She begged Doug not to buy it. Maybe, to get back at him for making such a decision without her blessing, she adopted the ghost persona to scare him away, to get him out of the home."

Fred made a contemplative grunt.

"Or... what if Doug is the ghost?"

"You lost me there. I could almost believe Kathleen, but Doug? Why?"

"Doug owes Victor Petrov a lot of money—money Doug doesn't have, because he can't find work. Also, Doug has a fondness for true crime fiction, and he expressed a desire to write books about the Vampire of Sacramento and the Dream Demon."

Fred chuckled. "Let me get this straight. You think he arranged a meeting with you, the investigator who cracked those cases, be- cause—" He held onto the last syllable, waiting for me to cut in and finish his sentence.

"Because he wanted me to investigate his house... and fail."

"Fail?"

"Fail."

"Repeating the word doesn't catch me up on your thoughts."

"I have established my credibility debunking the supernatural with previous cases. If I can't debunk his haunted house, he can use my failure to solidify his story of the haunting. He can write a book, claiming his supernatural experience as fact, even if it's not—even if he's the ghost haunting the home to create an illusion of a haunting. He'll write the book and market it like the *Amityville Horror* and make boatloads of cash, relieving himself of his debt."

"It'll take him writing the book, though," Fred said. "That's the hard part."

I shook my head and turned away from the window to assess the rest of the living room. "The hard part is having his story heard by the right people—finding an audience. After he speaks with media and news outlets about what happened, that's when the book deals come. If he can't write it, they'll employ a ghostwriter. Either way, it's his name on the book. It's his money."

"That's a lot of ifs," Fred said.

"Yeah, well, he had little else going for him. He needed—needs—money. Desperate times and all that, right?"

"Man, I don't know. Robbing a bank sounds easier than hoping all the stars align to get a book deal."

I padded through the living room, taking in the complete destruction. Vandalism was painted across over the plaster, painted in big, red, dripping letters, threatening Doug's family to leave the house or die.

When Doug told the story, I envisioned one large warning sprayed over the mantel. That existed, as did dozens of other warnings and drawings. Stick figures hung from nooses or holding their pumpkin heads in their one-dimensional arms. The word KILL was painted at least two-dozen times, as was DEATH and LEAVE and BURN. A television lay on the ground, the screen shattered and the frame bent. Only the furniture covered in drop cloths remained unscathed.

"Doug did all this?" Fred asked after a moment.

"It's just a theory. I mean, the Lutz's made a fortune, right?"

"Who?"

"The family from the Amityville home."

"Do they make money off the movies and stuff?"

I shook my head and poked out my lip. "I would think so, wouldn't you?"

"I never thought about it."

I shuffled across the hallway, to the dining room and kitchen, two rooms Doug had emphasized in his story.

The chandelier lay broken in a million pieces on the floor—the faux diamonds scattered across the ground like shattered glass. The chandelier's heavy frame had slammed into the overturned table, splintering the thick wood. Chairs lay in pieces, crushed against the ground like an over-hyped rockstar slamming his guitar against the stage.

The dining room opened into the kitchen, which was a disaster—a vision of destruction. Broken dishes and glasses and the contents of spilled cartons and chucked food carpeted the floor. Jars of jam and bottles of syrup and sauce and condiments puddled on the ground, oozed down the walls. The drawers were pulled out of their sockets. Silverware and cookware scattered around the countertop and were shoved into the sink's garbage disposal. The dish towels lay like lily pads across the wet, sticky, debris-strewn floor.

"Doug did all this?" Fred asked.

"Are you going to keep asking me that?"

"It just... it seems farfetched, no? How could he do all this, all that in the other room, without waking up Kathleen?"

"Maybe they planned it all together. If I remember correctly, the Lutz's planned their haunting with a lawyer."

"What about the possession? They planned for Emily to lose her mind?"

I bit my lower lip and shook my head, unsure of what to think about the possession. It felt heavy and unreal—an unfathomable, unprecedented weight. In my experience, the paranormal didn't exist. Humans wore the masks of monsters to achieve their selfish ends.

With that truth bright and constant in my mind, I saw only three explanations.

Kathleen handled the perpetuated haunting, driving her family out of the house to get back at Doug for forcing them into it.

Doug, with Kathleen's knowledge and help, orchestrated the entire affair to create the perception of a haunting to write a book and sell a bazillion copies.

Victor Petrov ordered his men to torment and harass Doug and his family for not paying back his debt in a timely fashion.

Despite my experience telling me one of those options likely stood as the answer to this riddle, I couldn't convince myself of them. Each scenario had its flaws and holes, and when questioned, the motivation or the rationale fell apart.

That left one explanation, which made the least, yet, somehow, the most sense of all.

The spirit of Vernon Nowak haunted the house.

He had killed his family at the dinner table. After that, whoever had taken residence inside the house had died at the dinner table. If Doug and his family hadn't escaped, would they have died, too? Would Emily, possessed by the vengeful spirit of Nowak, poison herself and her parents?

Why would the house, if haunted, drive them away, then? That differed from the history of the home. Every other family had died together. Yet Doug and his family fled.

Why?

If I could answer that, I would be on my way to solving the case.

"What're you thinking about?" Fred asked, leaning over and plucking a wrapped granola bar from the kitchen floor. "You have that distant look in your eyes, like you're figuring something out. Did you solve the mystery already?"

"Just weighing my options."

Fred ripped the wrapper from the bar, crumbled it, glanced around the kitchen as if searching for a trashcan, and dropped his garbage on the floor. "And?"

"None of my theories tip the scales against a legitimate haunting."

"What are you saying?" Fred shoved the granola bar into his mouth and chewed for a few seconds. "This house, is it actually... haunted?"

"Probably not."

"That's not the resounding and comforting no you offered earlier."

"It just... a haunting holds about as much water as my theories. So, if I'm reluctant to dismiss those, why would I dismiss a haunting?"

"For my peace of mind."

I offered a closed-lipped grin. "Do you want to lead the way upstairs so we can finish this walkthrough and get out of here? Haunted or not, this place gives me the creeps."

"Not a chance," Fred said. "You lead the way."

I shrugged and went to step forward, but stopped and cocked my head. A scraping sound, like a shovel grating against cement, rang throughout the home.

"What's that?" Fred asked.

In response, a destructive hammering, like a sledgehammer against stone, pounded out a constant rhythm.

"Where's it coming from?" I shuffled forward and listened, hoping to pinpoint the source of the noise.

"I know where it's not coming from." Fred remained rooted in place. "The car. It's not coming from your car, or from the office. I say we go there, to the place it's not at."

I shushed him and closed my eyes, a futile attempt to narrow the echoing blasts.

"Someone is here," Fred said.

"What?"

"In the driveway. A car pulled up."

I opened my eyes and hurried to the broken living room window overlooking the driveway. Sure enough, a brown-ish Honda Accord parked beside my Honda Civic. Behind the wheel sat a middle-aged woman. She had her phone to her ear.

The hammering ceased. A probing silence worked through the home. Chills sprinted up and down my spine; goosebumps rose on my skin.

After a handful of seconds, the woman lowered her phone and stared at the house.

Fred removed his phone from his pocket and glanced at the screen. "Someone is calling me. Should I answer?"

"Sure."

He swallowed. "Hello. Oh, hi. Yeah, we're here, looking around. Oh. Yeah, okay. Okay. I'll let him know." Fred slipped his phone back into his pocket and looked at me with a cheesy grin. "That was Doug. He said that's Kathleen."

"Why is she here?"

"In their rush to escape the house, she forgot to grab her daughter's medicine."

Out the window, Kathleen stepped out of her car and walked toward the front door. She spared a courtesy knock, though the house belonged to her.

"Come in," Fred said, inviting her into her home. "It's unlocked."

Kathleen opened the front door and stepped inside.

I stepped forward to greet her. "I'm August Watson, and I'm sure your husband told you already, but I'm investigating what happened here."

"Thank you." She dove into my arms and hugged me. "Thank you for doing this."

"A business trade," I said. "Doug agreed to install some media for me."

"Still, thank you."

I broke away from her embrace. "Do you have a few moments? I would like to ask you a couple of questions?"

Kathleen crossed her arms and glanced around her overturned home. "Do we have to do it in here?"

"Would you prefer to step outside?"

"If you don't mind. I need to grab a few things first, but I'll meet you by our cars in a few minutes."

Fred and I still needed to finish our walkthrough by checking the upstairs portion of the house, but it could wait until after speaking to Kathleen. She played a pivotal role in this madness, and I wanted to hear her perspective on the matter.

Kathleen wasted no time collecting whatever she needed to pick up.

As we waited, Fred and I leaned against the hood of my car, neither of us speaking. I watched the attic window, the one where I assumed Doug noticed a face.

Kathleen's feet crunched over the gravel as she approached. "Sorry about that," she said, brushing a strand of hair from her face. "You wanted to ask a few questions?"

"Questions Doug didn't know the answers to," I said.

"Okay."

I glanced at her hands, which held a half-dozen bottles of medication. "All for Emily?"

"Yeah."

"Do you mind if I ask about her illness?"

"Does it pertain to your investigation?"

"It could," I said.

"How so?"

I popped my lips and exhaled. In my search for the existence of the supernatural, I spent countless hours studying myths, legends, and the occult. Information usually varied, changing from one telling to the next—which proved both a curse and a blessing. In the driveway of a haunted house, I used the inconsistent information to string together a quick answer to her question.

"Well, certain illnesses, both physical or mental, can have profound impacts on the fortitude of a person's mind and, ultimately, their soul. It's possible Emily's condition allowed a dark entity to latch onto her. The more I know, the more I can help."

Kathleen licked her lips, hesitating before answering. "We're not sure what's wrong with her."

"What kind of medication does she take?"

"She has an inhaler for her asthma, and an epinephrine pen for her food allergies. She takes medication for her heart and blood pressure, pills to help her digest her meals, and insulin for her diabetes."

"I apologize if this sounds insensitive, but I'm ignorant of these matters. Does your daughter suffer from a single ailment, or from a legion of them?"

"The doctors have only identified symptoms, but not an overarching cause. We don't know why she has so many disorders."

I squinted, narrowing my eyes to focus and decipher words on the medical labels. Two of the orange bottles bore the name Barbara, one of which showed Acetaminophen as the drug.

"How long has she been sick?" I asked.

"Her entire life."

"I'm sorry. That must be tough."

"It is."

I sighed and returned my attention to the house. "What do you think? Is your house haunted?"

Kathleen glanced over her shoulder, back at me, and nodded. "I saw a monster in there. I saw my daughter do things she physically can't do because of her condition. The house is haunted, and it's evil, and I'll never step foot in there again."

"I'm sorry to take your time, but thank you for answering my questions. I'll be in touch soon."

"Thank you again, Mr. Watson." Kathleen ducked into her car and drove away, leaving Fred and me in the middle of the driveway.

"We ready to go?" he asked.

I grinned. "We still have the entire upstairs to walk through."

Shared Meal. Tuesday, October 24th. 1227hrs.

THE INTERIOR OF THE McDonald's buzzed with activity as customers filled the brightly lit space, and the aroma of freshly cooked burgers filled the air.

Alina bypassed the short line, buzzed to a table occupied by a single patron, and sat across from him. "You really need to rethink your eating habits. You're going to die young. Well, young-ish."

Detective Kyle Vanek had a McDonald's cheeseburger halfway in his wide-open mouth. Ketchup smeared over his upper lip like poorly applied lipstick. The rail-thin man wore civilian clothes, and he had a not-so-concealed weapon on his hip.

"This is Rhett," Alina gestured to Rhett, who had slid into the bench-styled seat beside her.

"Her boyfriend," Rhett said.

"He's a friend with benefits."

Vanek choked and coughed on the bite. He set his burger on the red tray and dabbed a napkin over his lips.

Rhett snorted an amused laugh. "If by benefits, she means occasionally responding to me, then sure. It's not the universal understanding of the word. She's—"

"Sixteen," Vanek said, clearing his throat. "She's sixteen. Stop talking before I arrest you."

Rhett zipped his mouth shut. "You two do your mind-meld stuff. I'm a bystander. No more words from me."

"Can you, like, skedaddle?" Alina asked with a tight grin.

"Skedaddle?"

"I mean, I'm hungry." She dug into her wallet and removed twenty dollars. "Could you order me a cheeseburger and some fries?"

"You're not stealing mine this time?" Vanek asked. "That's a relief."

"Skedaddle?" Rhett asked again. "Are you a cartoon character? Do real-life people say skedaddle? What does it even mean?"

"To leave quickly," Vanek said.

"I have a learning app. I know what it means," Rhett said. "But who says skedaddle?"

"Rhett. Oh, my God." Alina had clumps of hair in her hand, pulling, wanting to rip them from her head. "Could you give us three minutes of privacy?"

"Yeah, sure." He shrugged and winked. "You'll tell me later, right? We don't keep secrets from each other?"

"Plenty of them."

"What? Seriously? But I told you about my sneeze."

"You willingly offered that story without me ever prompting for it."

"Because I thought we told each other everything."

"I'm getting hangry. I need a burger."

"Fine. Fine." Rhett threw up his arms and stood from his seat. "But I'm not paying for it. I'm using the twenty dollars you gave me, and I'm keeping the change."

"That's why... that's why I gave it to you. Never mind. Thank you for ordering my food."

"You want something to drink?"

"Just water."

"Right on." He skedaddled to the front counter.

The detective flashed an amused grin. "And I thought you were a lot. It seems you've found your match."

"He annoys me to no end. I can't stand him half of the time. Did you see me four seconds ago? I was about to rip out my hair. He drives me crazy."

Vanek snickered and picked up his cheeseburger. "Seems like you like him." He bit into it. "Does he treat you okay?" he asked, his mouth full.

"Like a freaking princess. It's disgusting. He also makes me laugh and feel all-around... happy about myself and my life. I don't like any of it."

"But you love it," Vanek said. "Do you love him, too?"

"Ew. No." Heat flushed into Alina's cheeks. "I'm sixteen. I'm not supposed to know what love is. Too young. Too dumb."

"I don't know if anyone has ever misplaced you in the too dumb category for anything. Considering you two are friends with benefits—"

"Don't say that."

"You said it first."

"I know. I hate myself for it."

"Well, if that's what you are, or if you two are boyfriend and girlfriend, or however you want to label it, I automatically like him. I wouldn't dare discredit your opinion of someone. So congratulations on finding a sliver of light in this dark world." Vanek raised his drink in salute and sipped the dark-liquid from his straw. "Why this pleasant surprise?"

"It's a pleasant surprise for me to crash your private lunch?"

"I think so."

Alina couldn't help but feel warm; she couldn't help but recognize the healthy support she had found in her young life. Between Fred, August, and Vanek, she had incredible, steady voices speaking wisdom into her life, filling the massive void her father had created.

"It's about Ronald Greene."

Vanek took another bite of his burger, followed by some fries, and he spent a few seconds chewing and staring out the window. "I thought so."

"Have you learned anything?"

"You're supposed to be in school."

"There's a missing student. You think I can sit in class and do nothing?"

"What about him?" The detective shifted his gaze to Rhett.

Alina turned around to look at her boyfriend. He strummed an air guitar to the song playing throughout the McDonald's, singing to the lyrics.

"You can't drag others into your poor academic habits, especially when he's trying to graduate and not drop out again."

"You just said you respect my decisions."

"With selecting those you fall in love with."

Alina reached across the table and pinched a few fries off of Vanek's tray. "You say things like that, you get fry-taxed."

"That's fair. Well, I'll tell you what I know."

"Really? Like that? I had an entire argument prepared."

"Like that." Vanek cleared his throat. "I can't share classified information pertaining to an ongoing case." Vanek raised a finger and cut off Alina as she opened her mouth to rebut. "I can't have you obstructing or interfering with the investigation. Our relationship doesn't permit you confidential information, and I still have protocols and laws to follow. Second, I can't risk putting you in jeopardy. I made that mistake once, with the Minotaur, and I won't do it again."

"What about August?"

"What about him?"

"Blue Moon contracts through your department."

"Ah, I see."

"I know an anonymous caller said Ronnie took Holly Hanson on a date. Holly Hanson died ten years ago. So, unless I'm confused, that sounds paranormal to me, which falls squarely into the jurisdiction of August and Blue Moon, and by extension, me." Alina crossed her arms.

"That brings me to my third point. I work for the Sacramento County Sheriff's Department. Ronald Greene's case belongs to the Sacramento Police Department."

Alina scoffed. "You said it yourself. I'm not an idiot. I know you're following the case given its strange nature; you're privy to the details of the investigation, your department or not."

"I'm not making the same mistake twice. Besides, no one has contacted August or the Blue Moon Agency about this case, so it's none of his business. By extension, it's none of your business."

"You're throwing my words back in my face?"

"I originally went to school to become a lawyer. Why do you think I'm divorced?" Vanek split his face into a ghoulish grin.

"You can't give me anything? Something the public might not know, but could learn with enough effort; something that's not classified? Just throw me a bone. You know I'll find it eventually, but let's give Ronnie all the help we can. Save me and him the time."

"You're too persistent for your own good," Vanek said. "And convincing." He drank again, sucking from the straw until emptying the cup. "Fine. You win. I'll give you one," he held up a single finger, "and only one bone."

"That's all I need."

Vanek reached for his crumpled napkin and dabbed his lips.

"You don't have anything, do you?" Alina asked. "You know as much as me."

The detective stood and brushed crumbs off his clothes. "Stay in school and out of danger."

"You said you would give me..." Alina trailed off as understanding clicked in her mind.

"Sacramento P.D. knows as much as you." A few breaths of silence passed between them, and realization dawned in Vanek's eyes. He sat back in his seat. "What do you know?"

"How the tables have turned."

"Alina, this isn't a game."

"But it is."

"Alina, no one can get ahold of Ronnie's dad. He's been missing since Saturday. This is a family issue. That's all."

Alina considered Vanek's news for a moment. "You ever hear of Mama Bird? That's what I know."

"Who's Mama Bird?"

"Not until you do me a favor," Alina said.

"Obstruction of justice. Withholding pertinent information pertaining to an active investigation. All that. You know how it works. Please, don't act like you have the upper hand here."

"One favor, since you lied about throwing me a bone."

"What's the favor?"

"I want a meeting."

"You're having one right now."

"Not with you."

"You're going to make me ask, aren't you? You're the one who pushed for saving time. Why can't you just say it?"

"Grace Volkman."

"Who?"

"The woman who murdered Holly Hanson ten years ago. She's in Folsom Prison. I want a meeting with her yesterday."

"Not possible."

"Not really yesterday. I know time travel isn't possible."

Vanek shook his head. "It's not possible for me to arrange the meeting with her at all."

"Ronnie's life could hinge on this."

Vanek sighed. "What's Mama Bird?"

Alina had asked for her favor. Vanek would either come through, or he wouldn't. Either way, he was right about one thing; Alina couldn't withhold the information from him.

"Mama Bird is a character who issues challenges to teens. According to what I found, she's a caricature, but not a person."

"What do you mean?" Vanek asked.

"I'm not sure. Maybe it's someone wearing a costume; maybe it's an animated rendering of a created character. Either way, she appears as a creepy head—like a Barbie head—with bulging eyes and an oversized, upturned smile creepier than the Joker's death grin. The person responsible for the avatar contacts teens, has them perform tasks that get progressively darker and more violent, and often end with the victim murdering someone and taking their own life."

Vanek slumped in his seat and stared at his lap. "I remember something like that from a few years ago. Didn't they deem it a hoax?"

"Ten years ago, and yes, but only because they had no proof it existed. Except, that's how Holly Hanson died. Grace Volkman received instructions to kill her with a cutlass. That's why I want to speak to her. I want to know more about the game."

"What does it have to do with Ronnie's disappearance?"

"The anonymous caller tipped he went on a date with Holly Hanson, right?"

"You're stretching there."

"It's a lead, though. Maybe it's nothing, but maybe it breaks the case open. Either way, it's too much of a coincidence to ignore."

Vanek's eyes shifted to the front counter. "Rhett's coming back with your food."

"Can you get me the meeting this afternoon?"

"I'll see what I can do and call with more details. Volkman has to agree to speak with you."

"Make sure she knows it's regarding Mama Bird."

"I'm back," Rhett said. "I'm announcing my presence, so you two don't accidentally share a secret I'm not supposed to hear."

"We're done," Vanek said, climbing to his feet. "It was great to see you, Rhett." He reached for the tray Rhett carried and grabbed a half-dozen fries from their carton. "It's a tax for crashing my lunch. Also, if you don't mind, could you clean up my mess?"

Alina sealed her lips and nodded, not upset but impressed with the detective's dramatic exit. "Well done, Vanek. I'll get you next time, though."

"I look forward to it."

Rhett turned to Alina after Vanek exited the establishment. "What was that about?"

"Top secret police business."

"You're not an officer of the law."

Alina grabbed her burger, inspected it, and took a bite. It tasted like her childhood, like moving from home to home, parent to parent, eating whatever was cheapest and fastest. It made her stomach hurt. She pulled the yellow wrapper around the cheeseburger and pushed it aside, sticking with fries. They, at least, always tasted good.

"What now?" Rhett asked.

Alina thought about their next step. Usually, she would call August and update him on their progress.

"August!"

"What?"

"He sent me a text message hours ago, and I never responded." She fumbled with her phone, scrolling to her contacts and calling him.

"August," he answered on the second ring.

"Who is it?" Fred's voice boomed in the background. "Is it Maya? Tell her she owes me a hundred dollars, and that she can't run away from her debt forever. I'll find you, Maya! I have a very specific set of skills. Skills I have acquired over a very long career. Skills that make me a nightmare for people like you!"

"It's not Maya," August said.

"Oh. Why didn't you say so?"

"It's Alina."

"It's Alina? Let me talk to her. No, scratch that. I'm not talking to her right now. I'm mad at her. Tell her Roshambo isn't a fair game for battle. I'm four times her size, and I would crush her like a bug. She cheated."

Alina remained muted on the other end of the line as they went back and forth. She considered hanging up, wondered if they would notice she had ended the call. Before she could press the red circle at the bottom of her screen, August told Fred to stop talking.

"Hey," he said. "I'm sorry. He's worked up from our most recent case."

"With the Sheriff's Department?"

"I accepted a client."

"Really?"

"A client who can't pay him!" Fred shouted. "He's working for free because he's a bloody bleeding heart who can't say no to a damsel in distress."

"It's a haunted house and demon possession," August said. "With Maya out of state and unavailable for me to lean on, I'll need your help with this. Of course, school comes first. If you have spare time, though, I could use your mind."

"Yeah, okay. Of course."

"Want to meet at the office when you're done with classes?"

"I'll be there."

"Thank you."

"Tell her I sent the LARP organizer an email already, detailing why she shouldn't have won. I'll make sure they change the rules for next year, and then we'll see who the champion really is."

"Fred, let it go," August said, disconnecting the call.

Alina placed her phone back on the table and grinned at Rhett.

"What?"

"I just think you're really cute."

"You think I'm cute? What about me is cute?"

"You make me laugh."

"You think I'm funny, then?"

Alina smirked and nodded.

Vanek suddenly reappeared, looming over the table like a fleshy skeleton, panting for breath. "I almost forgot. It would've bugged me all day, too. What's the story with Rhett's sneeze? I have to know."

Alina bit her lip and side eyed Rhett.

"No," he said. "You can't tell him. I told you that in confidence, because back then I thought we told each other everything, though I was obviously and wildly incorrect to assume that."

"I have to know," Vanek said. "I'm a detective. It's in my DNA to know secrets."

Alina snickered. Vanek hadn't barged into the McDonalds from a deep-rooted sense of curiosity which he couldn't satiate. He returned out of plain silliness and comfortability with Alina and Rhett. To her, his coming back inside marked the evolution of their friendship.

"Rhett, I swore not to tell anyone, but I think Vanek deserves to know."

"Deserves to know? What did he ever do for us?"

Alina closed her eyes, expressing her dissatisfaction with a simple blink. "He saved our lives. Without him, we would still be on that island."

Rhett sighed and slouched, defeated. "Fine, but you tell him."

"I would love to." Alina, bearing the world's largest smile, turned to Vanek. "Last year, Rhett had a crush on an older, attractive female."

"Older, as in a year or two," Rhett said. "She was a freshman in college."

"Anyway, deciding to turn on his irritable charm—"

"Irresistible," Rhett said.

"What did I say?"

"Irritable."

"Oh, yeah. That's what I meant. Deciding to put on his irritable charm, he confidently walked right up to the young woman. Now, mind you, he suffered from a head cold."

"My nose was like a swamp—muddy with snot."

Vanek grimaced at the description.

"That's too much," Alina said, touching Rhett's forearm.

"It's true, though."

"Anyway, they were inside a Target, or something like that."

"A Walmart. You won't catch me inside a Target. I don't have that kind of money. Wait." Rhett snapped his fingers. "You're right. It was a Target. I went there for a Starbucks."

"It doesn't matter," Alina said.

"It matters. It characterizes the woman as classy and sophisticated."

Alina sighed and rolled her eyes, more out of amusement than irritation, though. "Am I telling the story, or are you?"

"Go ahead."

"Rhett walked up to her and went to introduce himself. Before he could get out a word, he felt a sneeze. He turned to not sneeze on her, but didn't realize his proximity to the refrigerator doors or the force of his sneeze. Ah-Choo! He head-butted the glass door, cracking it. Not only that, but he cleared all the snot from his sinuses with that single explosion. Green tendrils hung from his nostrils and over his lips, and it had stuck like giant slugs to the glass doors."

"I fell," Rhett said.

"The impact of his head butting against the glass knocked him to the ground. He sneezed so hard, he head-butted a glass door, cracked it, and nearly knocked himself out."

Vanek started with a low, throaty chuckle, which grew and crescen-doed into bent over peels of laughter. After a moment, he slapped Rhett on the shoulder. "I needed that today. Thank you for sharing. Did you get the date?"

Alina laughed with utter enjoyment at the question. "She didn't even ask if he was okay."

"She said, 'Ew,'" Rhett said. "As I wiped the mask of snot from my face, she hurried away, fleeing so quickly that she left her cart behind. It was full of knickknacks and paddy whacks." Rhett shook his head. "On the bright side, she purchased herself a little Starbucks treat, and it sat nearly full in the cart's cupholder. With her having abandoned it, well, I couldn't let it go to waste."

Vanek snickered and tapped on the table with his knuckles. "Get back to class."

Getting Together. Tuesday, October 24th. 1616hrs.

ALINA ENTERED THE BLUE Moon office, followed by Rhett. I glanced at Fred, who frowned at me.

"What's he doing here?" I asked.

To be clear, I didn't have a problem with Rhett. He made Alina happy, and that spoke volumes about the young man. However, he padded after her everywhere, like a lost puppy, following his owner from room to room. She condoned it, too, which meant he spent way too much time at my office and at my house. Again, nice kid. He made Alina happy. But he had an unfiltered personality, which was a lot when I was exhausted and beaten down.

"Good to see you, too," Rhett said with his cheery grin. "You look incredible today. What did you do differently? New haircut? Is that a fresh shirt?" He pinched my shirt between his thumb and index finger—a shirt I wore at least once a week for the past year. "I like this color on you. It really brings out your eyes."

"Alina, why is he here? This is a business meeting. Last I remember, I'm not paying Rhett."

"Flimsy argument," Fred said from his desk. "You're not paying me. Does that mean I'm not a part of the team? Because if that's true, no more haunted house visits for me."

Rhett hopped onto the ledge of the high counter Fred sat behind, his legs dangling a few feet from the ground. He reached into a bowl filled with Jolly Ranchers and plucked out a blue one. "A haunted house? Was it creepy?"

"Beyond creepy," Fred said. "We almost died."

"That's not true," I said.

"Don't listen to Fred," Alina said, crossing the office and plopping into her chair at her desk. "He can't even beat a tiny, little, pathetic girl in a fistfight."

I rubbed my temples and sighed. I didn't have the power to prevent the inevitable. For Alina and Fred to move past this ridiculous argument, I had to let them fight.

Fred roared to his feet. "She didn't beat me in a fight! She beat me in a game of blind chance and luck. You really think a hundred-ten pound little half-elf rogue girl can defeat the powerful Ghan the Gruesome?"

Well, that's a relief, I thought. They argued about their characters' abilities to beat each other up, not their actual, real-life abilities. For a second, I thought their dispute was sheer ridiculousness. Now, I realized, it was only ridiculous.

I allowed their bickering to unfold, to complete its natural course. When I sensed they both wearied of the hypothetical argument, I cleared my throat to draw their attention. Both of them appeared relieved I provided an excuse to change gears.

"We have a case, as I'm sure we're all aware of now."

Rhett dropped from his perch on the high counter, landing on his feet and leaning against the wall. "I'm not aware."

I glanced at Alina, and she shrugged off my annoyance. "We're investigating a supposed haunted house."

"A ghost might haunt it for real," Fred said.

"I'm going to bullet point the details, so we're up to speed on the situation," I said. "Doug Kosar moved his wife and stepdaughter, who has some unknown or undiagnosed condition, into the house.

Kathleen, his wife, expressed her concerns about the home, and her displeasure with her husband about buying the home without her consent. Her words landed somewhere in the abyss of his ability to care. Doug, who's floundering in his career and has no money courtesy of a gambling addiction, moved them in. Over the past eighteen days, they experienced a slew of paranormal events."

"The vibe of the place makes it difficult not to believe it's not haunted," Fred said.

"To complicate matters," I said, pushing forward in my brief of the case, "our client believes an evil entity possessed his stepdaughter. Emily has displayed erratic behavior, including self-harm and speaking in a variety of voices and accents."

"She also climbed her bedroom wall like a spider," Fred said.

"What?" Rhett asked, his eyes going wide as he looked from Fred to me to Alina. "I don't think this job is for me."

"It's not, because you don't work here," I said. "Emily punched holes as hand and footholds to hang on the wall."

"Do we have a lead or any evidence that it's not haunted?"

"I have a few working theories. My main suspicion falls on the husband, our client. He's an aspiring true-crime writer."

"Ah," Alina said, nodding her head with understanding. "He's also broke, right? You think he fabricated the haunting and the possession to create a media stir, a panic, interest, whatever, and that he plans to capitalize on the haunting by writing a book in the style of the *Amityville Horror*."

"It makes the most sense to me. The wife didn't want to move into the home, creating an imaginary rift between them, a dispute to make the haunting more believable."

"Their made-up disagreement will create credibility for their story?" Alina asked.

"If they're at odds with each other, but agree on the haunting, it will make their story appear more credible to the public."

"What about the daughter? She has some undiagnosed medical condition. Will people suspect the possession isn't a possession, but a sign she's getting sicker?"

"She's in a wheelchair," I said. "Yet, she scaled the bedroom wall."

Alina scrunched her face, trying to calculate that tidbit of information. "I don't get it. How's that possible?"

"Her possession is the one detail I can't explain."

"There's also the gambling debt, right? Does he owe someone money?" Alina asked.

"Big time."

"So maybe that guy is harassing him?"

"Could be," I agreed, though I doubted that scenario. Victor Petrov, based on preliminary research, didn't seem like that kind of man to orchestrate a haunting to scare his clients. "It gets weirder, and weirder in a way that aligns with the haunting being legit."

"What do you mean?"

"The house has a dark history, one that has repeated itself through every owner, beginning with the original builder. Every family to live inside those walls has died from a poisoning incident while at the dinner table, all the way to the family renting it two or three years back."

"Yet... our client escaped?"

"The pattern broke with their stay."

"Why?" Alina asked.

"I can't figure that out. The house, if haunted, allowed no one to leave; instead, it claimed their lives, keeping them inside that house forever. But not our client."

Alina tapped her finger against her desktop for a few seconds. "Anything else?"

"One other detail. I'm not sure how important it is to the home, but it's important to our clients and their personal history. The wife was in a cult fifteen years ago. She was, in fact, married to the leader."

"That's where her kid came from?" Alina asked, making connections with ease. "The cult leader?"

"Marshall Nix was his name, and he founded the Children of Eternity Cult—a starvation-based group. His autopsy showed he had died through thallium poisoning."

"And the house's previous inhabitants all died of poisoning, too?"

"Yeah."

"Thallium?"

"Cyanide."

"Jesus," Alina said, combing her fingers through her hair and sighing. "So where do we begin? How do we discredit a haunting and find the monster responsible?"

"I think we have to dig," I said. "Deep, too. We dig into the personal histories of Doug, Kathleen, and Emily. We dig into the histories of Vernon Nowak and his family, and of every family who lived in the house after him."

"Do you think there's a possibility it's haunted?" Alina asked.

I scowled, swallowing the thought that plagued my mind—swallowing the idea that a legitimate haunting made more sense than anything else. "If it's haunted, we're way out of our depth, and we do what Doug asked us to do."

"Which is?"

"Vouch for him and his family in a plea to have the Catholic Church investigate and perform an exorcism."

"But the supernatural doesn't exist," Alina said. "Isn't that our motto? Isn't that our default? Haunted houses don't exist."

"That's why we have to dig as deep as possible." My phone rang. I glanced at the caller, saw my mom's name showing on the screen. I muted the vibration, ignoring her call for the moment and addressing Alina and Fred. "If we dig deep enough, we'll find the buried skeletons."

Down the Rabbit Hole. Tuesday, October 24th. 2112hrs.

Bagley greeted me at the door when I got home. My dog, a double doodle a few months old, ate a late dinner with me and lay on the bathmat as I took a too-long shower. We collapsed onto the couch together—he sat off to the side, and my laptop rested on my thighs.

Before I researched my latest case, I returned my mom's call.

"Where have you been?" she answered, her tone akin to a mother up all night worried sick about her teenage kid. "I called you three hours ago."

"I'm taking on a few more cases. I was working."

"You're taking on more cases? I thought you quit."

"I never quit."

"Gussy, it's dangerous. You've been shot, stabbed, put in the hospital. People have…" she trailed off, not finishing the sentence.

Not that she had to. People have died. That's what she meant to say. Cambria had died during one of my previous investigations.

I licked my teeth, unsure of how to proceed.

"I spoke with Truman's mom earlier. Do you remember Truman?"

He and I graduated high school together, though we never said more than a dozen words to each other. My mom had a pilates class with his mom now. According to Mama Truman, her son became a veterinarian.

"Vaguely. Did he wear the eyepatch and pirate hat?"

"He's a veterinarian, and he's married, and he has kids. Now you tell me you've returned to a life of unpredictability? Why can't you settle down? Find a wife, have a big family, work a boring, safe job?"

I entertained the idea of settling down and living, as she said, a boring, safe life. The biggest hurdle presented itself as a woman, or lack thereof one.

Glacia, a past romantic interest, lived in Oregon, and she refused to move to Sacramento, where I preferred to stay. Lauren, a brief fling, had drifted out of my life. I'm not sure I ever broke things off with her, if we had spoken about ending things, but too much time had passed now, and I couldn't go back and right those wrongs.

Then, of course, there was Maya.

I had, for the better chunk of our friendship, had feelings for her. Though our relationship had changed and evolved, my feelings hadn't faded. To complicate the situation, she now pursued her journalistic endeavor, which carried her around America. More challenging, after falling in love with her last boyfriend, which ended catastrophically, she swore off relationships until she could figure herself out. Knowing Maya, who had spent the last decade, if not longer, figuring herself out, I would have to wait another ten years for her to jump back into the dating game. Even then, would she give me a chance? Or had she placed me front and center of the friend zone?

The most problematic issue, if I had to be honest with myself, was that I didn't know how to meet new people. I refused to put in the effort required for online dating—filtering through woman after woman until I found someone compatible. Also, I abhorred the idea of sliding into someone's DMs, as Alina and Fred recommended. I didn't drink, so I couldn't meet anyone at a bar. Outside of my small friends' group, I had no social or public life.

My dating possibilities had narrowed to near-oblivion. So, I had consigned myself to complacency with being single.

"Gussy?" My mom barked my name.

"Hm?"

She sighed. "I'm sorry."

"Hm?" My tone changed with the questioning hum, touching on abject shock. My mom, Kimberly Leigh Watson, apologizing to someone? Maybe the house was haunted and Emily was possessed. Maybe the world had turned inside out, upside down, and was coming to a cataclysmic end. "Did you say sorry?"

"I'm trying to butt out, as your sister says, of your personal life."

A bright explosion detonated between my eyes. Excitement billowed through my body and tingled my skin. "Is that why you're calling?"

"What?"

"Did Rachel have the baby?"

My sister was due with her first child, my mother's first grandchild, any day now. We all waited to break out the cigars and Champagne and pink balloons.

"Oh, no. Actually, she has a doctor's appointment scheduled on Thursday to see if she's dilated and to discuss an induction. Her due date is Halloween, though. With it being her first baby, who knows, she might not deliver until November."

"November?" I asked, thinking about when I saw Rachel last week. She was miserable, ready to pull the baby out herself. "Can she wait that long?"

"She'll have to."

I shivered at the idea of pregnancy, of labor, of delivery. "Thanks for making me a boy."

"I had no choice. Your dad said he would leave me if I had a girl."

I thought of the haunted house, and my fingers itched to move across the keyboard and dig into some research.

"Everything else okay?" I asked, dismissing my urge to place work before my family. Even if my mom had called to chat about nothing, I could push off my investigation to do that. If I had learned anything over the past ten months, I learned family and friends mattered more than anything else in life.

"Other than your brother driving me up the wall, everything is cherries over here."

I smirked. Adam, my brother, twelve years younger than me, was kicked out of his private university for smoking weed. He moved back home with mom and dad, enrolled in community college while he figured out what he wanted to do with his life, and he played hours' worth of online video games.

I could have advised my mom to force him to get a job and pay rent, or to move out of the house, but I knew she would never go for that. Besides, my mom hadn't called to hear unsolicited advice.

A year ago, I would've ignored her call, annoyed with her complaints about a problem she could fix without trouble. Now I understood she called to vent, to release stored up pressure. She didn't want Adam out of her house. She wanted something to talk to me about.

"Dad's doing okay?"

"Working more than ever. I think he's keeping himself out of the house to avoid seeing Adam always in the house."

I snickered. Before I knew it, I spoke a thought that I hadn't quite considered enough to process and understand the full implications. I spoke more out of banter than anything, to keep the fun going. "He can come live with me."

Silence.

Not offended silence, either; not angry silence. A contemplative silence that overtook our conversation, as if my mom was mulling over the idea.

"You're serious?" she asked after a moment.

Silence again, this time on my end, as I mulled over my unsolicited suggestion and reprimanded my stupid mouth for acting out of order. That's why I always thought before I spoke.

"Gussy, if you're serious, that would be incredible."

What had I done?

"He wants to transfer to Sacramento State from Cosumnes River College. If he stayed with you, he could save money on housing. That's not to say he wouldn't pay you rent, but I'd rather pay you rent than the university or a random apartment complex. Besides, you can keep him on track. Keep him focused on school and graduating. What do you think?"

My jaw hinged for a moment, and my tongue flapped as it struggled to latch onto words. "When would he move in?"

She gasped. "You're okay with it?"

No.

How did I say no? I owed my parents so much. If opening a room to Adam helped them out, even a little, how could I refuse?

After a second of contemplation, realizing I couldn't deny my mother after accidentally offering the house, I consented. "I'm okay with it."

"Really?"

"Sure."

"He's going to be so excited!"

I thought of Alina, of how I promised her my spare bedroom, of how I planned to turn it into a movie theater as a surprise. "Alina has claim to the spare bedroom," I said. "Adam will have to take my office, which is fine, because I don't use it, anyway. It's mostly an empty room right now."

"You're sure?"

"Positive. But, hey, I have a call coming in, and I have to take it. I'll call you tomorrow to work out the details."

"Thank you so much, Gussy. I love you."

"Love you, too, Mom." I held my breath as I switched lines, exhaled, and answered. "Hello"

"August Allan Watson," Maya said. "I hear you're back in the saddle, riding that bronco. And I hear you have a rough ride."

"I'm doing good. How are you?"

"Dandy."

"You spoke to Alina?"

"Oh, no. All she ever wants to talk about is Rhett. I can't stand it."

"She brought him into the office today."

"Gross."

"She really likes him, then?"

"I don't know," Maya said. "It's her first legit boyfriend, and she hasn't had the most positive relationships modeled to her. I'm not sure how she feels about him. She's always calling and asking me if she really likes him, or if she likes the idea of liking him, of having a boyfriend, or if she's forcing it."

"She's calling you, asking for relationship advice?"

"What's wrong with that?"

"That's like me calling a turtle for speed advice."

"Such an elementary analogy." I could almost see Maya rolling her eyes through the tone in her voice. "You completely missed the mark, failed to land the plane, swung and went wide with the punchline."

"You got my point, though."

"Not really, because turtles probably offer amazing speed advice. It's all about learning from what they can't do, learning why they can't succeed. Do the opposite."

I closed my eyes and cleared my mind. I had to right this ship before Maya hijacked the conversation and steered us off a cliff. "Fred called you, told you about the case?"

"Said you're taking it for free."

"Apparently, I'm running a charity these days. I'm also letting Adam move in with me."

"What?" Maya shouted the question. "No way."

"Yes way."

"Why?"

"Because I forgot how to say no."

"And I'm out of town and can't take advantage. Bummer."

"Bummer."

Maya blew air through her vibrating lips. "Well, I'm here to save the day and your charitable investigation."

"You solved it?"

"No, but I'm more equipped—because I'm smarter than any of you—to solve it. Spread the buttery details on my sliced bread."

"I don't like that analogy."

"Spill the tea."

I provided a quick summary of the case. Maya interrupted occasionally, asking clarifying questions. When I finished, I sank further into the couch, petting Bagley's head. I waited for her to respond.

"You're looking at it from the wrong perspective," Maya said.

"What do you mean?"

"With all your theories, there's a single constant—one we can't deny. You find the answer to that mystery and you'll solve the case in no time, Sherlock."

I narrowed my eyes and thought hard about what she referred to. It took me a few seconds, emphasizing my intellectual delay compared to Maya, but it crashed into place. "The possession."

"Bingo. If you figure out what's possessing the girl, if you figure out how she could use her unusable legs, you solve the mystery of the haunted house."

"Any ideas?" I asked.

"I would look into her medical history and pinpoint, or at least ballpark, what's going on with her. You said the doctors couldn't diagnose the condition, right?"

"Yeah."

"Figure out why. Figure out what kind of medicine she's taking and how long she's been sick. Does it connect to mental health, such as schizophrenia?"

"What about every inhabitant getting poisoned while eating dinner, but my client fleeing and escaping?"

"That's strange, too." Maya clicked her tongue. "I don't know what to tell you, other than if you figure out the possession, I'm sure the other answers will snap into a perfect position."

"Last question."

"Shoot."

I looked at the ceiling, watching the fan spin in lazy circles. "What are you looking into up there? Anything good?"

Maya chuckled. "It's sexy."

"A man?"

"A ship off the Alaskan coast drifted into shore. No living crew, though their belongings, fresh food, and fishing gear remained onboard. No record of the ship anywhere. We don't know what the ship is, what it's used for, who it's registered to, or who was on the crew. All we know is that there's a handful of people missing."

"You going to turn it into a podcast?"

"If I can come up with enough content. Right now I have a pilot, but I need more to stretch it into six episodes. I'll do some investigating and see what I come up with."

"How long will you be out there?"

"I don't have a return flight."

I nodded, knowing she didn't have a date in mind. "Well, I'm here if you need a sounding board."

"I might take you up on that, especially since Alina won't talk about anything but Rhett. Anyway, got to go. I have a date with a man named Jack Daniels at a seedy bar. I'm hoping to learn a few local secrets."

"Stay safe, yeah?"

"Safe is my middle name."

"I thought it was Mylene?"

"Bye, August." Maya ended the call.

I opened my laptop. Since I couldn't research Emily's health history without speaking to her or her mother, I had settled by diving into the history of the home and all who lived inside of it, spending most of my time on Vernon Nowak.

After serving his country overseas and seeing combat as a marine in World War Two, Vernon returned to California a different man. His mother, in an interview held after the tragic poisoning incident, said, "He was a happy and kind man, always willing to help someone else. The man who came back from the war... that wasn't my son."

I dug up other articles featuring other quotes from his mom, his dad, and his siblings. They all said similar things about Vernon—he had changed overseas after seeing combat. He rarely spoke, never smiled, and laughed even less than that. He was paranoid about Russia, about their rise in nuclear power, and the Cold War.

The Nowak family lasted twenty years before Vernon lost his mind and poisoned his wife and adult children. I read through the police reports detailing the incident. Apparently, the neighbor found the family dead. She went to investigate after hearing a baby screaming incessantly for most of the morning. Apparently, Vernon's son and his wife had a three month boy who napped during the fatal incident.

Two years later, the Sagers moved into the home—a newlywed couple focused on striking it rich rather than creating a family. They died of poisoning two years after purchasing the house.

After their deaths, the Lincolns moved in—a retired couple hoping to be closer to their kids and grandkids. They died two years later, poisoned.

The Nelsons purchased the house, lived in the home for ten years before they died of cyanide poisoning. Instead of selling the home after inheriting it, their children rented it out for forty years. Of the six families that had come and gone, only the last pair of tenants died of poisoning. After their deaths, the house sat abandoned for almost three years, before the Kosars purchased it.

What was I missing? What wasn't I seeing?

I read and reread the articles and reports and interviews until something—a glimmer of possibility—formed in my mind. My newfound thoughts didn't explain the possession, but it provided a new theory about the haunting.

I glanced at the clock, noticed the time had ticked deep into the night—0009hrs.

With a half-baked plan on how to proceed, I crawled into bed and fell asleep before my head hit the pillow.

The Visit. Wednesday, October 25th. 0900hrs.

DETECTIVE VANEK PULLED A few strings and called on owed favors to coordinate an early-morning visitation between Grace Volkman and Alina Moore at Folsom Prison. He called Alina late the night before the appointment.

"You owe me," he opened the conversation.

Alina couldn't help but release a short, gleeful scream. "You did it?"

"I cashed out a favor from the Sheriff. That's right. I had a favor owed to me by Sacramento County's Sheriff Jones. Not anymore."

"Well, now you have Alina Mylene Moore owing you a favor, and that's infinitely more impactful than Sheriff Jones. If you ever need anything, call me, and I'm there. No questions asked."

Vanek scoffed. "What could I need from you that's anywhere close to being better than what Sheriff Jones could've done for me, my career?"

"You're a conniving little squirrel. I'm sure you'll think of something."

Alina had to skip school again to make the meeting—only her second absence of the semester, which included her absence the day before. The high school allowed three unexcused absences to each student before enforcing disciplinary action.

Rhett dropped Alina off at the prison, and he waited in the parking lot. "You owe me," he said in a rare tone of seriousness. Even his face didn't bear his usual happy-go-lucky grin. "I plan to graduate high school, and I can't do that skipping class every day."

"I know," Alina said, cracking open the passenger door.

The prison guards questioned Alina, but she recited what Vanek told her to say. They made a few calls to confirm her story, and eventually allowed her into a visitation hall with a glass partition separating the visitor from the prisoner.

After Vanek had called the night before, Alina couldn't sleep. To combat rolling restlessly around in bed, she researched Grace Volkman. In high school, Grace had greasy brown hair, pale skin dotted with acne, and big, round, bright-brown eyes covered by thick glasses.

Sitting across from Alina in the visitation center, Grace appeared more pale, almost translucent, and her greasy hair had become a matted, tangly nest. She sported a thin, shadowed mustache on her upper lip, and her acne had remained into adulthood. Grace was no longer skinny, though, nor was she fat—she had the bloated, ballooned appearance of someone on a high-sodium diet. A sheen of sweat covered her brow, and she appeared out of breath, as if her walk from the cell to the metallic stool had winded her.

Alina grabbed the phone from the cradle and placed it against her ear.

Grace mirrored her action, but she didn't speak into the receiver. She stared through the smudged glass, glowering at Alina.

"I'm Alina Moore. I'm a junior at Pleasant Valley High School." She swallowed back a wad of nerves and waited for Grace to react to their connection. After a few beats, Alina continued. "Thank you for meeting with me."

Grace placed the phone on the shelf, removed her glasses, and wiped the lenses on her prison shirt. She took her time. When she finished cleaning her spectacles, she fit them around her face and picked up the phone.

Alina scratched the small area of skin behind her ear. Nerves riddled her stomach, and doubt crept into her mind. What if Grace refused to say a word? Alina hadn't considered the possibility. What if this was feckless, a waste of Vanek's, Rhett's, Alina's, and Ronnie's time?

Again, she swallowed the fear and pushed forward. "A student from Pleasant Valley went missing Saturday night. According to an anonymous source, he went on a date with..." Alina trailed off, licking her lips before inhaling. "He went to dinner and a movie with Holly Hanson."

Alina studied Grace's reaction. The woman was marble. She barely blinked at the name of the girl she had murdered.

"You murdered Holly Hanson," Alina said.

Grace shrugged. "It's a common name." The simple comment came off her lips in a calm breath. "Maybe there's a Holly Hanson at another high school, or at a college. Maybe the missing boy went out with a living Holly Hanson."

"Maybe," Alina said. "I don't think so, though."

"What do you think?"

"Mama Bird contacted someone and gave them a task involving Ronnie, our missing person."

Grace sucked on the inside of her cheeks and stared at her knees.

"Mama Bird told you to kill Holly Hanson, didn't she?" Alina asked.

"No."

"No?"

"She told me to kill someone popular."

"And you just did it?"

"I didn't have a choice."

Alina had read the police and court recordings of Grace's testimony, and she knew what Grace would say next. The woman's story never changed or evolved. Still, Alina allowed Grace her moment to speak, knowing that the more she spoke, well... the more she spoke.

"Mama Bird sent video recordings of my family from within our house. She said she had Baby Birds everywhere—that's what she called us. Baby Birds. She said if I didn't complete the challenge, my family would fall victim to her next challenge."

Alina nodded, debating how to proceed. Though Grace had steadfastly stuck to her version of events, evidence didn't exist to corroborate her claim of the threatening videos, pictures, or messages.

To complicate and shadow her defense in further doubt, Grace had multiple run-ins with Holly Hanson.

Holly circulated amongst the more popular crowd in high school, and she had earned, rightfully, the unfortunate reputation as a mean girl. Grace was a loner; she didn't have friends, and she navigated high school as an outcast. Holly, on three incidents documented by the school, though more unreported incidents doubtlessly occurred, had taken a predatory dislike to Grace. Multiple testimonies existed from multiple sources detailing similar stories—Holly harassed Grace at every opportunity, bullying and ridiculing her in front of other students.

Though Grace's retaliation and murderous action shocked the community, most students understood the motivation behind her abhorrent act.

Revenge. A tale as old as time.

Despite people understanding why Grace lashed out, no one believed her story about Mama Bird. Even when a handful of students stepped forward—all of them loners, kids misunderstood by their peers—claiming they had interactions with Mama Bird, people dismissed them, too.

A simple and unescapable fact remained. There wasn't any evidence of messages from Mama Bird on anyone's phone or email. No videos or photographs proved Mama Bird's existence.

The Mama Bird phenomena lasted a few weeks, but ultimately went down as an urban legend and hoax.

Alina stared through the dirty glass partition at Grace Volkman. "I believe you," Alina said.

"What?"

"I believe Mama Bird existed, and she's still out there."

Grace's exhausted, weathered face brightened, and youthful features—those that might have survived had life not buried her deep in the mud—surfaced for a moment. "You believe me?"

"Yes."

Tears filled her eyes and streaked down her cheeks.

"I need your help, Grace. I need to find Ronald Greene, Mama Bird's latest victim. How can I contact her?"

"You can't. She contacts you."

"How do I get on her radar?"

"I don't know."

"Why would she hurt Ronnie?"

"Was he popular?"

"Yes."

"Mean?"

"Not that I know of. He was a stand-up guy. Smart, athletic, kind."

"There has to be a reason."

"Say there is a reason," Alina said. "How does that help me? How would that help me find him?"

"Mama Bird knew I hated Holly. She knew I hated myself more. She manipulated me, used my feelings against me. If you learn Ronnie's reason, you might learn who he once hurt—who would want to hurt him."

"Which will give me his abductor."

"Maybe."

Alina tapped her fingers against her thighs, her mind reeling with excitement. She had a lead, though she didn't know where it led her to. Still, Grace had provided her with a direction.

The guard hadn't stepped in to end the visit, so Alina took advantage of her time with Grace. "Do you know anything else about Mama Bird?"

"Like what?"

"How did she contact you?"

"Through email. We spoke on and off for a while. I now know she groomed me to become her puppet. Back then, though, while angry at the world, I was too willing to listen."

"What was the first challenge?"

Grace snickered. "To draw a momma bird feeding a worm to a baby bird while in a nest. I asked what kind of bird, and she said she didn't care. She also said it didn't matter their location. I could place the nest on the ground, in a tree, on the moon. It didn't matter. It only mattered that I sent a picture to her when I finished."

"What kind of bird did you draw?"

Grace half-smirked through the smudged glass partition. "A dodo."

"The extinct bird? Why?"

"Because it can't fly. I thought it represented me. I couldn't fly, and I envied that it no longer existed."

Alina held Grace's gaze, refusing to shy away despite the heaviness of the last statement. She empathized with Grace, but she also felt sorry for her. "How many challenges did you complete before murdering Holly?"

"Eighteen."

"Does that number mean anything?"

"One for each year I lived. When I killed Holly, I was supposed to… to kill myself. That was the challenge. Take her with me. I couldn't complete the entire assignment, though."

"Why a cutlass?"

"I don't know. That's what Mama Bird told me. Use a cutlass on Holly, then turn the blade on myself."

Alina shivered at the image of the instruction. "Do you remember the other challenges?"

"All of them. Some of them repeated."

"What do you mean?"

"On three separate occasions, I had to cut myself. One of her tasks had me skip school and watch horror movies all day, from four in the morning to midnight. Mama Bird provided me with every movie I watched. Some challenges were ridiculous. I had to listen to the same song all day, on repeat, without pausing."

"How did you prove you completed them?"

"I was so deep into the game at that point, I wouldn't have skipped a challenge. I think after I cut myself the first time and sent a photograph proving it, both Mama Bird and I understood my commitment."

"What else?"

Grace closed her eyes, as if falling back into a memory, recalling the tasks she had performed for a deranged, unidentified person on the other end of a message chain. "One time," she said, her eyes still closed, "Mama Bird had me eat a bowl of worms. I recorded myself and sent her the video. Another time, she had me go to the highest point around this area—a building, a tree, a cliff—and watch the sunrise. Once, she had me go an entire day without eating. Another time, I had to go an entire day without speaking to anyone." Grace opened her eyes again, blinking softly.

"You did everything?"

"Except for the last. I didn't turn the cutlass on myself."

Alina sighed. But before she had the chance to push forward with more questions, a guard tapped her shoulder, signaling her allotted time had expired. Alina thanked Grace for speaking with her.

"I hope you find him alive," Grace said.

"Me, too." Alina hung up and left the prison.

Invasion of Privacy. Wednesday, October 25th. 1112hrs.

Rhett exercised his right to the silent treatment, proving passive aggression was the least effective and most irksome form of communication. He not only refused to speak to Alina, but to look at her. Despite his display of obstinance, he still complied with Alina's latest request to drive to Ronald Greene's house.

Alina glanced at her phone, confirming the address on her navigation. "Park over on the corner." She pointed across the street, four houses away from Ronnie's home.

Without a word, Rhett drove forward, made a U-turn, and parked where Alina had suggested. When he cut the ignition, Alina unbuckled and faced him. "It's been over twenty minutes. You haven't said a word."

Rhett curled his lips inward and widened his eyes, shaking his head.

Alina reached across the center console and grabbed his hand. His palm was rough and warm and much larger than hers. "Rhett, I really, really like you." She thought of her conversations with Maya and August, about what they had advised about her and Rhett's relationship. "But." She stopped, biting off the rest of her sentence and sighing. "Rhett, I've been part of terrible relationships, beginning with my relationship with my father. I'm a mess, and relationally, I'm still learning the ropes. But I don't have the patience to tolerate someone treating me poorly. I've tolerated that too much over the years, and I'm done with it."

"I'm treating..." He trailed off, swallowing whatever he meant to say.

"You not only make me happy." Alina paused, thinking he might add something inappropriate, as was his juvenile nature. It stung when he continued to hold his silence. "You not only make me happy, but you make me feel light, like the burdens of my past weigh nothing. Like I can float. I want us to work, because I like how you make me feel. But if I'm not making you feel the same way, if something I did is forcing you to bite your tongue, to not speak to me, well, that's a problem. Not only do I deserve to know, but you deserve to let me know so I can do better."

It took him a few seconds, but said, "Okay."

"Okay?"

"I'll speak."

"I'll listen."

"I wrote a poem about you."

Alina hadn't expected that. She leaned into the headrest and frowned. "Really?"

Rhett dug into his back pocket, removing his wallet, opening it, and pinching out a folded piece of college-ruled paper. "Do you want me to read it to you?"

"Yes."

Rhett nodded as he unfolded the lined paper. He cleared his throat and read at a record speed, as if he had the poem memorized and wanted nothing more than to finish his recital of it. "I saw the sunset the other night, and I cried, I cried with all my might; I cried because I knew that meant the day had died. It was a good day, too—one warm and bright and blue. Most of all, Alina, it had you. I watched the sky turn from blue to red to purple to dark, wondering, pondering, what will happen to my heart? If you walked away and made my world dark, would my heart fall apart? It scared me, being in the dark. I wanted, needed, the sun to rise, to see it in the sky, to see it illuminating everything before my eyes. I waited all night, sitting in the dark, holding my heart, hoping you wouldn't depart. Then, the sun rose, chasing away the dark, turning the sky purple to red to blue. And sitting in the sky, smiling at this guy, there was you, warming me all the way through." Rhett finished and inhaled. He offered a soft, almost embarrassed, smile and brushed away a tear with his knuckle.

Alina didn't know what to say, but she said the worst thing. "Thank you."

Rhett nodded his head, as if he expected the response. "I didn't write that poem for you."

Alina narrowed her eyes, confused. "You just said you did."

"I said I wrote it about you. I wrote it for me, to help me work through what I'm feeling. Do you know what I'm feeling?"

Alina considered his question against what she remembered of his reading. "Scared?"

"And lost, like I'm in the dark. You're the sun, right? You warm and brighten my day, but you also... like today and yesterday, you abandon me."

"Abandon you? I've been with you nonstop since yesterday."

"Emotionally."

"I don't understand."

"I know you're not an emotional person. I love that about you. You're strong and independent. And that's great. I'm sensitive, though, and I'm emotional. I'm also, while in relationships, a pushover. It's difficult for me to recognize my needs as independent and as important as the needs of the person I'm dating."

"I'm not meeting your emotional needs?"

"I don't know."

"Don't shut down."

Rhett focused on his breath for a second. "I dropped out of high school for a year. I came back because you convinced me to finish and graduate. You inspired me, made me believe in myself. These past few days, you ripped that belief away from me. You've made me feel inferior to what you want, even to what Ronnie needs. I know it's silly, because his life is in danger, but you've gone about this in a way that completely disregards me. Now look at us. We're parked in front of Ronnie's house, preparing to break into his room, all while we're skipping class. What if we're caught?"

"You don't have to go with me."

"That's not the point," Rhett said. "Of course I'm going with you. I'm not allowing you to do this alone. I'm only saying we could have gone about this vigilante investigation differently, like after school or on the weekend."

"I'm sorry," Alina said after a moment. "You're right. I've acted like a selfish ass. I never thought about how this investigation might affect you."

"Honestly, it's fine. I'm just, like, sensitive. Usually, I hide my soft interior behind a rough exterior, rugged handsomeness, and a disarming humor, and that's enough to bury how I feel. I don't know. It's silly. I'm silly." He chuckled and opened the truck's door. "Let's forget about any of this."

Alina pulled him toward her. She leaned over the console and kissed his cheek. "Your feelings aren't silly, and we definitely shouldn't forget if I made you feel inferior or forgotten. Thank you for saying something. I promise, in the future, I'll work harder at hearing your perspective."

They climbed out of the truck and jogged across the street.

Alina had picked up a few tricks from Maya pertaining to breaking and entering a home. She hadn't ever engaged the tactics until that late morning, and her inexperience cost about a minute of fiddling with the back porch's deadbolt. Finally, it unlatched, and Alina pushed open the door.

"Voila," she said, turning to Rhett with a grin.

"You terrify me sometimes," he said. "But in an awesome way. Like dying while skydiving."

"I'm not tracking the example."

"Well, imagine how terrifying it would be when you pulled the string and your parachute didn't open. Imagine the thrill you would have falling through the sky, though. Terrifying, thrilling, and exhilarating, all braided together to create an exciting death."

"I'm not sure you're speaking to a choir on this one."

"How would you want to die?"

"In my sleep, where I don't have to experience dying. It just happens, and I drift away, none the wiser."

Rhett scowled. "I don't buy it. You dying peacefully? Nah."

"What does that mean?"

"We're breaking into someone's house right now, while investigating their disappearance after going on a date with a girl who died ten years ago. You live for danger, and you're telling me you want to die in your sleep."

Alina giggled, shrugging casually. "People say you die how you live. Well, I'm a contrarian by nature."

"You really argue about everything, don't you?"

"You like it."

"I like you, but that doesn't mean I like all the things you do. Such as illegally entering a home."

Alina smirked and illegally stepped into the Greene residence.

She didn't bother searching through every corner of the house. If Ronnie kept any proof of why someone would want to hurt him, he would hide the evidence in his room.

His bedroom didn't have any posters on the white-painted walls. A desk sat in the corner, cleared of any clutter, apart from a family picture, his closed laptop, and a bookmarked copy of *The Picture of Dorian Gray*. He had made the bed in a rigid, military style, and he put his clothes in drawers or hung them in the closet. Nothing appeared out of place.

In Alina's estimation, that fit what she knew of him.

Ronnie collected A's on his report cards. He volunteered his time, played sports, sang in the choir, played in the band, worked an internship, and took a college class. To keep track of his life, Alina suspected he had a hint of organizational skills.

Unfortunately, she wasn't too sure if that would play in her favor. If he had a secret, he either filed it away, or rather, he destroyed any evidence of it. Alina leaned toward the latter option, believing they wouldn't find anything.

Still, they had to try.

"I'll search through his room," Alina said. "Can you keep watch in case anyone shows up?"

"I think I can handle that job," Rhett said. He moved into the room across the hall and peered out the window overlooking the driveway and street.

Alina checked Ronnie's closet, opening shoe boxes, sliding her fingers into his jean pockets, and looking inside of his shoes. After finding nothing of importance, she moved to his nightstand.

She found a journal.

Alina opened it and flipped through the pages, one by one, skimming over the meticulous daily entries. None of them mentioned anything about his date. The installments ended Friday, the night before he went missing.

Most of his scrambled, incoherent thoughts detailed his daily activities—his breakfast, how songs on the radio made him feel as he drove to school, the biggest takeaway from each class, the highlight of his day, his mood and speculation on why he felt happy or sad or angry, and how to replicate positive feelings or eliminate negative ones.

As the entries encroached closer on the actual date, they grew monotonous. The last ten passages were almost carbon copies of each other.

I ate Cheerios for breakfast. I'm not sure why? A craving, perhaps? It differed from my normal high-protein breakfasts, though, and I felt the nutritional shift in my energy level, my mental sharpness, and my emotions. Then again, during breakfast, I saw my dad. So, I can't say with any level of certainty if the cereal or my father blunted my ability to function at a high level.

Last class was theater. As usual, diving into the story, into another life, into another world helped me drown away my life and world. When the class ended, I simultaneously felt elated and deflated. I know that's a contradiction. Yet, the high of the performance lifted me off the ground so that I floated, but the knowledge of going back home, of seeing him again, acted like a slow-burning leak. I wish I could live here, on stage, lost in another life and world. Maybe Roy will know how to make me laugh.

Home. I missed Roy, so he didn't make me laugh. On the bright side, Dad's not home. If I wanted to make a quick dollar, I would bet everything he's at the bar with his buddies, getting drunk and making trouble.

Life is nothing more than a circle. It's tedious and bland and repetitive. What's the point of it all if we do nothing but run in circles like a caged hamster? Progress is nothing but an illusion. Life is nothing but a scam.

Setting his journal back on the nightstand, Alina moseyed over to the desk and opened the drawers.

When her search once again brought up nothing of value, she massaged her temples and exhaled, thinking of where he might hide a clue.

His computer?

Alina opened the laptop, but it had password protection. She closed it, not bothering to waste her time with random guesses. Absentmindedly, she grabbed the book penned by Oscar Wilde, and she stared at the cover, depicting the cover artist's vision of Dorian Gray. Alina had seen the movie, had seen all of them, had even read the book a year ago, so she knew the story well.

Did Ronnie read the novel for fun, or did he read it as a class assignment? Did it matter?

Alina opened the book to the marked page and read. She continued reading, skimming through half of the chapter before she dropped the book back onto the desk and stared at nothing in particular. As she looked inward, visualizing her thoughts, replaying the information she had collected about Ronnie and Mama Bird.

Without realizing it, she suddenly stood in the bedroom doorway across the hall. "We have to go. I know where Ronnie is."

Rhett turned to her, fear masked across his face. "Um, a police officer just stepped out of his car, and he's walking up the driveway."

Alina leaned into the room a few inches and tilted her head. "What? You didn't care to mention that when you saw the cruiser approaching?"

"Honestly, I was responding to a text message and didn't see it until you came in."

"Who were you texting?"

"Does it matter to who? I think we have bigger problems now."

Alina growled beneath her breath. "Come on."

"To where?"

"The garage."

"What?"

"A security camera probably caught us breaking into the house, right?" Alina asked, speaking fast. "Ronnie's mom or dad most likely called the police, reporting our break-in. The officer will walk around the back. There's also, and I'm guessing, another officer waiting out front in case we run that way."

"That doesn't explain your garage idea."

"There's usually a side door in a garage leading to a side yard. We can hop the side fence into the neighbor's property and go from there."

"Why can't we tell the cops the truth?" Rhett asked.

"What truth? That we broke into someone's home to investigate illegally when we should have relayed any information to them?"

"That's what I told you to do from the beginning."

"It's too late now."

Rhett groaned. "Garage, then?"

"Garage."

They dashed through the house, slipping into the two-car garage. As Alina predicted, a side door led to a side yard where the Greenes stored their trash bins. Alina climbed on top of the recycling bin and hopped over the wooden fence separating the Greenes from their neighbor.

A woman flirting with eighty kneeled over a raised bed. She pulled weeds from a backyard garden, wearing a sunhat, despite the cloudy day, and stared at Alina and Rhett.

Before Alina could act, Rhett stepped forward, wearing a uniform of effortless charm. "Hello, Ma'am. We're with the Jehovah Witnesses.

We rang your doorbell, but no one answered. And you know how persistent we can be. So, we hopped the fence, because nothing stands in our way from spreading the news of Jesus Christ, our lord and savior." Rhett kneeled a few feet from the woman. "Do you mind?" He reached out his hand. "Can we pray together? We'll pray over this garden, that it bears a bountiful harvest, as we will pray for God to use us so we may bear a bountiful harvest in his name."

Alina held her breath, not believing that she believed Rhett's stunt might work.

"My husband had an affair," the old woman said, adjusting her sunhat and holding Rhett's eyes in hers. "I walked in on him last week. With my older sister. She's always been such a slut, always wanted to sleep with my Rupert. I saw how he looked at her, too. With hungry eyes. Now that he has dementia, he thinks he can get away with it. He said he didn't know. He thought she was me. I'll tell you this much. That's about the most insulting thing he ever said to me in our sixty years of marriage. You know what else?"

"I'm not sure I want to know," Rhett said.

"My sister gave him chlamydia, and he gave it to me."

"You walked in on him, though?" Alina asked, unable to prevent herself from asking the question.

"What does that have to do with anything?" The old woman glared at Alina.

"Why did you sleep with him after his infidelity?"

"I have needs, too."

"Should we pray for him?" Rhett asked, jumping back into character. "Should we pray for his... for God's judgement to befall him?"

"Yes," the woman said.

Rhett glanced over his shoulder, beckoning Alina to kneel with him. "What would you like to pray for specifically?"

"His slow and painful death," the woman said. "That the chlamydia rots off his joystick. Also, pray for my sister, please. Her husband passed away last month after a massive stroke."

Alina kneeled beside Rhett, saying nothing, allowing him to carry them out of the hole.

"Yeah, sure." Rhett grabbed the woman's bony, palsy-marked hand. "Close your eyes." He inhaled. "Lord, we, your faithful servants, come to you in prayer to ask for your favor and blessing over the life of..." He opened his eyes. "What's your name?"

"Helen."

"Over Helen," Rhett said. "We pray for healing over the sexually transmitted infection she's suffering, and we pray that her cheating, sleazy husband faces a slow, painful death, and his... that his joystick rots off his body."

"Tiny joystick."

"I'm not sure God cares about the size of his—"

Helen cut off Alina. "Tiny."

Rhett cleared his throat. "We pray his tiny joystick rots off his body. Also, please be with her slutty sister, as she mourns the loss of her late husband. I pray she can fill that empty void with something other than Helen's husband's tiny, rotting joystick. Thank you for hearing our prayer. Amen."

"Amen," Helen said, her face bright with joy. "Thank you for jumping over my fence. That was a truly healing experience."

"That's why we do what we do," Rhett said, standing and helping Helen stand. "Now, if you'll excuse us, we have to spread the love of Christ to the rest of the community."

Rhett headed toward the side gate. Alina followed him. They opened it, snuck across Helen's driveway to the other neighbor's house, back to the public sidewalk, across the street, and into his truck.

From where they sat, laughing with relief, they could see the police cruiser parked in the Greene's driveway.

"Holy smokes!" Rhett said, slapping his palm against the steering wheel. "I'm not sure what's more shocking—that my improvisation worked, or her story."

"Definitely her story," Alina said.

"Where are we going now?"

Alina looked at him and bit her lip. After a second of admiring Rhett, she leaned over and kissed him on the mouth. "Thank you for saving our butts."

"Even a blind squirrel finds a nut now and then, right?"

Alina smiled, feeling that familiar sense of weightlessness she often felt around Rhett.

"Where are we going, though? I think we should skedaddle while we're ahead."

Alina chuckled. "Skedaddle?"

"I learned from the best of them."

"We're going to the school."

"Our school?"

Alina nodded and sighed, knowing where they would find Ronnie. "Our school."

Running into the Dark. Wednesday, October 25th. 1216hrs.

Rhett drove at a far too slow and safe speed through Sacramento to Pleasant Valley High School. Alina held her cell phone to her ear, waiting for Vanek to answer her call.

"You going to drive faster?" she asked Rhett, her voice low and harsh.

"And risk a ticket? Nope. You know what they say. Slow is smooth, and smooth is fast."

"That's how I'm going to kill you. Slowly."

"Kill who?" Vanek answered, his voice strained and tired. "I hope that's a hypothetical murder you're discussing in one of your how to get away with murder classes."

"I don't have time for a lecture," Alina said. "But I wouldn't ever skip that class, if it existed."

"Why aren't you back in school? The meeting with Grace should've lasted only an hour."

"I know where Ronnie Greene is."

"Where?" A shot of excitement piqued in his tone. "How? Also, I'm still upset with you."

"He's in the performing arts department at Pleasant Valley." A silence stretched out on the other end of the line. "You there?"

"Do I even want to know?"

"Know what?"

"I heard about a break-in at the Greene's. What am I going to see on security footage, if it's shown to me?"

Alina ran her fingers through her hair. "Does it matter? We found him."

"Jesus, Alina. You can't break laws to solve an ongoing investigation. Even if you learn the truth, your involvement jeopardizes any criminal proceedings because of illegal activity leading to the defendant's arrest. There's a reason we have a system in place."

Rhett pulled into the school's parking lot behind the performing arts department and parked in a handicap stall closest to the building.

"I'm at the school now," Alina said. "I'm going after him. You can reprimand me later, but right now, let's save a life." Before Vanek could respond, Alina disconnected the line. She turned to Rhett. "He'll send a unit out here."

"Are we waiting for them?"

Alina opened the passenger door, hopped out of the truck, and headed toward the performing arts department, not bothering to see if Rhett followed. As she hurried, she watched for school staff who might question why she wasn't in class. Alina opened the door and stepped into the building. She navigated through the halls, into the auditorium.

"You're sure he's here?" Rhett asked from behind Alina.

Startled, she about jumped out of her skin and whirled around. "Don't sneak up on me like that."

"I was behind you the entire time. Pay attention." Rhett scratched the back of his neck. "You're sure he's here?"

"Yeah."

"Where?"

Alina hustled onto the stage, behind the curtain, and into the dressing area. She arrived at an concealed door in the room's corner, hidden behind a hanging rack holding an assortment of costumes.

"You're sure a cop will find this?" Rhett asked.

Alina rolled the disguises to the side, allowing herself an unobstructed path to the door. "What?"

"You told Vanek that Ronnie's in the performing arts department, but not where. This seems a little off the beaten path, no?"

Alina grabbed her phone and dialed Vanek's number. Her hands trembled with excitement.

"Someone is on the way," the detective said.

"Send them to the dressing room. There's a door in the back of the room leading into the basement."

"Where are you?"

"Bye, darling." Alina hung up and smiled at Rhett.

"He told you to hang back, didn't he?"

"Technically, no."

"You're going to disobey him?"

"He didn't order me to do anything."

"Let's work this out," Rhett said, wedging himself between Alina and the door.

"Figure what out?"

"What if we go down there and Ronnie's abductor attacks us? We don't have a weapon. How do we fight back? Doesn't it make the most sense to wait for the police to arrive? I know I'm not the sharpest Crayon in the shed, and I know you hate taking advice, especially from me, but it seems foolish to rush down there without a plan other than screaming, 'Hey, you!'"

"I was going to say, 'Hey, you, put down the gun.'"

Rhett threw up his arms in frustration. "That's not funny."

"It's a little funny." Alina smirked.

"What's the plan? We go downstairs, into the basement, and tell whoever abducted Ronnie the police are on the way? It makes no sense."

"Ronnie abducted Ronnie."

Rhett blinked a few times as he swallowed her words. After a second, he said, "Come again."

"Ronald Greene abducted Ronald Greene."

"He kidnapped himself?"

"Yes."

"Why?"

"Because Mama Bird told him to."

"I'm confused. What about the girl he went on a date with this past Saturday? Who was she?"

"I don't know."

"How do you know he's down there? How do you know he's still alive?"

Alina glanced over her shoulder and wondered where the cops were. Her chest squeezed so tight it made it hard to breathe. "His journal. He said he wished he could live here. It was his escape."

"I still don't get it?"

Alina thought of Grace Volkman, of how Mama Bird had instructed her to kill Holly Hanson before taking her own life. If Mama Bird had resurfaced, had contacted Ronnie, and if he murdered someone and himself, where would he want to spend the rest of eternity?

Alina knew it was loose logic, but when she read the highlighted passages in *The Picture of Dorian Gray*, it made perfect sense in her mind.

Alina thought of the anonymous caller saying Holly Hanson had taken Ronald Greene, and investigators had until Wednesday to find and save him. Now Alina believed Mama Bird had contacted Ronnie. He planned to murder someone, then himself. He was the Grace Volkman in this scenario.

Alina couldn't stand around any longer, waiting for the police to arrive, when two people could die any second. How did she slide by Rhett, though?

Acting on a whim, doing the only thing she could think of, Alina reached for the hanging clothes, grabbed a fistful of fabric, and chucked an armload at Rhett. The entire rack toppled, falling onto him.

"Sorry," Alina said, sidestepping her boyfriend, driving herself into the door, and throwing it wide open.

She scurried down the old wooden staircase into the unlit basement.

Behind her, Rhett groaned and grunted. A heavy clanking sounded as the costume rack crashed to the ground. Footsteps beat against the stairs as Rhett chased after her.

Alina had her hand on the cool wall of the basement, feeling for a light switch. For a second, she considered flicking on her phone's flashlight, but she abstained, preferring to remain hidden as long as possible, or until she illuminated the entire area.

Instead of relying on sight, she relied on her hearing and sense of smell. Apart from Rhett's elephantine stomps down the stairs as he chased her, a dark silence filled the basement. The silence unnerved her, made her imagine Ronnie and whoever he had taken down there with him lying dead and bloodied on the floor.

"Alina," Rhett said, whisper-yelling her name.

Without his trudging footsteps burdening the otherwise muted room, Alina assumed he made it to the bottom of the stairs. She didn't respond. Rather, she continued shuffling forward, deeper into the bowels of the darkness and silence.

Rhett had other ideas.

A bright-blue light burned through the darkness of the basement, casting forward from Rhett's cell phone. The edges of the conical light didn't touch Alina, but she saw her boyfriend's silhouette, along with the dark outline of another figure beside him, holding a shadowed weapon above his head.

"Watch out!" Alina screamed.

As if expecting an attack, Rhett dove forward, somersaulted, and rolled into a crouched stance. He ripped his flashlight backward. It illuminated the area before the stairwell.

Ronald Greene stood four feet from Rhett. He held a long, curved knife in his right hand. Dirt and blood covered his face and clothes. He panted to breathe.

Without warning, he dashed forward.

Rhett jumped back, but he kept his phone held high, his light burning through the basement. It tracked Ronnie's movement, followed him to the back corner of the basement.

Ronnie slid into position behind a kneeling body, slipping the blade against the person's throat, drawing a thin line of blood across his taut skin. "Stay back!"

Alina stepped forward, bathing herself in the cone of light. She raised her hands in a sign of surrender. "Ronnie."

"Who are you?"

"My name is Alina Moore. Behind me, that's Rhett Jensen. We're here to help you before you do anything drastic."

"You can't stop me."

"You waited. You want to be stopped."

"Mama Bird told me to wait. She said to wait until the final bell today." Rhett showed a steely determination in his eyes. His red, curly hair sat in matted, sweaty tangles atop his head. "You shouldn't be here."

"The cops are on their way, Ronnie. They'll be down the stairs any second. I say we settle this before they arrive, just you and me. Okay?"

Ronnie pushed harder on the blade. The hostage moaned with pain.

"Mama Bird contacted you, right?" Alina asked, speaking faster now. "You can't kill him, Ronnie. Mama Bird said to kill him when the last bell rings. But not now. She had you call the police, right? You were the anonymous caller who tipped them off about Holly Hanson?"

Ronnie clenched his jaw, not responding.

Alina didn't need verification. She needed to stall him. The last bell would ring any minute—Wednesday was a minimum day, and school let out at 12:37. She didn't dare take her eyes off of Ronnie to see how much time they had.

She had to stall him, even if the bell rang.

A burning sense of pride filled her. What if they waited for the police to arrive? What if Ronnie, because of Alina's hesitance, killed the kid he held hostage?

"Did Mama Bird tell you to tip the cops?" Alina asked.

Again, no response from Ronnie.

"She had you wait in here for four days. What did you do? She sent you different tasks, right? You called the police, that was one task. But what else?"

"Shut up! You know nothing!"

"I know you don't have to go through with this."

"You don't know! She'll tell the world. She'll tell everyone."

Alina shrugged. "Who cares if they know?"

Ronnie chuckled, though not amused; he laughed like a madman who can't seem to get his point across to anyone else. "Who cares? I care. I've dedicated every second of my existence to getting into a prestigious university. That's over now, right?" Ronnie cackled at some unknown joke. "You don't know, do you?"

"You're gay, aren't you? That's who Roy is. Your boyfriend, right?"

"What does that matter?"

"You haven't come out yet."

"You think that's why I'm stuck down here, contemplating murder?"

Alina's mouth fell open. She had ended up in the right place at the right time, but she hadn't put the equation together correctly. She assumed Mama Bird had blackmailed Ronnie, using evidence of his secret sexual orientation to manipulate him. That wasn't the case, though.

As her mind reeled for an answer, the journal entries slammed into her. Alina squinted her eyes, and forced herself to discern the man who lay beneath Ronnie's blade. He was in his forties or fifties—bald, with deep crow's feet expanding from his eyes.

"Your dad?"

Ronnie growled deep in his throat. "Mama Bird discovered my grandfather, my dad's dad, and my dad have ties and leadership within a white supremacy group. She sent me the evidence, and then she said she would release it to every college I planned to apply for if I didn't follow her explicit instructions. Here I am, faced with a choice. Do I murder my father and kill myself? Do I end the life and future I no longer have? Or do I walk away and allow my entire existence to get flushed down the drain?"

"That's a simple decision," Alina said.

Ronnie laughed in disbelief. "I have nothing to do with my father's bigotry, but I'll face the consequences. I'll lose my future," Ronnie screamed with frustration. "There's nothing for me anymore. I've obsessed my entire life over my future, sacrificing my childhood for a successful adulthood. But now I have nothing."

"No one has to die."

Ronnie scrunched his face and yelled once more. "Someone has to die." He moved the blade from his father's throat and kicked him in the back.

The man gasped and fell on his face. He lifted his head and crawled toward Alina, sobbing. She watched him—a racist old white man, slithering toward her, a young black girl, on hands and knees, sobbing and begging for her to save him. For a terrible second, she wanted to kick him in the jaw.

Instead, she faced Ronnie, who turned the blade to his own neck.

"Rhett, get the pathetic old man out of here," Alina said.

"I'm not leaving you."

"I'm not asking you. Get him out of here, now." She fumbled in her pocket, removed her cell phone, and turned on the flashlight, highlighting Ronnie. "There's also redemption and second chances."

"Not with this," he said.

The dismissal bell chimed, partially muffled deep in the basement.

Alina dropped her phone from the sudden, jarring noise, and she sprinted forward, slamming her body into Ronnie, hoping he hadn't driven the blade into his throat. She flailed, scratching his face, slapping his arms, punching his torso. She lay on top of him, covering his neck with herself, shielding him with her body.

He struggled and fought back, using his athletic frame to toss her off of him.

Alina was relentless, though. She leaped back at him, wrapping her arms and legs around him, squeezing with all her might.

"On the ground!" A booming voice carried through the dark basement, and a bright, police-issued flashlight brightened the entire room. "Bellies on the ground! Kiss the floor! Both of you! Now!"

"He has a knife!" Alina called back. "He has a knife. Take it from him."

As the initial voice continued to bark orders, another person dashed forward and wrested the blade from Ronnie's hand.

Alina released from Ronnie and dropped to the ground. An officer planted his knee into her back and handcuffed her. She turned her head toward Ronnie, saw him lying on the ground and staring back at her. His face was wet with tears, broken and defeated... but filled with blood and life.

Stakeout. Thursday, October 26th. 0101hrs.

Fred had his back to me as he urinated behind a tree in the corner of the Kosar property. When he finished relieving himself, he grabbed his goodie bag of snacks, removed a Snickers candy bar, and ripped open the packaging.

I raised my binoculars and checked on the Kosar house. Most of an investigator's job is sitting around, waiting and observing. After my night spent researching the history of the haunted house, a new theory formed in my mind.

My efforts returned to Vernon Nowak—the supposed entity who lingered in the house and terrorized all proceeding inhabitants. A detail about his story stuck in my mind like a thorn in a sock.

When he returned from the war, he built the house.

As the Cold War ensued, his paranoia increased.

He eventually poisoned his family, everyone but a baby who napped in the other room.

The answer to Doug Kosar's haunted house lived in those details. How did they fit together, though, and what picture did they form?

"What do you think of Alina?" Fred asked, chomping on a mouthful of his chocolate snack.

I shook my head, shedding off my ruminations. "I don't know what to think about Alina."

Pleasant Valley High School had contacted me earlier regarding the incident with Ronald Greene. Apparently, Alina penned me as her emergency contact over Maya and her mother. I'm not sure how that slid through the system, but I received the call.

When I arrived at the school, Alina sat on the curb in front of the performing arts building, talking the ear off of a uniformed police officer. I recognized her principal, Mrs. Harley Brown, Detective Kyle Vanek, and Rhett.

I didn't bother to ask the principal, the responding officer, or Vanek about what happened. My sole concern lay with Alina. I sat beside her on the curb, listening to her one-sided conversation with the poor officer.

"...because he failed. Through his failure, Jigsaw, or John, found a new appreciation for life. His motivation for torturing and killing his victims was to inspire them to find a new appreciation for life by testing their will to live. Do you get it now? He didn't take pleasure from killing people, but he saw what he did as noble—as a necessary gift to remind people to be grateful for their life. The real question, Kramer, how have you not seen any of the *Saw* movies?"

"I haven't seen them either," I said.

"Yeah, well, you're a Neanderthal. I expect it from you. From Rhett, though? My boyfriend? Unacceptable. From Officer Kramer, a handsome young man... it's intolerable. What's society coming to?"

"What happened?"

"I saved someone's life."

Vanek whistled, catching my attention, and he waved me over.

I glanced at Alina and half-smiled, stood, and shuffled over to the detective. "You're working with Sacramento P.D. now?"

Vanek frowned and shook his head. "She called me before going into the basement. I showed up as a worried friend."

"Yeah, well, you're going to have to get used to that feeling. She told me she saved lives, though."

Vanek snickered. "I'll put it this way: Alina found a missing person."

I understood his meaning without him saying anything more. Alina worked contrary to advice, disobeyed orders, and had most likely broken a law or two in her search to solve whatever mystery had fallen into her lap.

"Is everyone okay?" I asked.

"Everyone is alive, thanks to her."

"I won't tell her you said that."

"Keep your phone near you. There's a potential case we may reach out about."

"It's always in my pocket," I said.

Rhett popped out from nowhere. "Gus, my man. Did you hear? We're campus heroes. Alina is in a lot of trouble, but the people love her. She's a local legend."

"She's the local idiot," I said.

"That's aggressive."

I stepped around him and sat beside Alina again. Officer Kramer had made his escape, leaving Alina and me alone.

For a while, I said nothing. A part of me wanted to dig into her, ask her what she was thinking—tell her she wasn't thinking. As I allowed my emotions to drain, as anger and fear trickled away, pride remained.

"You saved their lives, huh?" I asked. "I'm proud of you."

Alina looked at me and chuckled. She rested her head on my arm for a second before sitting straight again. "You're not mad?"

"I'm upset."

"But you're proud?"

"I can be both things."

"Ronnie would've killed his father, possibly himself. I saw it in his eyes. He was afraid and desperate and backed into a corner."

"Mama Bird? Who is she?"

Alina shook her head. "I don't know... yet."

I stared at the overcast sky. "You're going to find out, then?"

"I have to. She's caused too much harm and death for me to ignore."

A brisk breeze sent a chill down my spine, drawing me back to the present, to the night, to the task at hand—catching a ghost. Through my binoculars, I watched an empty house. Beside me, Fred chewed fervently on whatever new snack he conjured. My phone vibrated in my pocket.

Maya showed on my screen.

I set down the binoculars and tapped the screen. "It's one in the morning. What if I was sleeping?"

"I didn't think you ever slept."

"What can I do for you?"

"I got bored waiting around for something to happen, so I did a little research into your haunted house case."

"Oh, yeah?"

"Found some juicy information."

"Did you?"

"Yup."

"You going to tell me?"

"Not until you tell me how smart I am, and how lucky you are to have me in your life."

I glanced at Fred and frowned. "You're super-duper smart, and I'm so lucky to have you in my life."

"Gross," Maya said. "You sounded desperate."

"I am desperate."

"You ready for this, then?"

"Hit me."

"Don't tempt me. Are you sitting down?"

"Quit stalling and tell me what you know."

Maya cleared her throat. "Vernon Nowak went crazy. Cuckoo. He lost his mind and his marbles. He came back from the war with PTSD. However, we didn't know how to treat the disorder—barely knew how to recognize it back then. His constant paranoia, compounded with the impending threat of the Cold War, drove him beyond bonkers. He spent his time working on the house, just like that Winchester place."

I held my breath. Maya spoke about the points I had circled, meaning I was on the right track; she was just smarter.

"According to local gossip, Vernon stopped trusting big government, including banks. He put his fortune—which was a lot, thanks to his daddy's steel fabrication company, which had a massive contract with the government during both world wars—into the walls of his home."

I hadn't uncovered his fortune. The wheels and gears in my head clicked and turned. House renovation paired with paranoia paired with a vast fortune. Where did that leave us?

Maya drove forward. "That's when the poisoning happened. Gulp, gulp. Dead, dead. Two years later, the same poisoning happened. Two years after that, the same poisoning happened."

"Unless Vernon's spirit poisoned everyone, I'm not following?"

"We don't have an evil spirit, you big oaf; unless you consider a money-hungry serial killer an evil spirit."

I stared at the ground, stumped beyond coherent thought. Had she said serial killer?

"What do you mean?"

Maya chuckled. "Cue Dennis Lundgren, the Cyanide Killer."

I rattled my brain, but the name eluded me.

"Police caught up to and arrested him in Southern California shortly after the third family died of cyanide poisoning in the Nowak home. Apparently, according to police reports, he kidnapped prostitutes and fed them cyanide. He never confessed to any of the family poisonings, nor was he ever charged for them, but there is firm evidence of him being in Sacramento when each of the poisonings occurred."

"He heard about the rumor of the Nowak fortune buried in the home, poisoned the family, and searched for it? When he didn't find it, he skipped town, returned a few years later, repeated the process?"

"I don't know, but if I had to put money on a theory, I would say that's what happened. He's dead now, so there's no way anyone will ever know the truth. He died in prison about twenty years ago. Heart attack."

"What about the family poisoned three years ago? The renters?"

Maya popped her lips a few times. "I don't know about them. It seems no one took the rumor of the buried fortune as anything more than rumor. I mean, who knows? Maybe Vernon Nowak lost every marble in the old bag and poisoned himself and his family, and his spirit now tempts anyone who moves into that house to do the same."

"You didn't look up the Nowak fabrication business?"

"Of course I did," Maya said. "That's true. There's just not a reliable record of Vernon inheriting it, or stashing it in the walls of the home."

"What about the possession?" I asked, thinking of Emily.

"No idea how to explain that one."

I sighed, fitting together everything Maya shared with what I already knew, searching for a way for it to all fit. "Thanks for the update," I said.

"Tell Fred I can hear him chewing all the way in Alaska. He eats like a blender mixing gravel."

I shared Maya's thoughts. "Tell her she's mean, and just because I'm big and muscular doesn't mean I don't have feelings."

"I'm not acting as the middleman for you two to have a fake argument." I spoke to them both.

A natural silence fell over the conversation. In that exact moment, a heavy thump crashed within the house—like someone taking a sledgehammer to the wall.

"That's our cue," I said.

"What cue?" Maya asked.

"I have to go."

"Go where?"

"Where are we going?" Fred asked.

I hung up on Maya and looked at Fred.

"We're not going into the house, are we? You just scolded Alina for doing the same thing."

"This isn't a criminal investigation. We have permission to be here, and the police aren't looking for a missing person or trying to solve a case. You coming or not?"

"If I don't?"

"You'll be outside, alone in the dark, with who knows what kind of ghosts lurking on this property."

"You don't even believe that's true. Plus, you're not funny. Also, wait up."

We blitzed across the property to the front door, pausing before it. I checked the handle to make sure no one had locked it. It twisted and unlatched, and the door creaked open.

The demolition from within the house continued.

I stepped inside, careful not to make much noise and alert anyone to my presence. In my pocket, I carried a kubaton stick. It wasn't much of a weapon, but in close combat, it had its advantages without being deadly.

I gripped it. "Change of plans."

"What?"

"You're going to wait here."

Fred swiveled his head back and forth. "It's not a plan if it won't happen. It's an idea, and it's a terrible one. I'm not waiting anywhere alone."

Fred stood well over six-four and weighed something north of two-fifty, with all of his mass coming from pure muscle. Maybe, and I'm stretching my estimation, he had nine percent body fat. Still, I couldn't discredit his fear of the dark or the unknown or the paranormal or bugs and insects or clowns or heights or tight spaces or, most irrational, balloons. His long list of fears seemed to never stop growing or evolving depending on the situation.

"I need you to call Doug Kosar."

"It's one in the morning."

"Send him a text, then. Give him an update on what we're doing. We're at the house, investigating an odd noise. If we find anything, we'll keep him posted."

The idea of having Fred contact Doug was a trap. I needed to eliminate Doug as a suspect. If Fred called and updated him, if the demolition ceased thereafter, it would help prove Doug had performed as the ghost. Though I doubted it, I wanted to cover all my bases without leaning on an assumption.

If Doug knew about the hidden treasure, why would he drive out his family? Why not find the cash discreetly and use it to pay his debts? Why create the haunted house and draw more attention to the home?

Because Doug didn't know.

Still, I had to be sure.

"I sent him a text," Fred said.

"Thank you. You're going to wait here and keep an eye out for anyone coming or going. If I accidentally alert the ghost, and he runs, I need you here to catch him."

"You think I'm going to run headfirst into a ghost?"

"I do."

Before he could argue any further, I closed the front door and isolated myself inside the house.

The Boy Who Lived. Thursday, October 26th. 0118hrs.

I HAD TO KEEP three things in mind as I navigated through the house.

One. Not a ghost, but someone desperate to find a hidden fortune haunted the home. Honestly, that scared me more than a supernatural spirit. That person had already forced a family from their home through violent displays of property damage. If caught, if cornered, how would they react?

I gripped the kubaton tighter and moved past the kitchen.

Two. According to Maya, Vernon Nowak, for all his paranoia surrounding the Cold War and a nuclear holocaust, had added to the home continuously. I would bet he hadn't only added rooms and square footage, but hidden passages leading to a bomb shelter or a safe room.

Three. Someone digging for the hidden fortune used the secret layout of the house to move around. They knew how to disappear into the walls, as witnessed by Doug. I didn't have that knowledge. They knew the home. I didn't. They knew the terrain and the layout. I walked into the fight blind and unprepared.

With those three points highlighted, cycling on repeat, I continued treading through the home, searching for the source of the constant hammering.

It continued, about one smashing blow every thirty seconds. I couldn't discern the source of impact, though. It bled from the walls, coming from everywhere at once.

I climbed the stairs and moved into the guest bedroom.

Doug mentioned the ghost disappeared after entering the room. Since I didn't believe a ghost or evil entity haunted the house, I suspected whoever tormented the family had dipped into a secret wall panel to vanish. I circled the guest bedroom, applying pressure to the walls and searching for a switch.

After five minutes of fruitless activity, I stood in the center of the room and turned a slow circle.

Moving boxes, both empty and unopened, filled one corner of the room. A bed sat against the back wall. Two square nightstands flanked the bed. An armoire covered with a drop cloth stood against the wall opposite of the bed. According to Doug, all the furniture in the home came with the purchase.

With visions of Narnia—albeit a dark and violent Narnia—in my head, I moved to the armoire, cast off the drop cloth, and opened the double doors. An acrid stench slammed into me, like opening a crate for the first time in years.

I curled my nose and grimaced, and my excitement dulled. The armoire didn't hide a secret door.

I turned, pressing my back flat against the ornate wood, and I stared blankly at the bed. How could someone run into the room and disappear in seconds, leaving no hint of how they disappeared?

Another heavy slam rocked the home.

I had to keep moving and figure out how to infiltrate the hidden spaces. I moved through the Jack and Jill bathroom, inspected the shower and cabinets for a secret door, finding zilch.

I entered Emily's bedroom. In their eighteen day stay at the house, Emily had done little in the way of personalizing her room. Except, of course, for the holes she punched into her wall to climb it and hold herself in a spider-like position.

I rubbed my neck, massaging out the built-up tension and stress, turning my head to the side and stretching the tightness from my shoulders. That's when I saw it.

Emily's closet door. It was shut.

I know that's not an abnormal occurrence, but it piqued my curiosity. Had the door stood open, I might have glanced inside from where I stood across the room. However, with it closed tight, it drew me forward, beckoned me to open it and step inside.

I slid the hanging clothes to the side and cocked my head, inspecting the wall behind them. It looked, by cursory inspection, like any wall, except for a skinny line running the length of it. If someone didn't expect a hidden door, they might mistake it for a crack in the drywall. That's if they saw it at all.

I planted my palm on the wall and pushed. A panel depressed inward and clicked, popping open.

My throat constricted, and my hands sweated. I wiped my palms on my jeans and inhaled. Butterflies skittered around my stomach, making it feel like I plummeted thirty feet.

I fished my phone from my pocket and texted Fred, letting him know I found a secret passage and where I found it. Before he responded, I returned the phone to my pocket and reasserted my grip on the kubaton.

After a second of collecting my bearings, I shouldered the half-door open and climbed through.

I appeared in a vein—a narrow hall—that ran the length of the house. I followed it as it shaped the exterior outline of the home. It led me to a steel ladder set inside a chute going up and down. I climbed down, coming to the first floor landing. The steel ladder continued to a lower level, but my curiosity led me to explore the first floor.

I walked through the narrow hall, noticing a knob every five feet. Curious, I grabbed one, turned it, and pulled.

Nothing happened.

I pushed.

Nothing.

After a second of consideration, I slid the door. It glided on tracks, moving into a carved pocket, opening into the dining room.

The custom walls that Vernon Nowak built slid open. That's why I couldn't find a switch or hidden door earlier—I had pushed. I hadn't thought about sliding the panels into carved-out pockets.

As I crouched in the hidden door, footsteps thumped down the hallway. A second later, Fred appeared. He walked by me, then he froze. His head turned until he faced me.

He inhaled and bellowed out an ear-piercing scream. It lasted all of three seconds, before his mind must have processed and comprehended I, not a ghost, stood inside the wall.

"What are you doing?" he asked, speaking far too loudly.

"Shh-shut up," I whispered, covering my lips with an index finger.

"You scared the piss out of me." He glanced at his pants, not dark with urine. "Well, almost. Why are you inside of the wall?"

"I found the secret door."

"You said it was in Emily's room. Not the dining room."

"There's a door in every room. Watch." I stepped back into the secret hallway, away from the opening, sidled sideways a few feet to the next panel, and slid it open. "Boo! See. Secret entrances all over the house."

"Did you find the money?"

"No."

"Where do the passages go?"

"That's what I'm trying to find out. Why are you in here?"

"You texted me and told me to come upstairs."

"No," I said, shaking my head. "I said I found a door upstairs. I'm updating you on the situation, not asking you to abandon your post. Go outside."

"I don't want to move through a dark, hidden hallway anyway. That sounds like the last thing I want to do."

"Everything sounds like the last thing you want to do."

"Not true. First thing I want to do is eat a giant, juicy cheeseburger covered in avocado and bacon, with a large side order of dirty fries."

How did I always get sucked into these nonsensical conversations? I was thinking the problem wasn't Fred or Maya or Alina, but me. That idea hurt.

Without another word, I slipped into the hidden hallway and continued navigating around the house.

I found another ladder inside a chute, and I climbed down. I arrived in a basement illuminated by a naked bulb. Exposed wires ran along the cement walls. Concrete rubble and dirt lay in heaps in the center of the basement or bomb shelter or panic room.

Opposite from where I stood, a lumberjack had hacked away at the far cement wall with a twenty-pound sledgehammer. The solid steel head rested on the ground. He leaned over, his thick forearms gripping the long shaft. He breathed and panted, building up his willpower and strength, before lifting the sledgehammer, allowing his bearish hands to slide down the handle, throwing incredible power behind the blow.

Dust and fragments exploded off the wall. The sledgehammer dropped to the ground. The man used his hands to chip away loose stone, to widen the gap he bludgeoned into.

"You look like you could use a break," I said. "Want me to step in and take over for a while?"

The man turned to face me. He had a thick black beard and thick black hair tied in a bun. He didn't wear a shirt, and his muscles bulged and rippled. If Fred looked like a gladiator, this man looked like a barbarian—wild and unhinged.

If I were a hair smarter, I would've bid him farewell, climbed the ladder, and went on with my life. Though I'm not stupid, I am occasionally dumb.

Instead of leaving, I painted a forced smile over my face and stepped deeper into the basement.

"I know what you're thinking," I said, "and there's nothing to worry about. I'm not here for the buried fortune." As a show of honesty and nonchalance toward the subject, I shrugged. "I don't care about money. I'm only here to banish a ghost from this house. As I understand, you're the ghost I have to banish." The kubaton seemed more than insignificant beside the bestial man wielding a massive sledgehammer. It felt like I had brought a twig to a tank battle.

"Who are you?"

"August Watson. You?"

He grunted, gripped the end of the sledgehammer, and stepped toward me, dragging the head of the demolition tool behind him.

"Twenty questions it is. Yes or no, are you a Nowak?"

The man stopped his slow, dreadful advancement.

"Grandson to Vernon?" I asked, holding my position, hoping to stand tall and not show the fear radiating through my being.

It's not that I couldn't fight—I had years of hand-to-hand combat training, learned through years in law enforcement. I also had a layer of muscles through countless hours in the gym. Despite my physique and combat experience, I wouldn't pick a fight with Fred, only because he had a hundred pounds on me and, when angry, could rip a stop sign from asphalt.

For the same reason, I didn't care to engage the man in a fight, especially while he had a sledgehammer. Honestly, I wished I hadn't stationed Fred in front of the house. Why hadn't I had him tag along with me?

Hindsight is always twenty-twenty.

My only advantage was to keep him from attacking me until I could think of a plan to escape and call for help. One option presented itself—an option I wasn't too gifted at. Gab. Hopefully, I had absorbed a few tricks from Maya and Alina after all the time we spent together.

I licked my lips, greasing and preparing them to handle a verbose amount of words, and I removed the filter separating my thoughts from my tongue. I let loose and vented. Honestly, it felt fantastic to speak to someone, to unburden myself to a stranger.

It also provided me with an odd clarity to the case as I recounted the details.

"Before you do anything impulsive, hear me out," I said. "Grandpa Nowak, he didn't kill his family. He didn't kill your mom and dad. A serial killer did... probably. There's not any proof of that. But there are some loose circumstantial events that say it's a possibility. The Cyanide Killer—look him up—was captured by police six years after your parents ate their last meal with Grandpa Nowak. He was from this area, and he skipped town immediately after their deaths. Other victims who died from cyanide poisoning appeared wherever he went. When he returned two years later, guess what? He poisoned the family who lived in this house."

The man's stoic face never shifted. Information like that could shatter the foundation of someone's identity. His parents hadn't died by Grandpa Nowak, but by a serial killer.

That would at least warrant a question, right?

The man didn't blink at the knowledge.

My question about Maya's information crashed into my mind. *What about the family poisoned three years ago?* If the Cyanide Killer died in prison, who murdered the renters?

"You already know about the Cyanide Killer." I stepped back as pieces, now clear as day, fell into place.

"I heard about the Cyanide Killer," he said. "Heard he was from the Sacramento area around the time my family died. I looked him up." He lifted his broad shoulders to his ears in a shrug. "Maybe he killed my family and the other two families. Maybe he didn't."

"It doesn't matter to you?"

"They're all dead. What would it matter? It doesn't bring them back."

"To identify the killer and seek justice for what he did to your family."

"I was there the night my family died. I was sleeping in the other room—a baby, three or four months old. That's what the officer who found me said when I was old enough to ask about it."

"That doesn't change the fact you could've sought justice and closure."

"This is my justice. My closure." He spread out his arms and gestured around the basement.

In his momentary state of vulnerability, I almost jumped at him. But he closed up and regained a ready position before I could make the move.

"The hidden fortune," I said.

"It's buried in this house. I found letters proving it's here, somewhere."

I licked my lips. "That's why you murdered the renters a few years back? You learned about the fortune. You came home and poisoned the couple living here. The market and media hyped it as a haunting. No one suspected the boy who survived the original massacre."

The man narrowed his light-brown eyes. I spoke on a developing hunch, though I had nothing substantial. His response all but proved my thinking.

"You had three years," I said. "Why didn't you dedicate your time to searching for the fortune then? Why wait until the house sold?"

"A past crime caught up to me. I had to serve five years. They released me after thirty months for good behavior. I came straight here. The next day, the new family arrived."

I threw out another theory, one that I hadn't entertained but had crossed my mind. "That's when you went into cahoots with the girl, right?"

He didn't respond, which, again, said a lot.

"I found a secret door in her closet. You used it, didn't you? At least once."

"I used a lot of the secret doors."

"But you used her closet. Emily was bedridden through most of her stay, meaning she probably saw you. Yet, she said nothing to her mom or step-dad. That leads me to believe... you two worked out an arrangement. Did you agree to split the fortune? Was she going to help her step-dad pay his debts?"

"She didn't give me a reason. She said she would help get her parents out of the house."

I considered the information for a second. "One more thing." I raised my free hand—the one not holding the kubaton—into the air, forming a fist. "Roshambo."

"What?"

"We'll play a game of Roshambo."

"Why?"

"If you win, I'll leave my wallet and phone on the floor and walk away. I don't have my car here. I took an Uber. So, without my phone, I'll have to walk into town. That'll give you plenty of time to escape. You never shared your first name, so I don't know who you actually are."

"If I lose?"

"I get ten percent of the fortune."

"I thought you didn't care about the money."

"I lied."

"Ten percent?"

"Off the top. You and the girl split the rest fifty-fifty. That'll buy my silence about this whole affair."

"Roshambo?"

"One game. Do or die. Otherwise, what's the alternative? We fight? If you kill me, well, there are people who know where I am, who suspect secret tunnels in the house. I left a few passages open. It won't be long until someone finds my body, until forensics comes back with fingerprints or DNA that lead to you. If I defeat you, well, I defeat you. No fortune. No more freedom. You're back in jail, this time for trespassing, vandalism, destruction of property, murder... and the list goes on and on." I raised my eyebrows. "Roshambo is a win-win. You get your money, win or lose."

Much to my surprise, the man built like a fictional lumberjack released the sledgehammer, allowing it to topple onto the ground. He stepped forward and raised a fist.

Our knuckles were six inches from each other.

"Ro. Sham. Bo."

He went with scissors.

Instead of going with rock, paper, or scissors, I went with the kubaton, stepping forward and uppercutting him square in the jaw. I followed the strike with a wide left hook that connected with his temple, and a stiff right jab that broke his nose.

The mountainous man dropped onto his butt. He grabbed his face as blood poured from behind his hands.

I leaped forward and grabbed the sledgehammer, and I held it in a threatening position that signaled I wouldn't hesitate to shatter his kneecaps if he moved. With my other hand, I fished out my phone.

"Did you find the ghost?" Fred asked, answering the phone.

"Broke his nose."

"How do you break a ghost's nose?"

"You're going to have to trash your complaint to the LARP Committee."

"What do you mean?"

"Apparently, Roshambo is a viable battle technique."

Fred went silent. "I don't want to know, and you can't ever tell Alina."

404

Happily Never After. Thursday, October 26th. 0319hrs.

SACRAMENTO COUNTY SHERIFF'S DEPARTMENT cordoned off the Kosar house, deeming it a crime scene and preventing anyone from entering. Lights flashed across the cloudy, lightless night. The storm hadn't arrived yet, but it rained at a light trickle without ceasing.

I stood outside in the wet, huddled with Fred, Doug, Kathleen, Emily, and a detective who worked the opposite hours of Vanek. She differed from Vanek in most every way—short, chubby, and tanned, where he stood tall, skinny, and pale. He had a quiet authority about him, but she bellowed her position.

The lumberjack, Lyle Nowak, sat in the rear of a police car.

After I called Fred, he squeezed through a panel—if Lyle could fit into the hidden passages of the home, Fred could as well—and made his way into the basement. I traded spots with him, handing him the sledgehammer and tasking him to watch Lyle while I called the police. Lyle had a lengthy criminal record. Since he was breaking his parole by committing a crime, the officers arrested him, though they waited to take him to jail. I'm not sure why.

Doug, Kathleen, and Emily arrived forty-five minutes after the police interviewed us and arrested Lyle. The lead detective, Jasmine Sanchez, asked the Kosars a series of questions while Fred and I remained to the side.

Eventually, after another thirty minutes, we reconvened in a big huddle.

I hadn't met Emily, so I focused on her. She was sickly pale, with matted, greasy hair and a growth of bright-red pimples over her cheeks. She sat in a wheelchair, though she bounced her heels up and down.

"Nervous tic?" I asked.

"What?" Doug asked.

"I'm talking to Emily. Is that a nervous tic? Bouncing your leg?"

She stopped and glared at me. "What do you mean?"

"When did you meet Mr. Nowak?" I stared right back at the young girl. She didn't intimidate me, no matter how hard she scowled. I had spent the past ten-ish months navigating Alina. If I could survive that, I could handle Emily—possessed or not.

"Who?"

"Emily, this will go much quicker and easier if you answer my questions without asking questions you already know the answer to."

"I don't know what you're talking about."

"What's he talking about?" Kathleen touched her daughter's shoulder.

"I said I don't know."

"What are you talking about, Sir?" Kathleen asked.

"Your daughter schemed with Lyle Nowak. They worked out a plan to split the fortune. I'm not sure why she needed the money, but she cut a deal with him." I focused on Emily, gauging her reaction to my insinuation. "Did you want to pay your step-father's debt?"

"Emily is sick, Mr. Watson," Kathleen said. "She needs help. She couldn't scheme or plan or plot with that man. What do you think happened? She faked being possessed? Emily can't pull off such a stunt."

"Oh. My. God," Emily said. She shrugged her mom's hand off of her shoulder, and she stood from her wheelchair.

Kathleen covered her mouth and gasped. "Emily."

"Shut up. When you speak, you sound so stupid. Look at me, Mom. I'm standing. Do you know why I'm standing? It's because I'm not sick. That's why. You're sick." She jammed her index finger into Kathleen's chest. "You're a sick, demented woman."

Kathleen's hand darted forward and slapped Emily across the face.

Two deputies must have noticed; they approached the scene, though with little haste or worry.

"Don't you speak to me that way," Kathleen said. "I've sacrificed everything for you."

Emily rubbed her cheek and chuckled. "Did you? Or did you use me as a Get Out of Jail Free card? I mean, you're responsible for dozens of deaths, right?"

"You don't know what you're saying."

"You stole their money after you killed them."

"I didn't kill anyone!"

"You murdered my father. Marshall Nix. You poisoned him, didn't you? I don't know what happened after that, but something in you snapped—or maybe it was always broken. Either way, you appointed yourself to take care of me no matter the cost, even if that cost was harming me, so I would always have to rely on you."

"You're delusional," Kathleen said, but she sounded less than convincing.

"A month before we moved into the house, I saw the truth, Mom. I saw your search history, your research. I saw the bottles in the trash. You're not treating a disease, you're fostering one. You're making me sick."

"Liar!"

"You forced my potassium levels to spike, causing mild paralysis in my leg. You created my diabetes diagnosis, and you're giving me insulin for the fake disease. That's why the doctors don't know what's wrong with me. There is nothing wrong with me other than you."

"Stop talking," Kathleen said.

"When I found out, I stopped taking your medicine and supplements. I would store them between my gums and spit them out when you weren't looking. Guess what happened? I regained feeling and strength in my legs. I had more energy. Crazy coincidence, huh, Mom?"

"You did all this. You ruined our family."

"You ruined our family. You murdered my father, along with dozens of other people. Don't think for a second you were innocent in the cult activity. I blame you as much as him for all those deaths. Then, for whatever reason, you possessed me, too."

"What?"

"A demon never possessed me." Emily chuckled. "I was possessed with hatred toward you, and I wanted to make you suffer. I hacked into your bank accounts, drained all the blood money from them, and donated it." Her laughter bubbled, intermixed with her words. "I donated it back to the survivors of your cult." She glanced at Doug. "She wouldn't pay for a hotel room because she didn't have the money, but she couldn't admit that to you. Not after you learned she had a fortune, and not after she insulted you for losing all your money. She's too proud and pathetic."

Kathleen's face was a sheet, a snowy slope, a marble counter. Her lips fluttered, but no words escaped.

"I stopped showering, eating, sleeping, using the toilet," Emily said, continuing her onslaught of verbal jabs. "Lyle ran around with a mask, using the hidden panels to sneak from room to room and destroy the house, to make you believe Vernon Nowak's ghost haunted it." Emily laughed again. "You are gullible. But I'll give you credit. You lasted far longer than I expected. Even when I loved trying to make you miserable, you still made me miserable by hanging around."

Tears streaked down Kathleen's face. "You're sick. You're possessed."

"Lyle said Doug saw him in the attic the day we toured the house. Well, when you walked into the house with the agent, Lyle slipped out. I saw him leaving, and he saw me. That's when we made the deal. We would split the fortune, move to Mexico or Thailand—move as far away from you as possible, where you could never find me. We would live our lives without a worry in the world."

"I knew I saw someone up there," Doug said, almost absently, as if he had heard none of Emily's story apart from the face in the window.

"Shut up, Doug," Kathleen said, directing her anger toward her husband. "None of this would've happened without you. You're responsible for all of this... this mess."

"You didn't have the money? Emily said she drained your accounts. That's why you refused to pay for a hotel room. The Perrons, what, did you lie to them?"

One of the officers hovering nearby stepped into the circle. "This has gone on long enough." He removed his handcuffs from his belt and placed them around Kathleen's wrists. "You're under arrest for inflicting bodily harm to your daughter and for the murder of your late husband, Marshall Nix."

"What?" Kathleen asked, incredulous. "You can't arrest me. Who will take care of Emily? Who will take care of my baby?" She struggled as the deputy led her away.

Fred, with no food to dull his nerves, chewed on a fingernail. "Huh. I didn't see that coming."

"Neither did I," I said, completely baffled by the turn of events.

"I'm not sure I understand what happened," Doug said.

I looked at him, not knowing how to proceed. "Quick question. What happened to the dog? Frank, right? Where is Frank?"

Emily snickered with obvious pride. "At Lyle's place. We planned to take him with us."

"There you go," I said. "It's not neat, but it's wrapped. We exorcised a demon from your stepdaughter and cleansed your house of ghosts. Also, I think there's a small fortune hidden in your basement. If you find it, you can use it to pay back your debts. I think it's yours, since the owner can't claim it. Maybe get a lawyer, though."

Doug smiled and shook his head.

"Also, I completed the job. You owe me a home studio," I said. "I'll be in touch."

Unidentified Flying Object. Thursday, October 26th. 1938hrs.

The sky opened, and rain fell in sheets over the Sacramento region. It was the perfect excuse to sit on the couch and read a book. Well, I had planned on finally reading a book that sat on my to-read list for a decade—*The Road*, by Cormac McCarthy, one of my favorite authors. Bagley curled into my lap and kept me warm.

Alina had other plans for one of the last few nights I had alone before Adam moved into the house. She waltzed into the living room (she had a spare key) with a smile and popcorn.

"Why are you here?" I asked, looking up from page eleven.

"Hello to you. Congratulations on solving your case, and thank you for recognizing I also accomplished something huge today. It's time to celebrate."

"I am celebrating."

"Ew. Don't. Really?"

"What?"

Alina plopped onto the other side of the couch and curled her legs beneath her. "You're not celebrating by reading a book, are you?"

I opened the book and continued to read.

"They made a movie off that book, you know? And before you get all high and mighty and say the book is better and the movie sucks and you can't compare the two, the movie stars Viggo Mortensen, Charlize Theron, Robert Duvall, and Guy Pearce. What's the point of reading the book with a cast like that?"

I eyed Alina, her carton of popcorn, and an uneasy dread settled over me. "Did you go to the movie theater to buy that popcorn?"

"The oldest trick in the book—movie night requires the best popcorn."

"Movie night?" I asked.

"It's raining. It's dark. We deserve to sit on the couch and relax while watching a terrifying, gory movie."

"I'm sitting on the couch, relaxing, reading a book."

"Books aren't relaxing," Alina said around a mouthful of popcorn. "They're work. You've already done enough work today, and it's time to chill out, bro."

I knew I wouldn't win the argument, and I knew she would pester me until I agreed. Either way, reading was no longer within the realm of possibility. I moved Bagley off my lap, set the book on the end table, and walked into the kitchen.

"I'll take a soda," Alina called after me. "Do you have Sprite?"

I returned with a bowl. "My house, couch, and television; also, my night ruined with a horror movie. Pay the popcorn tax."

Alina snickered and dumped half of her popcorn (extra butter) into the bowl.

I collapsed back onto the couch and flicked on the television. "Is it streaming or do I rent it?"

"I already rented it from your account. All you have to do is hit play."

"We're going to have a long, serious talk about respecting the boundaries of privacy. But first, since you're getting up to grab a Sprite, get me one, too."

Alina glared at me with a pouty expression. She set her popcorn on the coffee table and stood, though. "I don't like this snarky version of you."

"Wait until you see the surprise I have in the works for you. We'll see how much you like this version of me then."

"I'm not sure how I feel about that."

I chuckled and sank further into the couch, navigating to the movie rental. *Saw*. Of course.

As I waited for Alina to return, I thought about Doug's case and the many complications and intricacies it possessed, the twists that I hadn't solved. I pieced together the hidden doors leading into hidden rooms. Beyond that, though, everything else fell into place with little mental effort on my end.

Sometimes, an inch of progress makes all the difference. It can often take you another hundred miles.

The thought of a hundred miles—or hundreds of miles—my mind drifted to Maya.

I glanced at my phone, considered calling and updating her on the case. She would like to know how it unfolded. Also, I wanted to hear her voice. I scrolled through my contacts.

"Who are you texting? Someone sexy?" Alina collapsed onto the couch, leaned over, and handed me a can of soda.

I clicked the phone to dark and looked at the young woman sitting three feet away from me. "Speaking of someone sexy—"

"Please don't use that word around me," Alina said.

"How's Rhett?"

"You have a serious, untreated mental condition, don't you? Did you just refer to my boyfriend as sexy?"

I stared at Bagley, who slept beside me in a heap of puppy rolls and fur. "I did, and I don't like myself for it," I said. "It felt weird, and on reflection, it remained weird. Also," I lifted my attention to Alina, "did you say boyfriend?"

"No."

"You did."

"Shut up."

"Alina and Rhett, sitting in a tree, K-I-S-S-I-N-G."

"Grow up, loser. He's not my boyfriend."

I shrugged and shoveled popcorn into my mouth. "I never said he was your boyfriend. You did. I wonder... what would Maya think if she knew you two were official? Or Fred?"

Alina pinched a couple of popcorn kernels and threw them at me. "Stop being lame."

I chuckled beneath my breath and stared at the paused movie for a moment. "If he asks me to be a part of the wedding, I'm going to say no."

"August!"

I raised my hands in surrender, in a surrender of the topic. I had beaten the dead horse long enough. "Quick question about the Ronnie Greene case, and then I'll play the movie. Well, two quick questions. Ronnie abducted his dad, meaning his dad was missing for three days. Why didn't anyone report him as missing?"

Alina shrugged and tossed another popcorn kernel into her mouth. "Ronnie's parents divorced a few years back. I'm not totally sure how the story goes, but he doesn't really have a nine-to-five. He's always missing—gone, I guess, doing one thing or another. I guess the investigators believed he took Ronnie, and that's the theory they chased."

"And the girl he went on a date with? That part makes no sense to me. You mentioned he was gay, so why would he tell everyone he went on a date, have dinner, and see a movie with a girl? Who was she? Why didn't she step forward and provide any insight into his disappearance?"

Alina slowly shook her head. "Ronnie won't speak to anyone, so he hasn't shared that part of his plan."

"No guesses?"

"I think it was a Mama Bird task, but I'm not sure." Alina swiveled her attention from me and stared out the rain-slick window. "It gives me an uneasy feeling, though. Who was she? What happened to her? Why did Ronnie take her out?" Alina returned her focus to me. "I don't think we've seen the last of Mama Bird."

Before I could respond or press play on the movie, my phone vibrated. I checked the caller. Kyle Vanek. I considered ignoring the call, but I answered at the last second.

"Hey."

"Evening," he said. "You busy?"

"I am."

"I'll make this quick, then. We didn't finish our conversation at the school."

"The new consulting case?" I asked.

"This one is strange—it's probably the strangest mystery I've ever seen."

"Mama Bird?" I asked, glancing at Alina.

Vanek grunted. "That one is strange, too. But no."

I tapped the speakerphone icon, allowing Alina access to our conversation. "Do you have any leads? I mean, can you dig into Ronnie's phone records, read his texts, emails, whatever, now that he's arrested?"

"We know Mama Bird contacted Ronnie through a self-deleting messaging service. Once he reads the message or watches a video sent to his account, it deletes forever. It's untraceable. As with ten years ago with Holly Hanson, we have no proof of Mama Bird's existence beyond what Ronnie says—and he's not saying anything."

I scratched Bagley's sleeping head. "What's your strange case?"

"Do you believe in extraterrestrials? In Unidentified Flying Objects?"

I blinked a few times, considering the question. I didn't believe in the supernatural. But were extraterrestrials supernatural? The Pentagon recently came out and confirmed the existence of UFOs, or, in the modern vernacular, UAP—Unidentified Aerial Phenomena. Did that mean I believed in them?

"I'm not sure," I said. "I have put little to no thought into the subject."

"Would you like to put some time into familiarizing yourself with the reality of aliens?"

I glanced at Alina. She aggressively nodded her head.

"When do you need me to start?"

The End.

Blue Moon Appalachia

Investigate weird goings on for a living? What kind of nutbag would do that?

Well, the kind with bills to pay, actually.In the quiet seclusion of the Appalachia mountains, something evil stirs. Home to generations of witches, the entire region knows the lore, and everyone knows someone with at least a suggestion of the supernatural in their family.

So when Edgar Corey, one time FBI field agent and all-round recluse, is called upon to help the sheriff with what sounds like a supernatural case, he automatically turns him down.

Or wished he had because all too soon he's up to his neck in a case that throws everything he believes into question. Is there something ancient and malevolent in the woods? Can he stop it if there is?

With darkness descending, Edgar must fight to get to the truth and one thing is for sure – they all wish Millie Nettles had left the thing she found in the ground.

Investigate the paranormal? Why didn't he just say no?

Blue Moon Boston

A coven of witches bent on murder, a cult of hidden figures raising a leviathan to smite the city ... sound like a regular Wednesday morning for Boston PD's supernatural division.

Chloe Mayfield is a career cop, but when a high-profile bust goes spectacularly wrong, she finds herself assigned to the losers in Blue Moon ...

... and discovers a world she never knew existed.

Get ready for high-stakes supernatural action.

The Original Series

Fight a demon, investigate a werewolf biker gang, have tea with mum ... it's all in a day's work for England's #1 paranormal P.I.

When a master vampire starts killing people in his hometown, paranormal investigator, Tempest Michaels, takes it personally ...... and soon a race against time turns into a battle for his life. He doesn't believe in the paranormal but has a steady stream of clients with cases too weird for the police.

Mostly it's all nonsense, but when a third victim turns up with bite marks in her lifeless throat, can he really dismiss the possibility that this time the monster is real?

Joined by an ex-army buddy, a disillusioned cop, his friends from the pub, his dogs, and his mother (why are there no grandchildren, Tempest?), our paranormal investigator is going to stop the murders if it kills him …… but when his probing draws the creature's attention, his family and friends become the hunted.

Free Books and More

Want to see what else I have written? Go to my website.

https://stevehiggsbooks.com/

Or sign up to my newsletter where you will get sneak peaks, exclusive giveaways, behind the scenes content, and more. Plus, you'll be notified of Fan Pricing events when they occur and get exclusive offers from other authors because all UF writers are automatically friends.

Copy the link into your web browser.

https://stevehiggsbooks.com/newsletter/

Prefer social media? Join my thriving Facebook community.

Want to join the inner circle where you can keep up to date with everything? This is a free group on Facebook where you can hang out with likeminded individuals and enjoy discussing my books. There is cake too (but only if you bring it).

https://www.facebook.com/groups/1151907108277718